Mrs. Bennet's Sentiments

Pride and Prejudice and Perseverance

DORI SALERNO

ISBN: 1530968771
ISBN-13: 9781530968770

DEDICATION

For Joyce

ACKNOWLEDGMENTS

A special thank you to all who supported and encouraged my endeavor. I would like to express my gratitude to the many people who provided support, talked things over, read, wrote, offered comments, assisted in the editing, proofreading and design. To Katherine Elswick for her constant support and encouragement. To Susan Arnout Smith for her professional advice, the many proofing rereads, the constant meetings and never letting me take the easy way out. To Laura Summer for her pithy, PR skill. To Sally Stockton for slogging through the first draft. To Dominique Salerno, my toughest critic, for her initial encouragement. To Debra Armelino, my enthusiastic first reader. To Kris Russell for trying to capture my initial cover idea. To Caitlin Alexander for keeping me from looking like a fool. To Marti Kranzberg, Robert Salerno and Carol Pratt for their second pair of eyes, and especially to Thomas Sonandres for his vigilance above and beyond the call of duty. And to Kevin Kornburger for getting through the computer maze of publication.

CHAPTER I

Mrs. Bennet sighed in exasperation. Butter and jam were smeared on her good linen tablecloth. She turned to fill the teacup held out by her daughter. Her daughter took no notice of her mother standing there while she perused her book. The teacup slipped from her daughter's hand. Mrs. Bennet reached out to catch it but the teacup fell to the floor. Watching the delicate arm of the cup shatter, Mrs. Bennet felt something inside her shatter. She slammed the teapot back on to the sideboard.

"Enough, Enough!"

"Mother, it is just a tea cup," snorted Lizzy.

"Yes, there is no need for hysterics. It is not a crisis, a 'tempest in a teacup'," chortled Mr. Bennet.

"It can be glued back together," soothed Lydia.

"Just a teacup! Just a teacup! Everything is just something. Care needs to be taken, attention paid to what one is doing. Everything in this house is either broken down or needs mending."

She felt a wave of heat overtake her. Her neck flushed red with a feeling of heaviness in her chest. She couldn't get a solid breath. She had to get out. She bolted through the kitchen, shoved the door open and ran down to the pump. She vigorously pumped the rusted handle of the pump.

Mrs. Bennet dripped with perspiration. Even the cool water running over her wrists as she worked the water pump wasn't helping. She took a few deep breaths, straightened, and patted her brow with her dry handkerchief.

She'd take a short walk down to the gate—that was just what she needed to clear her cluttered mind. With five daughters—none married—a husband, the Longbourn household and the farm to manage, she was exhausted. Lately she had been feeling queerly, with a constant flushing and a sense of feeling over-heated. She had less patience than she should, she admitted, thinking of the way she'd snapped at her family this morning over a broken teacup, nearly weeping at the loss. She'd never before been prone to such frequent bouts of temper. She felt more inclined to speak her mind, as well, but then—she drew herself straighter—who wouldn't when Mr. Bennet retreated into his library, making no attempt to deal with their financial situation. She could barely contain herself from throttling him.

Her girls were of little comfort. Mary continually played her pianoforte with little expression, and Kitty stomped about with her moodiness, petty jealousies, and fits—it was almost more than she could bear. Lizzy, like her father, refused, absolutely refused, to notice the work that needed to be done, and buried herself in her books, turning her nose up. She was well aware of how Lizzy condescended to her. Still, she understood that it was the girl's age. She'd probably done the same to her own mother.

Mrs. Bennet let out a long sigh as she passed the overgrown vegetable garden. Then there were her eldest and her youngest. Jane, her quiet beauty, tried her best to help but was too dreamy for practical matters. Lydia, though, was a fine, stout, merry girl who always raised her spirits. Mrs. Bennet chuckled. The girl reminded her of her younger self: open and impulsive, full of energy, high spirits and expectation. *I pray she will not be as easily deceived in her marital choice as I was*, thought Mrs. Bennet. As a young man, Mr. Bennet had cut a fine figure, quoted poetry and seemed to have so much promise. Now he puttered around, making sarcastic observations, content to wallow, leaving his wife to manage it all.

Mrs. Bennet sat herself down upon a large stone near the gate. She closed her eyes and let the sounds of the meadow calm her. She pictured herself alone with her easel and box of paints, and gave herself over to the reverie, imagining her brush strokes creating a lush meadow alive with wild flowers and golden-throated birds with beautifully colored feathers.

If only I could be free of them all. She came to herself with a start. What a terrible thought for a mother to have! But it was difficult to manage a household with five nearly grown young women. With her small income she could not continue to support them all for much longer. The girls would have to start looking for marriageable prospects—or worse, go into service. At that thought, she started to sob.

Oh, what was wrong with her? To make matters worse, off in the distance she saw Mrs. Long rapidly approaching, like a large ship with green sails of cloth billowing behind her, her face and bosom a cracked, wrinkled version of a ship's figurehead, shaded by an absurd velvet hat with green feathers.

Quickly Mrs. Bennet dabbed at her eyes with the end of her apron and tried to smooth her countenance. Mrs. Long was no doubt eager to boast about some new accomplishment of her two nieces and lament the state of the Bennet girls. Quite out of breath and slightly red in the face from her rapid pace, Mrs. Long sat down, her girth pushing Mrs. Bennet to the ragged edge of the rock.

"I have some important news, my dear Miriam." Mrs. Bennet braced herself for the torrent of praise sure to come regarding Mrs. Long's nieces and their triumphs in London. Mrs. Long took a deep breath and with one great exhalation came the news.

"Netherfield has just been let to a young man from the North of England. He came down on Monday in a chaise and four to see the place, and was so much delighted with it that he is to take possession of it before Michaelmas, and some of his servants are to be in the house next week preparing it to host the Assembly. He is a single gentleman of large fortune, four or five thousand a year. His name is Bingley."

Though Mrs. Long looked an unlikely angel, this information, considering Mrs. Bennet's previous state of mind, seemed heaven sent. She turned and clasped Mrs. Long's green-gloved hand. "My dearest Eugenia, will you proffer an introduction?"

Mrs. Long removed her hand, straightened her glove and sniffed. "As my nieces are coming out this season I will be in London, but we will return in time to attend the Assembly. I may be able to introduce you then, my dear."

Mrs. Bennet read the private thoughts behind the eyes of her acquaintance. Eugenia Long enjoyed having the power of information and had every intention of pushing her nieces forward to this eligible bachelor, with absolutely no intention of assisting Mrs. Bennet with her five daughters. She thanked Mrs. Long for sharing the news and hurried back to the house. Here was an opportunity to settle at least one of her girls. She must motivate her husband to call on this Mr. Bingley. For everyone knew that a single man in possession of a good fortune must be in want of a wife— and, after all, there were five Bennet girls from which to choose!

Mrs. Bennet sat at her dressing table, preparing for bed. She remained a handsome woman in her middle age. With her figure still trim, fair hair swept up in curls, and her large clear blue eyes, gentlemen still tipped their hats in greeting and appreciation. As a young girl she'd had many suitors and her manners were lively and pert. Yet even as a child she'd often been overcome with deep emotion. Her painting served as her outlet for communicating the turbulent emotions trapped inside her person.

Most said she was the perfect match for Mr. Bennet. Mr.

Bennet, with his wry humor, poetic moodiness, and shy nature, settled her down and she, with her passionate nature, inspired him. Five daughters later and a small estate to farm left them both depleted with no time for painting or poetry. She channeled her passion for art into raising her daughters and creating a home. For his part, Mr. Bennett had withdrawn further into moody reverie as he aged, with occasional outbursts of sarcasm at his wife's expense.

In the glass, she could see Mr. Bennet, his dark head, now streaked with gray, comfortably settled on the damask pillow, pince-nez resting on his nose while he perused his book. She sighed and resolutely squared her shoulders, altered the ruffle of her dressing gown to expose more of her bosom, let a playful smile tease her lips, turned and flounced upon the bed. After the matrimonial duties were completed, she began her campaign. "My dear, just as we find some solace in marriage, I do so wish our girls will be able to marry."

Mr. Bennet turned onto his back and straightened the sheet. "Why would they not be able to marry, Miriam? They are fine, healthy specimens of womanhood."

"What I mean to say is to have the opportunity to marry." She sighed. "We cannot afford to present them in London." At that Mr. Bennet frowned, for what she stated was indeed true. Before he could sink into his usual state of melancholy, she countered quickly, "I have promising news. A single man of large fortune, four or five thousand a year, has taken Netherfield."

"What is his name?" Mr. Bennet asked. He nervously

picked at the threads on the coverlet.

"Bingley. And I consider him a fine prospect for marrying one of our girls."

"Is that his design in settling here?"

"His design? Of course not! But it is my design, dear Edward, as it is very likely that he may fall in love with one of them. Therefore, dearest, you must visit him as soon as he arrives."

"I see no occasion for that," grumbled Mr. Bennet. He hated social functions and avoided them at all costs. Only at the urging of his wife and her connexions did he occasionally entertain. He was a genial enough, if not an active host at his own table, but sought no amusement in the company of others elsewhere. In truth, he was shy and found it difficult to put himself forward in any venture.

"You and the girls may go, or perhaps send them alone, as Mr. Bingley may like you the best of the party." Here he proceeded to offer playful kisses of affection. But Mrs. Bennet would not be distracted from her purpose.

"My dear, you flatter me." She gave a throaty laugh. "I certainly had my share of beauty, but I do not pretend to be anything extraordinary now. When a woman has five grown daughters, she ought to give over thinking of her own beauty."

"In such cases a woman has not often much beauty to think of," Mr. Bennet murmured as he caressed her shoulder.

She settled her ruffled night dress to cover her exposed shoulders, trying not to succumb to his sweet compliments and tender caresses. "You must indeed go and see Mr. Bingley when he comes into the neighborhood. It has to be you. I cannot call with five daughters in tow. It would be unseemly. Propriety dictates that a Gentleman may call on a Gentleman to start a new acquaintance, but never may a Lady first call on a Gentleman."

"My dear, it is more than I engage for. You are over-scrupulous, surely. When you meet him, you can give him a note with my hearty permission to his marrying whichever girl he chooses, though I must throw in a good word for my Lizzy."

Now Mr. Bennet's teasing had gone too far. Mrs. Bennet could see his sole intention was to avoid a social duty that would discomfit him, without any thought of what would benefit his children. His preference for Lizzy and indifference to the other girls irked her. Could he not see that each girl was a composite of the best and worst of their parents? Jane had the beauty of her mother and the poetical, dreamy, shy manner of her father. Lizzy had the playful, pert manners of her mother, tempered by her father's wit and intellect. Lydia was the flamboyant, energetic charmer, a vision of Mrs. Bennet's younger self. Kitty had inherited the darker moods and tempers of both parents. Mary was an overly studious, shy girl just trying to find her place in the mix of all the Bennets.

"Lizzy is not a bit better than the others. I am sure she is not half as handsome as Jane nor half as good natured as Lydia, but you are always giving her the preference."

"They are all silly and ignorant like other girls, but Lizzy at least has something of a quickness that her sisters lack."

Mrs. Bennet felt her skin flush. She threw aside the bedcovers and stood at the bedside trembling with anger. The man's total insensitivity to the needs of the girls enraged her.

"Edward, you are a poor parent," she cried. "How can you abuse your children in such a way? Or do you simply take delight in vexing me? You have no compassion for my poor nerves."

Mr. Bennet turned to face away from her. "You mistake me, my dear. I have a high respect for your nerves. They are my old friends. I have heard you mention them with consideration for twenty years." He yanked the bedcovers up to his chin and slammed his head against the pillow. "Artistic temperament be damned!"

"You do not know what I suffer!" Mrs. Bennet, now flushed and sweating, grabbed her pillow and some bed linens and stormed out. She locked herself into the spare room and sobbed in frustration.

CHAPTER II

All five girls had heard the row. As they tidied their rooms, Lizzy made jokes, strutting about and proclaiming herself half as handsome as Jane. Kitty paced nervously. Lydia, busily stripping the beds, formulated a plan of making breakfast and taking it to their mother in bed. Mary, hugging her pillow, was crying and Jane was thoughtful.

"Do hush, Lizzy, it's not funny," said Jane as she handed Lizzy fresh linens.

"I think Mother is really ill," said Kitty.

"Oh she's not ill; she's just ridiculously dramatic to shout at Father like that. She enjoys working herself up into such a state." Lizzy snapped the clean sheet onto the bed.

"Yes, but what were they fighting about?" asked Mary.

"Oh you know just as well as I! Most likely it was over the fact that Mother does all the work and Father does absolutely nothing— the usual bickering."

"No, Lizzy, I don't think so," said Jane, as she smoothed down the sheet, slowly reviewing the argument in her mind. "Mother sounded fierce."

"Like a lioness," piped up Mary.

"Yes, like she was defending her cubs," agreed Jane.

"I know what it was about," said Lydia. "I heard from our aunt in Meryton that a new bachelor is moving into the county. I think Mother wanted Father to do his social duty and present us. Perhaps this young and single gentleman would turn out to be a suitable husband for one of us."

Jane sighed. "Father may not do his duty by us, and Mother is right to be frustrated."

"Frustrated, I understand," allowed Lizzy, as she struggled to stuff her feather pillow into its casing. "But screaming at Father like that?"

Kitty stopped her pacing. "Do you think Mother is suffering from some physical ailment? I saw her become very red and then overcome with perspiration. She was down at the pump, running the water over her wrists."

"Charlotte Lucas said her mother had some of these same symptoms recently. Perhaps it is a stomach upset going around. Mrs. Lucas seems to be fine now."

"Excuse me," Lydia interjected, tossing a pillow at Lizzy. "But the pertinent fact is that a new young bachelor has come to town, and Father must do his duty for us. Lizzy, you have the closest connection to him. Do prevail upon him to make a visit. I will take Mother some breakfast in bed and encourage her to sketch a little. That always seems to calm her."

"It would be best for Mother to stay secluded," said Jane, nodding. "If we heard the row so did the servants."

Mary had dried her tears and now spoke quietly. "I like Mother's sketches. I keep the one she drew of me in my room. I am curled up with a book and I look so studious."

Lydia laughed. "She drew one of me on a swing with my head thrown back to the sky, laughing."

"I have a charming one I keep of me gazing out the window with my chin resting just so on my hand," said

Jane.

Kitty giggled. "I have the oddest one I savor. It is of me standing on a cliff with storm clouds above."

"I have one," said Lizzy. "But it disconcerts me. She has me sitting in a chair, an open book in my hand, but I am gazing up archly, and in it I am only half as handsome as Jane." She chuckled. "But I must admit it is a true likeness."

Jane, crisply folding the corners of the blanket on her bed, reiterated their plan. "It is decided. Lizzy will approach Father about the visit. Lydia will attend to Mother. Girls, finish tidying your rooms. Let us make a quiet day of it, be cheerful and helpful, and act as if nothing untoward has occurred."

Lizzy searched for her father during the day and reported her unsuccessful efforts to her sisters. "He probably took himself off for a walk to Meryton to avoid any embarrassing encounter with Mother."

Later that evening, when all were seated by the fire, as Lizzy was busily trimming a new hat, Mr. Bennet looked up from his paper and remarked, "I hope Mr. Bingley will like it, Lizzy." All the girls' eyes turned upon their mother. Mrs. Bennet took a deep breath and replied to her husband's jibe in measured tones.

"We are not to know what Mr. Bingley likes since we are not to visit."

Lizzy, seeking to make peace, said, "But you forget,

Mama, we shall meet him at the Assembly. You mentioned that Mrs. Long has promised to introduce him."

"I do not believe Mrs. Long will do any such thing. She has two nieces of her own. She is a selfish, hypocritical woman, and I have no opinion of her."

Mr. Bennet's expression made plain his approval of his wife's estimation. "I have no opinion of her either and am glad that you do not depend on her serving you."

Mrs. Bennet's gaze remained on her embroidery hoop. She appreciated that he did not offer his usual reprimand about her tendency to reveal her opinions too readily, but being of like mind about a neighbor's shortcomings would not mend her feelings at present.

"When is the next ball to be, Lizzy?" asked Mr. Bennet.

Lizzy could not fathom why her father continued to pursue this topic. "Tomorrow fortnight."

"So it is," sighed Mrs. Bennet. "Mrs. Long does not come back till the day before, so it will be impossible for her to introduce him as she will not know him herself."

"Then you must introduce her, my dear."

"Impossible," said Mrs. Bennet as she stabbed her needle through her embroidery cloth, "I am not acquainted with him myself. Do stop all this teasing, Edward. I am quite sick to death of Mr. Bingley."

"I am sorry to hear that, my dear. If I had known that, I would not have taken the trouble to call on him today. We cannot escape the acquaintance now."

"Oh!" Mrs. Bennet was up and in her husband's arms, kissing him gratefully. The girls surrounded them, expressing surprise and joy.

"How good it was of you, my dear. But I knew I could persuade you. I was sure you loved your daughters too well to neglect such an opportunity." She continued to shower him with praise and affection almost to the embarrassment of her girls.

"Now, now." Mr. Bennet cleared his throat. But it was apparent that he enjoyed feeling the hero of the hour.

Mrs. Bennet's eyes shone. "What an excellent father you have, girls. I do not know how you will ever make him amends for his kindness. At his time of life it is not so easy making new acquaintances, but for your sakes he would do anything. How pleased I am, and it is such a good joke, too, that you should have gone this morning and never said a word about it till now."

Later that night, while Jane braided her hair, Lizzy, turning down the covers of their bed, remarked, "Papa likes to have his fun, such a good joke. He nearly drove Mama mad."

Jane sighed deeply. "Yes, but why? He isn't a cruel man. Why would there be so much fuss? Why did he push Mama to such extremes with his inaction?"

"You believe he did it deliberately to torment her. I cannot believe that of Papa. Mama just over-reacts to everything."

"Perhaps, but perhaps this is what she must do to force

Papa to perform his obligation. Think about it, Lizzy, the introduction does not particularly benefit her. Now Mr. Bingley will call on Papa. Mama then will invite him to dinner so we have a chance to meet him before the Assembly. She has to get the house ready, make sure we are all dressed well and encourage Papa in his role of genial host. I know you love Papa, but I believe Mama merits your affection as well. She is only thinking of us."

"Perhaps," was all Lizzy said. She squeezed Jane's arm. "Come now, to bed with us."

As the house drifted into quiet, Edward Bennet, seated by the fire in his den, was pondering his behavior as well. He enjoyed a good joke on his wife; it had been their love play during courtship. He would tease her, and she would laugh good-naturedly at his pranks; he'd always adored the instant rosiness of her smiles. But this time she had sought his assistance for their girls. It was time, he conceded, that they met young men and set up households of their own. Perhaps his reluctance was only that he did not want to lose them just yet.

CHAPTER III

On the bright fall day when Mr. Bingley came to call, the young ladies remained sequestered upstairs, peering furtively around walls and over banisters as Mr. Bennet made polite, if stiff, conversation in the comfort of his library. Mrs. Bennet spent the entire visit beneath the open library window, ostensibly clipping roses from the garden. She was pleased with how the conversation progressed. Soon after, she sent an invitation to Netherfield for dinner, which was promptly accepted. However, before the dining preparations could begin, Mr. Bingley's footman delivered a note that he must return to London. At this, Mrs. Bennet was quite disconcerted. She had looked forward to presiding over her table and presenting each of her daughters in the most amiable light, giving them the advantage of meeting Mr. Bingley before the Assembly.

Mrs. Bennet paced nervously. "Oh, Mr. Bennet, I do hope Mr. Bingley really intends to settle at Netherfield. If I can but see one of my daughters happily settled, it would be such a blessing."

Mr. Bennet sighed and shook his head. "Counting chickens, Miriam, counting chickens."

A week later Mr. Bingley returned from London, bringing with him a small entourage consisting of his two sisters, the husband of the eldest sister, and another young man. Preparations for the Assembly to take place that

Saturday kept the girls at Longbourn quite busy. Jane was to wear her pink silk with a lace shawl and matching gloves. Lydia chose a cerulean blue gown that enhanced the color of her eyes and was a complement to her coloring. Kitty's gown was of a similar style but of the palest sea green that offset her alabaster skin and auburn tresses. Mary, being so shy and there having been much discussion about whether she wanted to attend, finally settled on a simple sweet gown in ivory trimmed with a sprig of flowers at the bodice.

Lizzy, however, insisted on being obstinate. Mrs. Bennet had encouraged the choice of a wine colored gown to be worn with a garnet pendant at the throat. The gown displayed her daughter's figure well and brought out the rich tones in her skin, eyes and hair. Lizzy instead chose a dove grey dress with pearl beading. The dress was elegant in its simplicity and looked well enough, but Mrs. Bennet sighed in exasperation. "I don't understand you, Lizzy. Why choose something that, though pretty, is quite conventional? Why are you content to be the little brown wren? It does nothing to bring you out."

As soon as she said it, she wished she hadn't. She could see the quick look of hurt that crossed Lizzy's brow. "What I mean, dear, is that you are very attractive, and you shouldn't be afraid to show it. For all your pert and saucy ways I am surprised at your conservative choice."

"But don't you see, Mother? The more conservative the gown, the more license I can take with my behavior. If I were to wear the highly colored gown you like"—Lizzy grabbed a black lace fan and fluttered it coquettishly—

"which to my taste has a bit of the Spanish Gypsy about it, my manners and witty remarks could be interpreted as wanton!"

Mrs. Bennet laughed and said, "Perhaps you are right, my dear. But I insist on my string of pearls to be entwined in your lovely dark hair to match the pearl beading on the dress." She stroked her daughter's hair and kissed her cheek.

Leaving the girls to their preparations, she sought solace in the library with her husband. "Dear Mr. Bennet, I fear I have offended Lizzy while trying to choose a gown with her. She already doubts her beauty, and my comments may have made it worse." Her hands clasped as she fretted. "Do make some special mention to her about how well she looks in her finery, once we are all dressed. I know I complain that you distinguish her above the others, but I now see that perhaps you are right to do so. The gown she chose is elegant and simple, but with her hair up she should look a classic beauty. Make some remark to that effect."

"Of course, my dear, whatever you wish," said Mr. Bennet as he proceeded to light his pipe and rest his feet upon a low stool.

Mrs. Bennet nodded, satisfied, and turned to leave. Then she turned back. "My dear Mr. Bennet, you should be changing too."

"Miriam, I am not planning to attend. Please don't ask me. I did my duty. Let me stay here and read in peace. I will wait upon your return and hear all the news."

"Edward, you must go," she cried. "You have already met Mr. Bingley and this is the perfect opportunity to present your daughters. What was the point of meeting him before the ball if you were not going to proffer an introduction? He didn't dine privately with us, so there is no prior acquaintance with our girls."

"Nonsense. He will introduce himself now and ask for introductions to the girls. Sir William and Lady Lucas will be there also."

"Yes, but they will be concerned with their daughter Charlotte's introduction."

"Miriam, they are also our friends and will assist you with the girls if needed. I have asked Sir William to act in my stead. Besides, do you intend on dancing?"

"Of course not, Edward, this is an assembly for the young people of Hertfordshire. Chaperones sit on the side-lines."

"Exactly," said Mr. Bennet, puffing on his pipe. "You all chat amongst yourselves, observe the dancing and attend to the youngsters. You'll be so occupied with gossip you won't even miss me."

"Do as you please, Edward," sighed Mrs. Bennet. "You usually do. It's just that sometimes it is nice to have one's life companion chivalrously by one's side."

CHAPTER IV

Seated next to Lady Lucas, Mrs. Bennet had a most advantageous view of all at the Assembly. Netherfield, being the oldest estate in the county, had never looked better. The ballroom had been painted a dusky rose; the chandeliers sparkled, giving off a soft glow that improved the complexions of all. She nodded to Mrs. Long across the room, whose nieces, like her daughters, were enjoying the lively first reel. Their host, Mr. Bingley, looked quite handsome: tall, fair haired, in a well cut waistcoat. He displayed an easy, open countenance; his manners were the epitome of the gracious host concerned for the well-being of others. And he had brought an intriguing stranger along with him, a man almost as tall as himself, with thick dark hair and a close-cropped beard. Might he be engaged to Mr. Bingley's sister? Lady Lucas knew as little as she did, so she endeavored to inquire elsewhere.

Mr. Bingley's sisters were clearly ladies of London fashion, and their ball attire was much admired. On the pretext of desiring to know the origins of the lace on her gown, Mrs. Bennet approached Mrs. Hurst, the eldest sister, a tall, extremely thin woman who, when standing next to her short, stout, barrel chested husband reminded Mrs. Bennet of the number ten. After listening to an exhaustive discussion of lace making and a minute evaluation of the particular pattern created for her dress, Mrs. Bennet broached the subject of the handsome stranger. "Do you have two brothers?" she inquired, glancing over at the dark-haired man.

"Oh goodness no," said Mrs. Hurst. "That is Charles' lifelong friend, Mr. Darcy. They were in school together and although they are almost like brothers, we have no relation. Mr. Darcy is a single gentleman who resides at Pemberley and has care of his young sister, Georgianna." Mrs. Bennet waited, breath held, to hear if Mrs. Hurst would intimate an engagement between Mr. Bingley and the younger sister of Mr. Darcy, but none was forthcoming, only an inquiry about local lace shops.

So there are two eligible bachelors at this evening's ball—oh, what a fine opportunity! The evening was already quite a success. It was evident to all that dear, lovely, Jane was the most sought-after dance partner for Mr. Bingley. Mrs. Bennet looked about for a way to turn the situation now to Lizzy's advantage.

Lizzy had been dancing with a local boy for most of the evening. Mrs. Bennet knew him as pleasant, but far too young and dull to suit her quick-witted daughter. She took a seat nearest where they stood and, just as he moved to request Lizzy's hand for the next reel, she called out to him, "Tom, could you please fetch me some refreshment? I am quite parched." Lizzy was obliged to sit down and wrinkled her brow in irritation. Mrs. Bennet noted that Mr. Darcy stood quite nearby, his gaze trained neither on the dancers nor on the couple conversing next to him. In fact, the frown on his face looked quite intimidating and unapproachable. She gave a discreet nod to focus her daughter's attention on Mr. Darcy as a potential dance partner. Lizzy blushed.

Before she could think of a way to direct his attention to Lizzy, Mr. Bingley approached Mr. Darcy and offered an introduction.

Splendid, thought Mrs. Bennet, *things are going swimmingly!* Until she heard the words Mr. Darcy spoke in reply: "She is tolerable," he muttered to Bingley, "but not handsome enough to tempt me; and I am in no humor at present to give consequence to young ladies who are slighted by other men."

Mrs. Bennet gasped, for of course her daughter had not been slighted; she had only sent her partner off to get some refreshment, and with the very aim of freeing her to meet this discourteous man. She felt Lizzy stiffen beside her and turned to find her daughter staring straight ahead, a glassy smile upon her face and that same hurt expression sparked by her mother's earlier ill-chosen words.

At that moment, Tom appeared with the punch glass. "Why thank you, Tom," said Mrs. Bennet loudly. "How kind of you to interrupt your dancing pleasure." Tom bowed solemnly, looked over to Lizzy, extended his hand and Lizzy, with a wry smile and a nod to her mother, joined the reel.

Oh, that horrible man! Mr. Darcy, indeed. However could a man so polite, so kind as Mr. Bingley, have such an oaf for a friend? Mrs. Bennet wanted to take her folded fan and rap Mr. Darcy smartly across the face. To throw her glass of punch into

his face. To—

She stood. And as she navigated the chairs and passed in front of the man, she made a slight false step and spilled several drops of the red liquid onto his white shirt cuffs. "Pardon me," she said icily.

Mr. Darcy looked upon his sleeve in dismay and attempted to remove the stain by dabbing it with a small cloth. He spent the rest of the evening walking about and speaking only to members of his party. The local gentry deemed him as disagreeable as Mrs. Bennet did. He was discovered to be proud, thinking himself to be above his company, and above being pleased. It wasn't nearly the satisfaction Mrs. Bennet had hoped for, but it would do.

The girls arrived home in high spirits to find Mr. Bennet in the library, reading his book and awaiting the return of his family. Their stories tumbled over one another's. Kitty and Lydia were still breathless after having danced each dance; Mary was happy she'd had the courage to attend, and that she'd heard herself remarked upon as a highly accomplished young lady. Mrs. Bennet was pleased to have seen her eldest daughter so much admired by Mr. Bingley and his sisters, and was even happier to share the good fortune with her husband.

"Oh my dear Mr. Bennet, we have had a most delightful evening. Nothing could be like it! Mr. Bingley thought Jane quite beautiful and danced two dances with her. He first danced with Miss Lucas but did not seem to admire her. Yet he seemed quite taken with Jane, and just as you predicted, he inquired about her and got himself introduced." Mrs. Bennet glanced over to Lizzy and checked herself from any further effusive description of Jane's much admired beauty.

Lizzy noted this and promptly proceeded to deflect her mother's concern by launching into a lively and humorous rendition of her rejection by Mr. Darcy, portraying him as a proud peacock strutting about.

Mrs. Bennet scowled. "No one," she added pointedly, "suited his fancy. He didn't even dance with the females of his party. He was so high and conceited there was no enduring him."

Arm in arm, the girls tumbled and skipped up the stairs to bed, Lydia and Kitty still discussing every dance and dancing partner, Jane and Lizzy retiring to review the evening and its implications for Jane. Mrs. Bennet remained seated with her husband in the library. Once she was sure they were alone, she spoke vehemently, "I assure you, Edward, that Lizzy does not lose much by not suiting Mr. Darcy's fancy. He is a most horrid and disagreeable man and not worth pleasing. His hurtful comment, overheard by Lizzy—'not handsome enough to dance with'—was appalling."

"He said that?"

"Yes, Edward, he did. And though Lizzy makes a sport of it, she was cut to the quick. It was all I could do to stop myself from walloping him. I feel terribly guilty about it all."

"Guilty? Why should you feel guilty, Miriam?"

She confessed how she had managed the situation so Lizzy would be without a partner in order to give Mr. Darcy the opportunity to approach her.

"His rudeness is not your fault, dear."

"Yes, but if I had waited a little to observe him, I might not have encouraged the situation. If you had been there, Edward, you may have prevented it."

"How?"

"You would have taken the measure of the man and perhaps restrained me from my meddling or at least given him a proper set down."

"Are you now blaming me?" Mr. Bennet loudly tapped the tobacco out of his pipe.

She wrinkled her nose at the small mound of tobacco. "I just meant that your presence might have been beneficial for the girls and a support to me. When left to my own devices I can easily muddle things."

"You didn't wallop him, Miriam, did you?"

"Of course not! I merely put a blot of punch on his sleeve, something to annoy a proud, vain man such as he." She stood and leaned over to brush the offending tobacco ash onto a saucer and emptied it into the fireplace. "I am going to retire now. The Lucases are coming over for luncheon, and I must be up early to prepare."

A blot on his sleeve, Mr. Bennet mused as his wife left. Knowing Miriam, she'd probably walked about the room gaily conversing all the while putting a blot on his character. The whole village must abhor the man by now. He chuckled and stood to put out the fire.

♦♦♦

CHAPTER V

The Misses Lucas and the Misses Bennet were engaged in a lively round of discourse about the happenings of the previous night. Platters of cold meats and rolls with sweet butter were passed among the famished young ladies at the luncheon table. Lady Lucas, similar in stature to Mrs. Bennet, but with a robust, hefty figure, secured a roll in her meaty hand, slathered it with butter, took a large bite and pronounced the ball quite a success. Mrs. Bennet remarked kindly that Charlotte had been Mr. Bingley's first choice of partner and must feel gratified about that. Charlotte Lucas, ginger-haired and with a highly freckled complexion, was an intelligent woman of twenty-seven and a realist: plain, sensible and well aware of her status as the elder spinster of the village. She was Elizabeth's dearest friend and they shared an understanding of absurdities and wit.

"I believe, Mrs. Bennet, you have no cause to be concerned," Charlotte declared. "He favored his second partner most. I overheard him mention that he enjoyed the Assembly immensely and considered the eldest Miss Bennet to be the prettiest in the room."

"Handsome is as Handsome does," snorted Lizzy.

"Oh ho, don't be so sarcastic," laughed Charlotte as she bit into her sweet cherry tart. "My over hearings were also about you, dear girl. Poor Lizzy, to be only 'just tolerable'? Darcy is not nearly so worth listening to as his friend, is he?"

Mrs. Bennet's fork clattered against her plate. "Charlotte, I beg of you, do not put it into Lizzy's head to be vexed by his ill treatment. He is such an odious man that it would be a great misfortune to be courted by him. Mrs. Long said he sat next to her and rudely refused to speak to her."

"That's not true," said Jane. "I saw him speaking with her."

"Only because she finally turned to him and asked how he liked Netherfield, and he was forced to acknowledge her. She said he was very gruff in his reply."

"Well, Miss Bingley told me that he never speaks much, unless among those well known to him," said Jane.

"Perhaps you mean those comparable to him in financial stature. Everyone says he is filled with pride. We have learnt that he is the master at the Pemberley estate and has ten thousand a year. Perhaps he heard that Mrs. Long doesn't keep a carriage and arrived in a hack chaise and deemed her unworthy of conversation." Mrs. Bennet took her carving knife and sliced off a piece of ham quite savagely.

"Mama! You are quite agitated by this. I assure you it is of no consequence," soothed Lizzy.

"And you looked so lovely in that gray dress and pearls, the picture of elegance." Mrs. Bennet brandished her knife, pointing it in a scolding manner at Lizzy's nose. "Promise me you will not deign to dance with him if he asks."

Lizzy hid a smile behind her hand. "I can safely promise

you, Mama, I will never dance with him."

Mrs. Bennet nodded in satisfaction and took another savage slice at the ham. Though she wanted all her daughters to marry—she couldn't bear the thought that Lizzy might become the sort of spinster that Charlotte Lucas had—she did not want them to enter a marriage in which they would be continually condescended to. She thought of Mr. Bennet's witty sarcastic remarks made at her expense whenever she offered any opinion or suggestion. She had enough of that to contend with in her own sphere of matrimony.

"Have you ever seen a man look so handsome in a cap?" Lydia squealed.

Kitty giggled. "Oh, but what about all those medals? Did you see the one who smiled at me when I—"

"Enough! You two must be the silliest girls in the country." Mr. Bennet slapped down his morning paper on the table, interrupting them.

It had come to their attention some weeks earlier that a militia regiment had taken residence in the neighboring village of Meryton. Kitty and Lydia were in the habit of making frequent walks to the village and returning with much news about the officers.

Mrs. Bennet had passed her girlhood in Meryton. Her elder sister still resided in their family home with her husband, a Mr. Philips, who had been a clerk to their father, the local attorney. Mr. Philips had succeeded him in the firm and the house. Mr. Gardiner, Mrs. Bennet's elder brother, had settled in London and was a well-respected tradesman. Realizing she could not rely on Mr. Bennet for an introduction to the officers, she decided she would prevail upon her brother-in-law to introduce himself to the officers and entertain them. This might be a source of a suitable match for Lizzy, and perhaps for Lydia and Kitty as well.

At their father's rebuke, Kitty immediately quieted, casting her eyes downward and nervously twirling her napkin on her lap. Tears filled her eyes. Lydia squeezed Kitty's hand under the table and said, "But he's so handsome," and rebelliously continued her description of Captain Carter and her hopes of seeing him while they walked about the village that afternoon. Mr. Bennet sighed in irritation. Seeking to avoid a confrontation, Mrs. Bennet brushed the crumbs from Lydia's ample bosom and excused them from the morning table.

"Girls, go ready yourselves for your afternoon constitutional. Kitty, why don't you wear the bonnet with the green ribbon that matches your lovely eyes." A quick hug banished the girl's tears. Lydia slung her arm through Kitty's and they ran upstairs, giggling, to ready themselves for the expedition.

"Edward, why must you be so critical of the girls? I am astonished that you speak so slightingly of your own children."

"If my children are silly, I hope to be sensible of it,"

huffed Mr. Bennet. He raised his paper to commence reading again.

"But they are all very clever."

"On that point, Miriam, we do not agree."

"Edward, you must not expect such girls to have the sense of their parents. When they reach our age, I doubt they will think on officers any more than we do. I remember as a young girl I fancied a Red-Coat or two, and if a smart Colonel with five or six thousand a year should want to marry one of our daughters, you would not refuse him."

"I am sorry to have caused Kitty any pain, but your schemes about marriageable opportunities are becoming insufferable."

Mrs. Bennet snatched his paper away and glared at her husband. "What other options do they have, Edward?"

"Don't start, Miriam. You know I have no control over the entail on this estate. The law is the law. The entail cannot be superseded. If we had a son, we might have been able to challenge it."

"Well, we do not have a son, though with five daughters it was not for lack of trying. Your cousin might swoop down and demand Longbourn at any moment. So I suggest you at least tolerate my schemes. I am only trying to see the girls well situated." And with that, Mrs. Bennet scooped up the tea pot from the sideboard, leaving Mr. Bennet alone at the table to sip his cold tea.

CHAPTER VI

Later that morning, a footman arrived from Netherfield. When Mrs. Bennet called upstairs for Jane, all five girls came bounding down the stairs. Mrs. Bennet flushed with pleasure as Jane read the note addressed to her. "What does it say, my love? What does it say?"

"It is an invitation from Caroline Bingley. She wishes me to join her and her sister Louisa this evening for dinner."

"Will Mr. Bingley be there?"

"No, he is to dine out with the officers this evening."

"See! Even Mr. Bingley thinks it is important to entertain the regiment!" exclaimed Lydia.

Dining out—how very unlucky. There must be a way to extend Jane's visit so she could spend some time with Mr. Bingley. Mrs. Bennett frowned and paced in the foyer. While glancing at the open door where the footman stood, she raised her gaze upwards, noted the gloom of the day and the clouds overhead, and smiled broadly. "Jane, please send your acceptance; this man can't wait all day."

A grateful acceptance was writ and dispatched with alacrity.

"Mama, I will need the carriage," said Jane as her mother closed the door.

Mrs. Bennet turned and led her into the sitting room. "No, no, it is better to go on horseback."

Jane's pink lips pinched in confusion. "Why?"

Mrs. Bennet could feel Netherfield within Jane's reach, but all must be handled perfectly. "Because," she said, "it looks like it is going to rain and if it does, you will be obliged to spend the night. Then you would be able to see Mr. Bingley at breakfast and perhaps pass a pleasant afternoon in his company."

"That would be a good scheme, Mama, but what prevents them from sending her home in their own carriage?" teased Lizzy, looking up from her book.

"Because, dear heart, the gentlemen will have taken the carriage into town to dine with the officers."

"Mama, I would much rather go in a coach."

"Your father cannot spare the extra horses today. Can you, Edward?" She shot her husband a piercing look.

Mr. Bennet, seeing she was not to be thwarted, acquiesced. "Uh, no, unfortunately, Jane, they are needed on the farm."

During the day the clouds grew darker. Jane had ventured out on horseback not ten minutes and the downpour began. Mrs. Bennet sighed contentedly and congratulated herself on her triumph. The rain continued all evening, making a trip back to Longbourn impossible.

The next morning, another note arrived from Netherfield. Jane wrote that she was feeling ill with a cough and sore throat. "There now," said Mr. Bennet, "all your scheming in the pursuit of Mr. Bingley will be the death of her."

"Nonsense, Edward, healthy young girls do not die of colds. She will be well taken care of, and it prolongs her stay a bit. I would go and see for myself, but I believe the horses are still needed at the farm."

Lizzy, however, was quite anxious about Jane. She knew of a boy living in one of the cottages who'd fallen ill, initially with a cold which then developed into a serious complication of the lungs, and died. Lizzy declared she would walk to Netherfield.

Mrs. Bennet was appalled. "You will do no such thing. Think of all the dirt and mud. You will arrive looking disheveled and dirty. You will not go. It will only embarrass Jane. Let Mr. Bingley and his sisters attend to her. You are not to interfere."

Much to her consternation, Lizzy did not heed her. She left with Lydia and Kitty, walking with them as far as Meryton, and then continued on to Netherfield.

"Oh, Mr. Bennet, how can that daughter of yours be so intractable?" Mrs. Bennet paced the parlor, beside herself with frustration. "What will Bingley's sisters think of her unannounced visit? The absolute impertinence of it! Does she not see that her presence will divert care and attention away from Jane?"

Her husband shook his head, let out a deep sigh and raised his eyes heavenward. No words of censure for Lizzy or support of his wife escaped his lips.

Mrs. Bennet felt a rush of heat upon her neck and the sharp lightning bolts of pain that signaled a severe headache. She retired to her chamber, where Mary, deeply concerned, placed a cool cloth upon her brow and agreed that every impulse of feeling should be guided by reason. Mrs. Bennet sat up to look at her daughter who spoke such wisdom. She wished Edward had heard that remark from Mary. Mary may be the brightest of the bunch.

Mrs. Bennet did not have much time for repose the following day. The footman from Netherfield arrived yet again with a note, this time from Lizzy, saying Jane was ill, had spent an uncomfortable night, the apothecary had been sent for, and that Mrs. Bennet must come.

She called out to Lydia and Kitty. They must defer their plans of visiting in Meryton. No officer's tea today; Jane took priority.

The carriage was readied, and they set out for Netherfield. When Lydia and Kitty complained about missing the tea, Mrs. Bennet rubbed her temples. "Do be quiet, girls, my head still aches, and I must soon assess Jane's condition." The girls conspired amongst themselves, with Lydia trying to think of ways to engage the officers.

The day was still overcast and the gravel drive slick from yesterday's rain. The greenery and lilacs, which otherwise stood out in contrast against Netherfield's grey stone manor, appeared muted. As Mrs. Bennet stepped from the carriage, she saw Mr. Jones, the apothecary, approaching the house.

Mr. Jones was well known to her. She had turned to him often for relief from her symptoms. He was an elderly, severe looking gentleman in a plain black coat, with a sparse circle of gray hair upon his head and a gray beard grown into a small point beneath his chin, giving him a Mephisophelean appearance. But he was a kind and gentle soul, prescribing teas and suggesting she eat yams every day. Oddly, the yams did seem to relieve some of her frequent flushes of heat and perspiration. Mr. Jones was also an astute gentleman, aware of the stresses of her situation that resulted from five unmarried daughters.

He greeted her, and they made their way into the house, depositing Kitty and Lydia with Lizzy, who met them in the hall, the worry apparent in her expression. Together Mrs. Bennet and Mr. Jones entered Jane's bedchamber. She peered at Jane's throat while the apothecary took her pulse. Then she listened at Jane's back and chest while the girl took deep breaths.

Mr. Jones confirmed there was no immediate danger, just a slightly reddened throat and some nasal congestion. As he prepared to leave the sick room, Mrs. Bennet pressed his arm. "Mr. Jones, I do not think it advisable to move Jane just yet."

"Ah." Mr. Jones took her cue. "I completely agree, Mrs. Bennet."

Jane protested, but the apothecary prevailed. Mrs. Bennet smiled triumphantly, then turned to her next task. Mr. Bingley and the others waited in the breakfast room for news of Jane's condition.

Mrs. Bennet and the apothecary were ushered into the large room, where a long table held the remains of the morning repast. Lizzy, Lydia and Kitty were at the far end of the table. Mr. Darcy and Miss Bingley remained seated while Mr. Bingley rose and inquired with great concern, "I hope you have not found her condition to be worse?"

"Indeed I have," said Mr. Jones. "She is not to be moved."

Mrs. Bennet affected a woeful smile. "I am afraid we must avail ourselves a little longer of your hospitality, Mr. Bingley."

"Think nothing of it, my sister would not hear of her removal. You may depend upon it."

Mrs. Bennet looked to the raven-haired, shapely Miss Bingley, who nodded coldly. Taken aback, for she had certainly expected Miss Bingley to be endeared of her daughter, Mrs. Bennet said pointedly, "Though she is ill, Jane has the sweetest of tempers. I hope she will be of no trouble."

This remark did sufficiently embarrass Miss Bingley into offering assurances that Jane would receive every attention. Fearing that her cold manner was the result of Lizzy's presence, she sought to differentiate Lizzy's impertinent manner from Jane's. "Jane is so sweet and even tempered that I often tell my other girls they are nothing to her."

Lizzy rolled her eyes and sighed.

Seeking to make their exit on a cheerful note, Mrs. Bennet remarked on the beauty of Netherfield, specifically the arbor over the gravel walk. The colors and textures had made quite an impression on her. She then and there privately decided do a small sketch of it and present it to the Bingleys in thanks for their care of Jane. "I hope you will not be leaving soon, Mr. Bingley. I understand you have a short lease."

"At present I am quite settled here, but if I decide to leave I would go immediately, for whatever I do, I do in a hurry."

"You seem to pride yourself, dear sir, on your impulsive nature," teased Lizzy, "a quality that perhaps one should not boast. For what good is it to do everything in such a hurry? Would it not be best to be seen as a more serious gentleman, slow to make decisions, weighing them carefully before proceeding with any action?"

"Oh, you mean I must plod along like my elder friend Darcy?" Bingley gave Darcy a boyish punch. Darcy rubbed his arm.

Lizzy laughed. "Plodder or flibbertigibbet, which will it be?"

Bingley arched a brow and grinned. "So you are set on analyzing my character. What is your judgment? Am I simple or complex?"

"It is an intricate character," Lizzy mused, "playful yet compassionate, witty yet not silly. I must say that intricate characters, Mr. Bingley, are the most amusing. Don't you agree, Mr. Darcy?"

If it were possible, Miss Bingley's tight smile tightened further. Mrs. Bennet discreetly gave her daughter a light pinch fearing that Lizzy's reckless banter would ruin everything for Jane. "Lizzy, do not run on in so wild a manner," Mrs. Bennet chided.

But then Mr. Darcy, with a rising of the corner of his lip that, to Mrs. Bennet's painter's eye, displayed arrogance and a presumption of moral superiority, remarked, "I believe the countryside can in general supply but few subjects for study."

Lizzy regarded him. "All people change and alter, which would hold one's interest."

The beastly man assumed that those living in the country were just simple folk, beneath his notice! Mrs. Bennet choked back anger. "Yes indeed, there is quite a lot that goes on here as well as in town. I cannot see that London has any great advantage."

Mr. Bingley, attempting to appease both, said, "For my part, when I am in the country I never wish to leave and when I am in town I feel the same. I can be happy in both."

"You have the right disposition," Mrs. Bennet said, "but I see your gentleman friend seems to think the country nothing at all."

"Mama," Lizzy said, "Mr. Darcy only meant that there were not such a variety of people to be met with in the country as in town, which you must own to be true."

Mrs. Bennet again felt the rush of heat in her bosom. "Certainly, my dear, that is true. But Mr. Darcy was not really referring to numbers; he was referring to quality. We dine here with at least four and twenty families. I am sure that dining out in London could not number more. Else one would be exhausted, either in town or country."

Lydia, hearing the words four and twenty families,

prevailed upon Mr. Bingley to honor his promise of giving another ball. She clasped her hands, along with Kitty's, together in front of her.

Mr. Bingley, no doubt grateful for the diversion, agreed wholeheartedly to the scheme. "I am perfectly ready to give a ball, and when your sister is recovered, you shall name the day."

Upon the mention of Jane, Mrs. Bennet gathered herself and again thanked Mr. Bingley for his care of Jane. "Come, girls, Lizzy, it is time for us to be on our way."

"Excuse me, Mrs. Bennet," interrupted Mr. Jones, "but I believe that Lizzy should stay and attend her sister in the sick room until she is well enough to travel." He gave Mrs. Bennet a significant look and a subtle wink. Normally his acumen would delight her, for he too had clearly noted there were two bachelors at Netherfield. However his failure to ascertain her displeasure with Mr. Darcy's countenance and Miss Bingley's obvious dislike of Lizzy's manner diminished her appreciation of his efforts.

"Thank you Mr. Jones for your concern, but this is too much of an imposition."

"Nonsense," countered Bingley. "It is not an imposition at all. Jane must have her sister at her side to help her get well." Mrs. Bennet noted the tender concern in his voice.

Even Mr. Darcy chimed in and pompously declared, "Yes, she must stay for it is best for a sister to attend a sister in illness. I doubt dear Caroline has much experience in a sick room." Mrs. Bennet looked askance at Mr. Darcy. She couldn't decide whether he was insulting his hostess or protecting her.

Miss Bingley responded with her tight smile.

CHAPTER VII

Jane recovered, and on Saturday Lizzy sent a note home asking for the carriage, but Mrs. Bennet yet again wished to delay Jane's departure. After all, Mr. Bingley should see Jane well and thriving in her vitality. In the end, the Bingleys provided the carriage that Monday for Jane's safe return.

Mrs. Bennet had tea waiting for the girls, and endeavored to ascertain the success of the visit. It seemed that Mr. Bingley had been most attentive and appeared to have a deep interest in Jane. Lizzy reported that, for her part, it had been quite humorous watching Caroline Bingley court the favor of Mr. Darcy. She did allow that Mr. Darcy, when in a talkative mood—which was rare—was an amusing verbal sparring partner. Unfortunately, Caroline could never seem to follow the rapid exchange of wit in their conversations.

"Like goes to Like, Lizzy. Caroline Bingley with her proud manner is a good match for Mr. Darcy. I hope you have no designs on the man."

"Heavens, no."

"Just the same," Mrs. Bennet chided, "you might have annoyed Miss Bingley if Mr. Darcy was paying you particular attention."

As Lizzy reached for the pot to pour herself a cup of tea, she assured her mother that was not the case; indeed, Mr. Darcy hardly spoke ten words to her on Sunday.

Mrs. Bennet nodded, satisfied. Still, it would do well to keep Lizzy from Caroline Bingley. She hoped his sister's possible dislike of Lizzy would not reflect negatively upon Jane and ruin her matrimonial prospect with Mr. Bingley.

As for Mr. Darcy, that he should so cruelly taunt Miss Bingley by showing false interest in Lizzy—*well...* he sank even further in Mrs. Bennet's estimation.

The family was happily reunited at luncheon. Mr. Bennet proclaimed his hope for a fine dinner that night and announced that Longbourn would have an additional guest.

"I know of no guest, Edward, unless Charlotte Lucas is coming to see the girls. Charlotte is like family and will be happy with our table."

"No, Miriam, I mean a gentleman."

Mrs. Bennet looked over to Jane. "It must be Mr. Bingley. Jane! Why ever did you not warn me?" She started to rise from the table—she'd have to instruct the cook on additional preparations, the silver need to be polished, the dinner to be served on the good china, and—

Mr. Bennet interrupted her. "It is not Bingley. It is someone I have never met."

"Is it an officer?" inquired Lydia.

"No, not a scarlet coat, I am sure," replied Mr. Bennet, enjoying the game immensely.

"A tutor for me!" exclaimed Mary.

"No, it is not a tutor, my dear girl."

"Edward, I am at quite a loss as to who this mystery guest could be."

"Father, is it some sort of relation?" asked Lizzy as she eagerly speared the last piece of beef.

"Well done, my girl! It is a relation, my cousin, a Mr. Collins, whom I have never met, but who is the heir to Longbourn. He will be lodging with us during his visit."

A profound silence blanketed the table. Mrs. Bennet fixed her husband with a burning gaze. "It is an awful thing that your estate should be entailed away from your children. If it were up to me, I would have tried to do something about it, but you just acquiesced to circumstance. And now you wish us to entertain this man who, at will, can turn us out of this house!"

"Let me read you the letter he sent, my dear. You may feel differently," countered Mr. Bennet.

Mrs. Bennet settled her tea cup forcibly into the saucer and crossed her arms. "No, I am sure I will not. I think it is in extremely poor taste to call upon us for a visit. Most likely he is here to take stock of the estate, measuring and valuing all that we have which will be his own someday. I am sure it is a visit motivated by greed."

"The gentleman is a clergyman, Miriam, established at a valuable rectory. He writes of his patron, Lady Catherine de Bourgh, and his contentment with his situation, and now I quote, 'As my own father has recently passed away, I wish to establish peace with all families. The circumstance of my entail over Longbourn, I hope, will not become an obstacle to our relations and lead you to reject the olive branch. I do not wish to be the means of injuring your fine daughters and assure you to make them every possible amends."

Mr. Bennet looked pointedly at her, and she slowly comprehended that this was a man well situated and in search of a wife. Making amends would entail marrying a Bennet girl so the Longbourn estate would stay within the family. An alliance of the Bennets and the Collins would be most beneficial to both. If he were married to one of the girls, he could not very well turn out his wife's family from their home.

She rose from the table. "Girls, we will receive your father's cousin in sympathy and civility. It is no fault of his that the estate is entailed to him, and it is clear he is in search of family. As his own father passed away recently, and that elderly gentleman was the source of contention, perhaps now we can mend relations. Lizzy, Mary, Lydia and Kitty, do go change your frocks and refresh your appearance. We will dine with our new cousin tonight."

Kitty turned and asked, "What about Jane, shouldn't she change?"

"Jane looks well enough," said Mrs. Bennet. *Jane always looked well. She was for Bingley; now they would see who would be a match for Mr. Collins. And a match must be made!*

CHAPTER VIII

Mr. Collins appeared to be a fine young man, tall with wavy dark hair, serious dark eyes and a very formal manner.

"Thank you, Mrs. Bennet—cousin, if I may—for inviting me to join you for the evening repast at your table. May the good Lord bless our breaking of bread, the sustenance of life."

"So good to finally meet you." Mrs. Bennet extended her hand cordially. As he bowed, she considered that he strived perhaps a bit too much to present the image of the learned clergyman. He seemed merely to be playing at the role at present.

"I am so looking forward to meeting my five lovely cousins." At that, he blushed and stammered to add, "I have heard much about their beauty and accomplishments. As you may know, my father's passing has left me bereft of family. While administering to my parish flock keeps me quite busy, coming home at the dimming of the day to an empty house, no matter how well furnished and equipped, can leave one feeling a bit forlorn."

"Indeed." His words leaned to no other interpretation than that he was in search of a wife and hoped to find one amongst her daughters—*oh, how exciting this was!*

As they made their way to the table, Mr. Collins bowed to each daughter, shook Mr. Bennet's hand, cleared his throat and said somberly, "May I offer blessings for this family and this sumptuous feast provided by the fertile fields from the Lord's bounty?"

Mr. Bennet was quite taken aback, for his family rarely said any form of grace at table, but as this was a cousin clergyman, he acquiesced. Mr. Collins intoned in Latin, "In nomine Patris, et Filii, et Spiritus Sancti." Lizzy and her father, with heads bowed, snickered. Mrs. Bennet discreetly elbowed her husband and shushed Lizzy, for she discerned in Mr. Collins a good heart, and he seemed quite lonely in his present circumstances.

At dinner he was much taken with Jane's beauty, but Mrs. Bennet slipped into the conversation Jane's potential attachment to Mr. Bingley. She deftly steered his attention to Lizzy by drawing Lizzy into conversation that demonstrated her bright mind and entertaining personality. "Mr. Collins, what do you make of free will versus God's will?" challenged Lizzy as she passed him a plate of sliced venison.

Mr. Collins blushed as he accepted the plate almost reverentially. "'My will or Thy will,' it is an age-old question, Miss Bennet, one that I would welcome discussing with you further." There could be no doubt: Mr. Collins was captivated and had decided then and there to win Lizzy's affection.

As the meal wound to a close, Lydia and Kitty grew restless and begged to be allowed a walk to Meryton to catch a glimpse of the officers. Mary announced she would retire to her room for the evening, as she wished to engage in some serious study of a new philosophical text she was reading. Mrs. Bennet encouraged Mr. Collins, Jane and Lizzy to join Lydia and Kitty on their walk, and glad she was to get them out of the house. She needed some precious time to herself, for she wished to try her hand at recreating that lovely gravel walk and archway at Netherfield.

She set about putting up her old easel and jars of paint in the small sitting room near her writing desk, enjoying the familiar but much missed scent of linseed oil as she opened each jar.

Mr. Bennet sauntered in. Paying no attention to her activity, he said, "So, Miriam, what do you think of this Collins fellow?"

She continued to lay out her paints and parchments. Whenever she endeavored to paint, her husband inevitably appeared at her side with some necessity or some issue to distract her from her purpose. He never claimed need of her attention when she was managing the household accounts, working the menus in the kitchen or overseeing the needs of the garden. But as soon as she laid her paints upon the table, there he was, hovering about. She relented and put down her brush and gave him her attention.

"I think, Edward, that he is a young man, well settled in his parish, and he wants a wife, and I believe he has set his sights on Lizzy."

Mr. Bennet put his hands in his pockets. "I don't see how that would be a suitable match. He's much too pompous and full of himself. Lizzy would soon burst his balloon."

"He's young, and his posturing is insecurity. With a woman's guidance, he will become confident and mature into his position."

"Still, I don't think Lizzy will have him," Mr. Bennet grumbled.

"Well, she'd better take him." Mrs. Bennet emphatically snapped the legs of the easel into place. "Not only will it assure her a comfortable living, but it will secure Longbourn for the family. I hope she is not so selfish as to not see that. You must speak to her and encourage her to accept him when he asks."

"I will not ask my daughter to marry a booby just to secure a roof over my head," thundered Mr. Bennet. With that, he left in a sulk.

Mrs. Bennet sighed and looked at the blank canvas. *How else shall it be secured?* Her husband might be obstinate, but with or without his assistance, she would see her girls settled in households of their own. She squared her shoulders and resolutely picked up her brush and started to paint.

The walking party returned from Meryton in high spirits. Plans were afoot to return tomorrow evening for a dinner party at their Aunt's house. Lydia proceeded to give a full account of a new charming gentleman who was also an officer. "Oh, Mother, his name is Wickham. He is quite good-looking, with striking fair hair and the bluest of eyes."

Lizzy was busy removing her shawl, but there was a faint blush upon her cheek. Mrs. Bennet could see that Mr. Collins was watching Lizzy. He frowned.

Kitty agreed, adding, "He has a fine countenance, a good figure and very pleasing manners. Aunt Philips has invited him along with Officer Denny."

"It will be a merry group!" said Lydia.

"I would so very much like to see my sister," said Mrs. Bennet. "I will come and help with the gathering." Privately she thought: *Two more gentleman and two more daughters, Lydia perhaps for this Wickham and possibly Kitty for Officer Denny.* Granted, they were both a bit young, but an engagement could be procured for a year or two.

Still, her motives for attending had less to do with Lydia and Kitty and more to do with ensuring that Lizzy's attention stayed on Mr. Collins. She'd noticed Lizzy's blush at the mention of this new officer, Wickham. And that wouldn't do. That wouldn't do at all.

CHAPTER IX

"My dear!" Mrs. Philips enthusiastically embraced her sister. Though the girls often visited, the sisters found it difficult to take the time away from their household duties to indulge each other's company. Yet Mrs. Bennet always took comfort in the unchanging décor of her childhood home. Here, as they proceeded to the parlor, were the familiar heavy green velvet drapes striped with gold, with the matching bay window seat cushion from which she had spent so many hours gathering scenes for her paintings.

As they waited for the officers to arrive, Mr. Collins regaled them with tales of his patroness, Lady Catherine de Bourgh, and her daughter. The mention of Lady Catherine's daughter caused some concern, and Mrs. Bennet frowned and moved closer to the edge of her seat. "Mr. Collins, do you have hopes of an engagement there?"

"Oh no, Lady Catherine would never approve, and Miss de Bourgh is of ill health. Besides," he said, "my attentions are elsewhere," and he quite boldly, with a nod and a wink, indicated Lizzy, who was sitting prettily in the window seat. Mrs. Bennet sat back and smiled. "Lady Catherine always says—"

"Tell us about your house and the improvements you are making," interrupted Mrs. Bennet, thinking it might serve as an enticement to Lizzy. Now that she knew where Mr. Collins stood, it was time to work on her daughter.

"Oho!" A clatter of voices and boots arose from the entryway, and the officers entered amid much fuss with heavy cloaks hung and swords and pistols unharnessed and put aside. Mrs. Bennet could see that this Wickham was, in a word, breathtaking. Lydia was right: the bluest eyes on earth, with the look of Apollo about him. It was clear he was a cut above the other officers in manners and countenance.

At dinner, though, she was not pleased with the seating—whatever could her sister have been thinking? Oh, if only Mr. Collins hadn't gone on so long about Lady Catherine, perhaps she would have thought to check the name cards and arrange them into a more proper seating. Instead, Mr. Wickham was seated between Lydia and Lizzy with poor Mr. Collins seated near Kitty on the other side of the table. Lydia, to her credit, was a lively flirt and drew Wickham's attention easily. But Mrs. Bennet could see that Lizzy was annoyed and wished to converse with Wickham without interruption.

At the lottery table they were again seated together, Lydia, Lizzy, and Wickham, as they had no interest in the whist game being played by Officer Denny, Kitty, and Mr. and Mrs. Philips. Mr. Collins did not wish to play either, deeming it unseemly for a clergyman. Mrs. Bennet circulated amongst the tables, offering refills on muffins and drinks, but her main purpose was to maintain a cautious eye on Wickham and Lizzy. Lydia became so engrossed in the lottery game and her winnings that she allowed Wickham to be drawn off into conversation with her sister.

When Mrs. Bennet overheard the name Darcy coming from the pair, she lingered, trying to eavesdrop unobtrusively, slowly refilling their tea cups and placing extra muffins from her basket on their plates. She snapped her muffin tongs abruptly. What she heard only cemented her dislike for the proud Mr. Darcy.

This charming officer, Wickham, had actually been done out of his inheritance by the fellow—an inheritance left to him by Mr. Darcy's father! He spoke of his own father, a lawyer like Mrs. Bennet's, who had moved to Pemberley to become the elder Darcy's steward and manage the estate. The elder Mr. Darcy had treated Wickham as a second son and had intended him to have means to enter the church and be by this time in possession of a valuable living.

Mr. Collins was staring at Mr. Wickham as if he'd like to challenge him. Indeed, Mrs. Bennet chuckled that this young god should consider himself suitable material for a clergyman. He was far too lively and flirtatious for that profession. Most likely scandal would follow him if he chose that path. *No, the role of the dashing young officer suits you.* She moved to refill Mr. Collins' cup.

"Dear Mr. Collins, as a man of the church, perhaps you could explain to Lieutenant Wickham the duties you are bound to, which are so very different from the life of a military man." Her design of this interjection was twofold: first, to interrupt the intimacy of Lizzy and Wickham's conversation, and second, to draw Mr. Collins out on a subject she was sure he would present well.

Mr. Collins did not disappoint. "The clergyman's duties,"

he said authoritatively, "are to improve the Christian conscience of the community, provide guidance to those lost, offer comfort to those bereaved and celebrate the joys of the church community in baptismals and weddings."

Lizzy could not resist the bait. She looked at him with open curiosity. "How does one improve a community's conscience, Mr. Collins?"

"One improves the community through education, good works and by example, of course, Miss Bennet."

Even Lizzy could not poke fun at such sincere sentiments. Mrs. Bennet relished a feeling of satisfaction; Mr. Collins had demonstrated quite an admirable character.

Wickham, though, chuckled. "And now, Mr. Collins," he said, "you must allow me to outline the duties of one who takes regimentals. It is the duty of a soldier to not only protect and serve but to ride well, dance well and always win at cards."

Most of the party laughed, but Mrs. Bennet caught Lizzy's eye and hoped she could see that this young man was the perfect example of her oft-quoted maxim, 'Handsome is as Handsome does.'

CHAPTER X

Mr. Bingley and his sisters called on Longbourn the next day to issue their invitation to the Netherfield Ball. Mrs. Bennet could hardly temper her delight that they had made the visit in person, rather than sending a card. Even more gratifying, much attention was paid to Jane.

That was the sentiment Mrs. Bennet focused on. Though, to be honest, there was another: The Bingley sisters sat gingerly on the settee, presenting a picture of high fashion in their silk frocks and elaborate hats. They directed most of their conversation to Jane, and appeared to slightly snub Lizzy.

"Jane, we are so glad to see you well again." Caroline Bingley extended her hand.

"Yes, you look the picture of health, and I adore the lace collar you're wearing. Wherever did you get it?" inquired Mrs. Hurst.

"You must accompany us to the local shops and assist my sister in her obsessive hunt for more lace," chirped Caroline.

Mrs. Bennet watched her daughters, but Lizzy seemed unfazed by any chill that the Bingley sisters exuded. Mr. Bingley, for his part, was all charm. He asked for suggestions about the ball, making sure to include Lizzy as well as the other girls in the discussion.

Mrs. Bennet excused herself, and when she returned, she

carried the painting she had completed of the walkway at Netherfield. "Dear Mr. Bingley, Miss Bingley, Mrs. Hurst, allow me to present this little rendition of the sweet walkway and arch at Netherfield in thanks for your great care of Jane during her illness."

She could see the alarm in Lizzy's face, but she did not care. Her daughters were always anxious that their mother would mortify them in some way. It was usual for daughters their age to feel so, but she found it tiring. She was certain that this small landscape would not offend.

Mr. Bingley took the small canvas in his hands. "My word, this is extraordinary!"

Caroline Bingley rose to look at the piece. It was clear from her expression that she expected to be amused at Mrs. Bennet's attempt. Instead she gasped, "But this is delightful!"

Mrs. Bennet had the audacity to repeat the "but" with a slight chuckle. "But what did you expect, Miss Bingley?" The young woman colored slightly, but Mrs. Bennet was careful not to appear puffed up with satisfaction. Miss Bingley could present a problem for Jane. She needed to be taken down a peg and yet befriended.

"Miss Bingley," she said, "I am trying to refine my technique in portraiture. I wonder if you would pose for me. The gown you wore at our assembly, with all its intricate beading, would make for an interesting study." Miss Bingley started to protest, but it was clear she was flattered. "Please, Miss Bingley, you would be doing me a great favor."

"Capitol!" said Mr. Bingley after his sister had given her consent. "I would like to have a portrait done of my sister. Is there one of Jane?"

What a good sign was such a request! "I have some small sketches of Jane, but no formal portrait as yet." Mrs. Bennet then showed him a small miniature of Jane that sat on the mantelpiece.

"I say, that is very good, it almost captures her beauty." Jane blushed prettily from across the room.

"Would you like to have it?" asked Mrs. Bennet.

There was a hushed silence. All eyes were on Bingley as he huskily replied, "Yes, I would very much, if you can spare it."

"I have several sketches of all my daughters. I would be delighted to spare this one." She removed the miniature from its frame and watched as Mr. Bingley carefully slipped it into his breast pocket.

He patted it and said, "It is safe here close to my heart." His eyes traveled across the room to Jane's.

♦♦♦

Mrs. Bennet arrived at Netherfield the following week at a prearranged time and in possession of all her accouterments: easel, oils, and brushes. Miss Bingley was unsure about the best location for the sitting, and so Mrs. Bennet asked to see most of the rooms to check the light, requesting that Miss Bingley stand in the center of each room. Truthfully, she was thrilled to get such an intimate tour of Netherfield; now she could really see how fortunate Jane would be.

The front parlor was chosen for the best afternoon light. Miss Bingley changed into the much admired gown she'd worn at the Assembly, with its multicolored intricate beading that simulated peacock feathers from the empire bodice to the hem. Mrs. Bennet set about arranging her work station. It was decided that Miss Bingley would not be seated, as the detail on the dress and her figure would show to its best advantage standing.

The girl fretted over whether she could hold a standing position for long periods of time and so Mrs. Bennet concocted a perfect solution: she would sketch and then paint Miss Bingley's face, the position of the arms and her carriage. The dress could be brought over to Longbourn on her dressmaker stand, and Mrs. Bennet could then paint the details of the dress. Miss Bingley was delighted with the solution and complimented Mrs. Bennet on her ingenuity.

As they laughed together, the ice was broken. Miss Bingley insisted on Mrs. Bennet calling her Caroline, and Miriam graciously allowed the intimacy of first names in hopes of further cementing a bond. She was not unaware of how Caroline Bingley condescended towards herself and her family, but she would do all she could to win her over for Jane's sake. Caroline was quite pretty, and so it was easy to praise her good looks and graceful carriage. The young woman preened under the compliments.

As the sketching commenced, more civilities were exchanged and the conversation came round to marriage.

"What suitors are you rejecting, Caroline? You must be breaking the hearts of all our local gentlemen and officers."

"I care not for any local gentleman, but there is one close by but cannot be counted as local."

"Ah, a riddle. Let's see: One nearby but not local. Not residing in Meryton?" For it occurred to Miriam suddenly that perhaps the Apollo-like Wickham might suit. Caroline giggled and shook her head. "Oh, I think I know," Mrs. Bennet said gamely. "One who resides in this house and, it seems, a match well-suited for you."

Caroline clapped her hands in glee before remembering to maintain her pose. "Yes, our families suit and I adore Pemberley." They both laughed.

Both proud little peacocks. Mrs. Bennet adjusted the angle of her subject's chin. "I should have guessed. I saw him at your side for most of the assembly."

"Oh, yes, it was clear he had no interest in the local ladies." The way she said "local ladies" led Miriam to draw a slight sneer in the portrait's mouth. With all her vanity, Miss Bingley wouldn't notice, but a discerning eye might spot the artist's comment on the character of her subject. "I am hoping that at the next ball here at Netherfield, and he will feel comfortable enough to dance. As we dance he will understand through the movement of our figures, graceful and correct, that we are match. I am sure he will see that."

Despite the girl's self-possession, at the moment she seemed really quite young. "As he has been staying here so long with your brother, surely you must have garnered some inclination about his feelings?"

"Mr. Darcy is a proud man and disinclined to show much. He has complimented me on my appearance, though." But as she said this, Mrs. Bennet observed some anxiety in her countenance. "Mrs. Bennet, what are Lizzy's plans? Will she be attending the ball?"

Mrs. Bennet nearly laughed. Caroline was threatened by her Lizzy—and over Mr. Darcy, of all men! Well, there'd be no harm in reassuring her that her worries were misplaced—in fact, it would surely be just the thing to smooth the path for Jane. "Well, yes, she hopes to attend the ball. We are entertaining a distant relative at the moment, a man of the church whom I think is a very good prospect for Lizzy. Your brother was kind enough to invite him to the ball."

"How splendid!" exclaimed Caroline. The welcome news of a potential engagement for her rival had the effect of softening her whole countenance. "How is dearest Jane? You know she is our favorite."

"Jane holds you and your brother in the highest regard."

"And we her," sighed Caroline. "My brother is quite fond of Jane and carries that miniature you gave him with him everywhere."

Mrs. Bennet felt herself glow with pride. Oh, that all of her hopes for her daughters should be coming to fruition! Yet diligence and attention was still required. "Well, that is enough for today," she said, reaching for a piece of muslin to drape over the canvas.

"May I see it?"

"No, you may not. You know that is not allowed." She

wagged a finger. "I think just two more sittings are needed. Afterward, I will take the canvas with me, and if you send the dress over with its form, I should be able to complete your portrait in time for the ball. It would make a lovely display."

"Do you really think so?" asked Caroline, stepping forward.

"Oh, I do, indeed." And as she tidied up she began to think. *This might be a very respectable way to earn a livelihood. People would see the portrait and might want one themselves, or perhaps a landscape of their property and—*

"Do you think it would be too vain to display my portrait?" asked Miss Bingley.

Here, Mrs. Bennet saw her opportunity. "Perhaps it would be well to display the painting of the walkway I gave you, as well. That way you could say you were so charmed by it that you decided to show both works before you hung them." She placed the last of her brushes in her case and then turned to Caroline Bingley. "Now, no peeking."

On the carriage ride home, Mrs. Bennet ruminated. If Darcy admired the portrait, she assumed Caroline Bingley planned to offer it to him. If he accepted, then it was proof of his intentions towards her. Much the same as Charles Bingley's intentions had been clear when he had asked for that sketch of Jane.

Mrs. Bennet had Caroline Bingley for two more sittings. At each sitting she was able to probe deeper into Mr. Bingley's intentions toward Jane, though Caroline seemed more interested in discussing the loathsome Mr. Darcy.

Miss Bingley may have been besotted with Mr. Darcy, but the more time Mrs. Bennet spent at Netherfield, the more she was convinced that Charles Bingley would make his intentions known to Jane at the ball.

CHAPTER XI

There was much bustling about in the Bennet household as the girls prepared for the Netherfield Ball. New materials had been purchased in Meryton. This time, Mrs. Bennet succeeded in ensuring that the color and style of each gown perfectly suited the charms of each of her daughters.

In anticipation of a possible engagement announcement, she indulged herself as well. She wore a cream-colored gown with accents of blue to match her eyes. The pale blue pelisse added to the effect. She glowed, and in truth her daughters proclaimed her stunning. Mr. Bennet, after observing his wife's preparations and final dressing, returned to the parlor in full dress.

"Edward, you look wonderful."

"Thank you, my dear, I thought with you turning heads this evening, I'd best be at your side to make sure your head is turned my way."

Mrs. Bennet felt quite girlish as she clasped Mr. Bennet's hand and turned to look at their daughters. Jane, in a frothy blue creation, was the picture of feminine elegance. Lizzy was most striking, truly, in a peach gown flecked with subtle tones of gold. In fact, she thought that Lizzy's dark beauty outdid them all tonight. She had noted Mr. Collin's intake of breath when Lizzy entered the parlor. Perhaps there would be two engagements announced tonight!

Of the younger girls, Lydia looked lovely in a simple pale pink gown with white satin ribbon trim on the bodice and matching satin wrap. Kitty was a vision in yellow, her red hair piled high with pearls entwined in her curls. Mary, thank goodness, had finally consented to wear something other than white. A simple gown of lavender and lace with a matching lavender ribbon for her hair created quite a charming effect.

"Well, here are all my girls, the gentle colors of the rainbow. Quite an array, don't you think, Mr. Collins?" joked Mr. Bennet. Mr. Collins, struck dumb in admiration, stammered his approval. "All quite lovely, sir, perfection, really," he said. But his eyes were only for Lizzy.

Mrs. Bennet was thrilled to see her two paintings displayed in the foyer at Netherfield with a small elegant card underneath naming her as the artist. She received many compliments and inquiries about her work. "The execution of the gown is exquisite. Why it almost seems to shimmer as you gaze at it from different angles!" exclaimed Lady Lucas.

Mrs. Bennet was proud of her art on display and her art

at matchmaking. All was proceeding as planned. She could see Jane and Mr. Bingley in deep conversation. She turned to Lady Lucas, flushed with the success of both her achievements and raised her voice so she could be heard over the music. "I believe we will be celebrating a soon-to-be-announced engagement."

Lizzy shushed her. "Mama, do not be so indiscreet."

Mrs. Bennet turned to her. "I have it on good authority from his sister that he cares a great deal for Jane and has serious intentions towards her. Discretion is not needed when love is in the air."

She nodded meaningfully to Lizzy as Mr. Collins crossed the floor to take her hand for the two dances promised to him. Lizzy sighed and looked back at her mother to indicate her disapproval. Was that glance of scorn for her or was it indicative of her feelings towards Mr. Collins? *Mr. Collins has only offered his admiration and there is no cause to scorn him. Lizzy must be made aware of the importance of securing Mr. Collins' suit.*

The dance began, but soon her concern only increased. She could see that Mr. Collins struggled through the two dances with Lizzy. Lizzy unsmiling and silent, held herself stiffly and was clearly bored with her partner. She also seemed to be searching the floor, looking over her partner's shoulder toward the door. Was she searching for young Wickham?

No, she couldn't be. Mrs. Bennet had learned from Caroline Bingley that Wickham was not held in high estimation by Darcy and so most likely would not attend the ball. *A relief.* She distracted herself from her worries about Lizzy by searching out the rest of her girls.

Jane and Bingley looked like a fairy book picture of a romantic couple on the dance floor. Lydia and Kitty giggled among the circle of officers seeking their attention, while Mary was conversing with Mrs. Long's nieces. Miss Bingley, whose elegant magenta gown with black pearl beading nearly outshone that of the painting, danced with Mr. Darcy, but he did not seem particularly attentive to his partner's chatter.

After the first set, Lizzy returned to sit near her mother. "Lizzy," Mrs. Bennet hissed, "please show your cousin some consideration."

Lizzy's eyes watched the promenading couples. "Mother, I know what you hope for but it shall not be."

"How can you—" She quieted as Mr. Collins returned. Before she could pinch Lizzy's arm and force her attention to Mr. Collins, the next reel started and Mr. Darcy crossed the floor, bowed low and held out his hand to Lizzy. Mrs. Bennet was so startled she nearly blurted "No," but Lizzy, the spark in her eyes evidence that she was enjoying the affront to her mother and Mr. Collins, curtsied deeply and accepted his hand.

All eyes were upon them, for they did make a handsome couple. Lizzy's gown shimmered with every twirl and movement. Darcy threw his head back and laughed at some comment she made—perhaps the first time anyone of this company had heard the man laugh. Mr. Collins asked Charlotte Lucas to partner with him, and Charlotte, endeavoring to distract him from his cousin's rejection, gently guided him through the steps. Mrs. Bennet glanced over at Caroline Bingley. The girl had become quite pale and her mouth was quivering.

At the break from the next set of dancing, refreshments were served. Mary, at the piano, sang a Scottish aire. Though her voice was light and pleasing, the tone and pitch were a bit lacking. Miss Bingley stared scornfully at Mary; Mrs. Hurst was smirking. Mary took the polite applause that followed as a request for more, but as she opened her mouth, Mr. Bennet, disengaging from the group of cigar-smoking gentlemen on the patio, intervened, suggested that other young ladies be allowed to display their vocal talents. A collective sigh of relief circled the room. *Well,* Mrs. Bennet thought as the next singer, barely tuneful, began, *at least Mary was not the worst one.* The poor child was just seeking some attention to define herself; in one way or another. That was true of every young lady.

"Mr. Bennet," she whispered to her husband, "do dance the next set with Mary," and he readily agreed. To her horror, Darcy again requested Elizabeth's hand. As some of the elders were also dancing, Mrs. Bennet took it upon herself to seek Mr. Collins as a partner. This situation must be rescued.

They danced a few steps of the contra dance, a reel Mrs. Bennet had loved in her younger days. The steps were faster than she remembered, though, and before her breath could escape her, she said, "As you know, Mr. Collins, our girls must dance with the gentlemen hosts of the ball. It is only polite."

"Yes, I understand that," Mr. Collins replied stiffly. "But it appears that more than politeness is in evidence."

"Perhaps for Jane that is so. But I assure you, Mr. Collins that Lizzy actually detests the man she is dancing with almost as much as I do. I think he is trying to make up for insulting her at the last ball. He refused to dance with her."

"Why on earth did he refuse?"

Mrs. Bennet grasped Mr. Collins' left arm as she completed her turn from the circle. "I have no idea, Mr. Collins. Mr. Darcy seems a very proud man and thinks quite a lot of himself."

"Darcy!" replied Mr. Collins. His eyes widened with growing alarm.

"Yes," said Mrs. Bennet. "What is the matter?"

"He is the nephew of my patroness, Lady Catherine de Bourgh. I must pay my respects to him, Madam." He bowed to Mrs. Bennet as the dance ended. "I find myself most relieved to learn of his identity, for you see, I believe he is to be engaged to Miss de Bourgh, Lady Catherine's daughter. I believe that is Lady Catherine's wish."

How astonishing! Poor Caroline Bingley! Here was Mr. Darcy, presenting himself through friendship as a potential suitor to Mr. Bingley's sister, all the while dancing and blatantly flirting with Lizzy, and yet promised to another girl entirely. What a duplicitous, cold-hearted man!

Mr. Collins approached Mr. Darcy, bowed low and spoke of his connection to his aunt. Mrs. Bennet, from her seat across the room, observed the way Mr. Darcy condensed to Mr. Collins' remarks with an arrogant smirk and a curt nod. Lizzy, interrupted at the first opportunity, took Mr. Collins' hand and returned to her family table. Mrs. Bennet watched Darcy's eyes follow her. Caroline Bingley noted it as well.

The evening was winding down. "Oh, Mr. Bennet," Mrs. Bennet fretted as her husband gathered their coats, "what a trying evening. This has not gone at all as I hoped." The one bright light was Jane, who now stared wistfully across the room at Mr. Bingley as he acknowledged his departing guests.

As the guests made to leave, several crowded around the paintings on display. Mr. Bingley was exclaiming about the landscape and added that he adored the portrait of his sister—"Both well executed, don't you agree, Darcy?"

"Indeed, both seem absolute true renderings." He looked at Mrs. Bennet before saying, "Take, for example, Caroline's smile."

"If you truly admire the portrait, I will offer it to you, sir." Caroline Bingley's tone was light, but Mrs. Bennet could not miss the fury in her gaze when Mr. Darcy declined, declaring that it would not be proper for him to take it from her dear brother who adored it so. She felt a pang of sympathy as the girl attempted a gay laugh of indifference.

Lord Lucas admired the landscape and asked the price of getting one done of his family home.

Mrs. Bennet was gratified by the response. "Lord Lucas, you will be my first commission." Then she heard Mr.

Darcy murmur to Mr. Bingley.

"Surely she does not mean to accept remuneration for her artistry? Are you supposed to pay her for Caroline's likeness?"

Mrs. Bennet turned toward this most unlikable man. Her chest flushed, and she wished for a full glass of punch that she could pour down his vest. "The landscape was a gift of thanks for Mr. Bingley's tender care of Jane when she was ill; the portrait also is a gift, as I particularly requested Miss Bingley to sit for it as a practice of my skill."

"How long did you have to pose?" inquired Mrs. Long.

"Oh it was wonderful, she sketched and painted me in three sittings, and I didn't have to wear the gown while doing so. I sent the dress over on its dressmaker form, and Mrs. Bennet was then able to replicate it. It saved weeks of my standing in a heavy gown."

"I should like you to do the same, Miriam, for my nieces," said Mrs. Long. "I would love to have portraits of them in their coming out ball gowns. We shall discuss the price privately."

"So she does intend on charging and selling her work," Mr. Darcy said to Mr. Bingley. "Most unseemly!"

Mrs. Bennet drew her shoulders back as though girding herself for battle, ignoring the concern she could see on Mr. Bennet's face. "And what would you prefer, Mr. Darcy? After all, there is an expense of oils, canvas, brushes and time. And does not Mr. Reynolds, a well-known portrait painter, also accept remuneration for his commissions?"

"But that is his profession."

"And this may be my profession as well. Should I not be compensated?"

"He is a man and you are a married woman. Marriage is your profession."

Mrs. Bennet raised a brow. "And if a woman does not marry?"

"Well, then, she is supported by her family or may become a governess, I suppose, or a lady's maid, depending on her social standing."

"Ah, of course, Mr. Darcy, the social norms are unfortunately just as you say." Mrs. Bennet looked down at her feet demurely, appearing to acquiesce to this pompous man. But when she looked up, she made sure to catch the eye of every female in the group. A ripple of sympathy passed through the women. Charlotte Lucas lifted her head high; Lizzy pressed her arm in support. Caroline Bingley looked at her brother, and Mrs. Hurst was gazing resentfully at her husband.

Lord Lucas coughed and interrupted. "Be that as it may, Miriam, I really do want a painting of the family home. Will you come tomorrow and consider starting the sketch? We can discuss the particulars after dinner tomorrow."

"And my nieces are coming down to me again in a fortnight. Will you see them?" asked Mrs. Long.

"Of course," Mrs. Bennet replied. She turned to glance one more time at Caroline's portrait, her eyes traveling to the sneer in Caroline's mouth. Her eyes met Mr. Darcy's and she looked pointedly at his mouth before she turned away.

In the carriage, Kitty and Mary, exhausted, slept soundly. Mr. Collins and the other girls had taken the second carriage. Into the silence, Edward finally spoke. "You went too far, Miriam. You went too far. Why must you always speak your mind? There will be repercussions from this."

Mrs. Bennet responded gently. "Edward, even if we had all the money in the world, I would paint, and I would accept remuneration as a show of respect for my work. I am sorry that displeases you, but the revenue will help us in our situation." At his hurt look, she took his hand. "More importantly, I have come to realize that I want more than marriage and motherhood. I have returned to my authentic self and it makes me happy."

CHAPTER XII

In the morning, Mrs. Bennet found Mr. Collins pacing outside the kitchen door. She sent Cook out to collect the eggs and invited their cousin to sit and join her for tea. But he shook his head. "May I request, Madam, a private audience with your second daughter, Elizabeth?"

Oh, this was it! Everything was falling into place. "By all means, my dear Mr. Collins. After breakfast I shall arrange it in the front parlor."

When the family and Mr. Collins had breakfasted, Mrs.

Bennet asked Lizzy to search for the needlework, which she had left in the front parlor. As soon as Lizzy left the table, Mrs. Bennet gave Mr. Collins the nod and he followed in pursuit. By the time Lizzy turned with the needlework in hand, Mr. Collins stood before her. "I have something I wish to say to you, Miss Bennet."

Lizzy saw her mother at the door and tried to put Mr. Collins off. "Here, Mama, is your needlework."

Mrs. Bennet took the needlework. "Stay and hear him out," she hissed, then turned and shut the door.

She stayed outside the door, pacing as she listened to his plea. It was quite prettily said. Mr. Collins listed the qualities he admired in Lizzy: her spirit, her liveliness, her humor, her beauty. He pointed out the advantages he could offer her and the opportunity for her family to continue at Longbourn. He offered a nice, well-furnished home and a generous yearly income that would not cause her to want. There would be no need for any dowry or to enact the entail upon Longbourn until all her sisters were married and her parents settled in their old age, either in their home or one of her sisters'. What more could one ask for? *This is a happy day!* thought Mrs. Bennet. She leaned in to hear the response, but Lizzy's voice was so low she could not make it out.

Soon the doors flew open and Mr. Collins appeared, flushed. Mrs. Bennet opened her arms and said, "Let me be the first to wish you joy."

"There is no joy here, Madam, she has refused me."

Lizzy, behind him, was looking fixedly down at the

carpet.

"Surely not, Mr. Collins, perhaps Lizzy just wishes to be asked again. A lady sometimes refuses at first and wants more wooing. It was that way with Mr. Bennet and me," she soothed.

"If that be the case I shall entreat again," and he turned. "Miss Bennet, I—"

"Not now, my dear Mr. Collins." She gently, yet determinedly steered Mr. Collins toward the entryway and directed him to a walk in the garden. "Let me speak with her and then tomorrow you may pursue your suit."

When she returned to the parlor, Lizzy was seated looking out the window. "Have you gone mad, Lizzy? Mr. Collins is a fine young man, and he offers your family stability from the entail."

A moment passed before she met her mother's gaze. "Is that why I should accept him?"

"Well, it is one of the very good reasons. He is learned, good-looking, and comfortably well off."

"He has no wit, Mama."

"No wit, no wit!" Mrs. Bennet heard the screech in her voice. "What a spoiled girl you are, Lizzy. Whom are you setting your cap for? It best not be Mr. Darcy, for he thinks himself well above your station, my girl, and only flirts with you to torment Caroline Bingley. And even that poor girl is in for a shock as it is rumored he is to be engaged to his cousin, Lady Catherine de Bourgh's daughter!" She found that she had been walking from one end of the room to the other, and she halted. "And if Mr. Darcy did have a notion in your direction, I would not allow it, for there lies only unhappiness and inequality in such a match. Did you not hear him on a woman's profession as marriage?"

"And what are you promoting, Mama, but that very fact!"

This caught Mrs. Bennet up short, for it was true; she was promoting this marriage as Lizzy's way to stability and comfort. She sighed. "Yes, Lizzy, and I am sorry it is this way. We have very little recourse but to make a good match for our financial stability. As Mr. Darcy says, there is little left to us other than governess positions or a life in service. Please consider Mr. Collins's proposal. He is a good man, and perhaps you can teach him to appreciate your wit. He is a sincere, well-meaning person, Lizzy. You could not say that of Mr. Darcy."

"It isn't Mr. Darcy that is the obstacle. It is the person of Mr. Collins. I find him a bit ridiculous."

"He is a bit pompous," she allowed. "But it is because he is still young and insecure in his position. A good woman will help him grow."

"I have no desire to be his governess," snapped Lizzy.

"And if you don't accept him you may end up being someone else's governess." With that Mrs. Bennet went to seek the counsel of her husband.

"Well, Edward, Mr. Collins has proposed, and Lizzy has refused him."

Mr. Bennet, snugly ensconced in his favorite chair in the library, sucked his teeth in irritation at being interrupted in the perusal of his newspaper. "What can you expect,

Miriam, after your display last night? She seeks her own independence as well. Besides, he's a bit of a ninny."

"Edward! This young man offers your daughter a comfortable home, expects no dowry, offers our family a home in Longbourn until all our daughters are married, and offers to care for us in our old age. He is a good-hearted young man and your making occasional sport of his sensibility with Lizzy has not helped the matter. As for independence, Lizzy has no special talent to make her way in the world."

"She has wit and intelligence."

"And what will that get her, Edward?"

"Perhaps a more suitable match for her sensibility."

It was no use—her husband was blind when it came to Lizzy; he saw too much of himself in her. "There is another young man," sighed Mrs. Bennet, "an officer by the name of Wickham. He is witty, slightly sarcastic, and I am certain he appeals to Lizzy, but there is something of a rogue about him. Perhaps we should invite him to dine at Longbourn with some of the other officers."

"I am sorry if Mr. Collins is heartbroken," he said. "But we cannot expect Lizzy to barter herself in exchange for our comfort." As he spoke, Mr. Bennet glanced out the library French door and saw through the opening in the hedge, Mr. Collins in the Lucas's garden seated on a bench, with Charlotte Lucas sitting sympathetically at his side. "I'm sure Mr. Collins will recover quickly."

CHAPTER XIII

An invitation to a Bennet family dinner had been dispatched to Mr. Bingley, and now the footman was at the door with his reply. Mrs. Bennet opened the note and slowly sank into her chair.

"What is it, Mama?" asked Jane, seeing her mother stare distractedly out the window. Jane and Lizzy sat on the parlor couch working on their embroidery.

Mrs. Bennet struggled for some composure and tried to answer with a lightness in her voice that would disguise her anxiety.

"I have just received a reply from Mr. Bingley regarding our dinner invitation, and it seems the whole party is leaving for London tomorrow and he cannot venture a guess as to the date of his return. He says to pay his respects to all the lovely ladies of Longbourn, and he wishes them well."

Jane looked like she had been slapped. Mrs. Bennet rose to comfort her. "Dear girl, gentlemen are often called away on pressing business. You know he keeps a residence in London as well as here. I'm sure he will send you a private note, assuring you of his affection and his speedy return."

But no note arrived that day, and the party had quit Netherfield early the next morning. At dinner, the family gathered and the mood was somber. Blessedly, Lady Lucas had invited Mr. Collins to dine. "What could have caused them to leave with such alacrity?" Mrs. Bennet lamented.

Jane, with tear-stained cheeks, had no reply, but Lizzy answered in anger. "What could have caused this? My God, Mother, with the way this family behaved at the ball it is no wonder Charles is reconsidering his affection for Jane."

"Lizzy!" What do you mean?"

"Well, for one, Mary, insisting on singing her fool head off and Lydia and Kitty flirting shamelessly with the officers. Then there was you loudly boasting about Jane's potential engagement, and then Mr. Collins presenting himself to Mr. Darcy in a most supercilious manner. Finally, there was you again, Mama, having your wares displayed like a common tradesman, seeking commissions and expounding on your new profession as an artist for hire."

"Lizzy," Mr. Bennet intervened, "Mary sang only one song."

"Only because you were able to stop her," countered Lizzy. At that, her sister burst into tears and fled from the table.

"Thank you, Edward, for your defense of poor Mary." Mrs. Bennet rose slowly from the table, aware that the family expected her to flee to her room, claiming weakness, flushing with heat and migraines. Instead she shocked them all.

She turned toward Lizzy, keeping her voice low and measured. "Mary is your sister and deserves your support. Lydia and Kitty were dancing and conversing appropriately with officers of the regiment under the watchful eye of your father. Mr. Collins is a cousin and only offered you admiration and his heart. Miss Caroline Bingley, in our sittings, had assured me of her brother's deep affection for Jane; an engagement was expected. Miss Bingley is the one who wished to display my 'wares,' as you so dismissively title them. She had hopes of presenting her portrait to Mr. Darcy. His acceptance would have signaled his intentions towards her."

Lizzy began to protest, but Mrs. Bennet spoke over her. "However, Mr. Darcy was quite distracted during the ball. It was clear to all his attention was elsewhere. With your wit and charm you proceeded to mortify our hostess. You danced two sets with Mr. Darcy, making quite an impression, and you were engaged in conversation with him for most of the evening, until your cousin paid his respects to him and prudently escorted you back to the family table."

"It was I who escorted him back. He was making a fool of himself," sneered Lizzy.

Mrs. Bennet silenced Lizzy with an icy glare. *I have had enough of your impudence* "It appears to me that the cause of their sudden departure has been motivated by the actions of yourself and Mr. Darcy. Caroline Bingley obviously wishes to remove him from Netherfield in hopes of kindling his affection for her, though I doubt Darcy's indifference is because of you, dear girl. He is promised to his cousin, Lady Catherine de Bourgh's daughter. Still, your heedless behavior at the ball put at risk your sister's happiness!"

Mrs. Bennet moved to stand behind Jane and patted her shoulder. "Jane, I am sorry that Mr. Bingley has returned to London. And in a few weeks' time, perhaps you will consider visiting your aunt and uncle in London. Your paths may cross and you may revisit the affection you had for each other. Caroline will receive you as long as Lizzy is not present. I do not believe that Mr. Bingley could love you less because your sister sang a song or your mother was excited in her anticipation of an engagement and likes to paint. You heard how publicly he expressed his favor for the miniature of you and the likeness of his sister." She looked toward Lizzy. "There is no shame in what I am doing. The shame is in how you, dear Lizzy, hold your family in contempt."

Mrs. Bennet turned to her husband. "Edward, I promised Sir William I would meet with him today to discuss the preliminary sketching of his home."

She left the dining room steeped in chagrined silence and quietly made her way through the garden towards the Lucas estate. When she returned, Mr. Bennet had retreated into the library, Jane, Lydia and Kitty had retired to their rooms, and Lizzy still sat at the table, quietly sobbing.

CHAPTER XIV

In the privacy of their bedchamber that evening, Edward Bennet expressed his sorrow and dismay at all that had occurred. "Miriam, do you really think Lizzy was the cause of Bingley leaving?"

She sighed. "All I know is that I watched Caroline Bingley grow agitated by the attention Mr. Darcy was bestowing on Lizzy. It is clear that Mr. Darcy looks down on country families and dislikes women of strong opinion; on two separate occasions I have challenged his opinions. Between Miss Bingley's jealousy and Mr. Darcy's prejudice that his friend not marry into a country family, those two forces were enough to propel the whole party back to London."

"But what of Bingley? Has he no spine?"

"It appears that he is a gentleman who is easily influenced." Mrs. Bennet, seated at her vanity, carefully finished her last brush stroke. "He has such an agreeable nature, which I thought perfectly suited to Jane's. However, he is a gentleman who, wanting to please all, avoids any discomfort. My one hope is that in London, if Jane stays with the Gardiners, Bingley will meet my brother, a man with the greatest sensibility married to a woman of grace and accomplishment. He will see that a respectable tradesman in London is not an inferior connexion at all. Then he may resume his suit towards Jane."

"You were very hard on Lizzy, Miriam."

"Oh, Edward, she cannot have been unaware of Caroline Bingley's hopes! She was in that house for over a week, and Lizzy is a quick study of character. So I do fault her for her pride and not taking into consideration how it would affect Jane. Perhaps I am so angry over her rejection of Mr. Collins that it caused me to be more vexed than usual. However, Lizzy does have a tendency to sneer at us, especially me and, quite frankly, I am tired of it."

"But how will we all get on together?" asked Mr. Bennet. Mrs. Bennet fluffed her pillow and reached over to extinguish the candle.

"Edward, I will not apologize. She will have to make amends to me."

Walking the grounds with Lord Lucas, Mrs. Bennet noted the fine structure of the house, the weathered grey stone façade, and the cobbled walkways, all surrounded by glorious gardens lush in white and purple lilacs. It was a fine example of a country estate, simple and charming. As they turned past the hedge, they came upon Mr. Collins strolling with Charlotte Lucas. The couple appeared to be deeply engrossed in conversation, with attention only for each other.

Mr. Collins's continued stay with the Bennets was uncomfortable at best. She did not encourage him to repeat his request for Lizzy's hand, and Lizzy took every opportunity to avoid being alone in his presence. On her subsequent visits to sketch the Lucas home, Mrs. Bennet often saw Mr. Collins walking in the gardens with Charlotte. And soon Mr. Collins announced his engagement.

As the Bennets were his only living family, a small wedding was held at the local church, attended by the Bennets, the Lucases and six other families. Lizzy acted as Charlotte's attendant, and Mr. Bennet stood in for Mr. Collins. Along with a generous dowry, Lord Lucas bestowed on his daughter the lovely painting of her family home that Mrs. Bennet had completed.

After the wedding supper, the couple left for Kent. Lizzy said her goodbyes to her dearest friend, trying bravely not to cry. Mrs. Bennet watched, feeling sympathy for her heartache. As they walked back to Longbourn, Lizzy, with a catch in her throat said, "Mama, the painting you made of Charlotte's home was beautiful and I am sure she will take great comfort in it. Oh, Mama, I am so sorry to be the cause of so much unhappiness... Jane's heartbreak, and the possible loss of our home."

Mrs. Bennet brushed a tear from her daughter's cheek. "Sit here a moment in our garden with me, and let us make amends. You did not cause Jane's heartbreak. Bingley did."

"Yes, but he went away because of my..."

"He went away because he is easily influenced and is not yet a man who knows his own heart. If he cannot withstand an outspoken mother-in-law and a sister-in-law who sings off-key, then he is not man enough for Jane."

"Our home is still under the entail," Lizzy said. "I see

now how Mr. Collins' offer was more than generous."

"Lizzy, you cannot marry a man to save our home. It was wrong of me to expect that. Your father and I must do that. And if the home is entailed and we must leave, so be it. Right now Mr. Collins will be quite preoccupied with setting up his new household in Hunsford for his bride. I doubt he will exercise his ownership rights so quickly. Are you regretting the loss of Mr. Collins or of Charlotte?"

"Charlotte, Mama. With Jane preparing to go to London and Charlotte gone, there is not much left for me."

"I believe, dear Lizzy, that a few trips to Meryton might be amusing." Lizzy colored a bit. "With my artist's eye," chuckled Mrs. Bennet, "while at my sister's for dinner, I think I ascertained there was some interest in a young Apollo."

"Apollo?" asked Lizzy confusedly.

"My secret name for Wickham. He has wit, which, as I well know, is a priority for you," she teased. Here, Lizzy blushed furiously. Mrs. Bennet stood, put her arm around Lizzy's shoulder, and led her toward the house. "I think we should have several dinner parties for members of the regiment. I know that Officer Denny is partial to Kitty. And Lydia"—Mrs. Bennet laughed—"seems to like them all!"

CHAPTER XV

Mrs. Bennet made good on her promise and hosted several dinners and afternoon picnics where Wickham was in attendance. It was clear to her that this was where Lizzy's interest lay. Wickham certainly seemed partial to her, but he was such a charmer that he flirted with all, even Mrs. Bennet! Mr. Bennet frequently rolled his eyes, but he grew accustomed to the visitors and relaxed into the role of host when the mood struck him. He liked to see Lizzy happy, and Wickham seemed able to keep her in good spirits.

The other girls were fortunate as well. Officer Denny paid suitable attention to Kitty, while Lydia flirted with each new officer brought to the table. On one or more occasions though, Mrs. Bennet thought she observed some competition between Lizzy and Lydia for Wickham's attention.

Jane made an effort to join in the fun, but it was clear she was still pining for Bingley. Mrs. Bennet decided it was time to send Jane to visit her uncle in London. She had received two well-paid commissions for the portraits of Mrs. Long's nieces; Mrs. Long had been well pleased with the results and had sent the nieces back to Kent with their treasures. The resulting commission would support Jane's visit to London at least for a fortnight.

A shopping trip to Meryton was arranged. At the dressmaker, as Jane's new gowns were fitted, the seamstress entertained them with local gossip. "Oh, those boys of the regiment, they are the wild ones. One of them we calls 'the handsome hunter' has finally landed his prey."

Mrs. Bennet laughed good-naturedly. "I believe we know him. We dubbed him 'Apollo.' Pray tell what the name of his prey is, is she a pretty bird with lovely brown plumage?"

"I don't know about any brown plumage. Maybe he keeps that one in another cage." The dressmaker winked. "This one is a sickly looking dove with a pale eye and wheat-colored feathers. This one's cage is gilded."

Sickening suspicion swirled in her stomach, but she struggled to keep her voice light. "Oh, do stop talking in riddles. Your news is safe with us."

The seamstress laughed. "True enough, Mum, and I'll gladly share it for it won't be secret for long. That young blond officer, Wikem, I believe his name is, though perhaps he should be known more rightly as "Wicked," has proposed to Miss King, whose dear father has just passed and left her six thousand pounds a year. He was at her side providing comfort, if you get my meaning, Mum. Don't think the family is too pleased, though."

Jane, who had just stepped out of the final gown being pinned, hurried into her own garments. Mrs. Bennet likewise gathered her things as quickly as she could, trying to maintain her composure. The seamstress draped the gown over her arm. "Do you wish to wait, Mum, or shall I send them over later?"

"Please send them. Thank you."

Outside, Mrs. Bennet found she could hardly breathe.

Jane started to sob. "Oh poor Lizzy, Mama!"

"He is incorrigible," hissed Mrs. Bennet. "Wicked, indeed. And Lizzy will have to be told."

Jane clasped her arm. "Perhaps she can go to London with me?"

Mrs. Bennet shook her head, her mouth firm. "If you are to see Bingley at all, or his sister, Lizzy should not be at your side." After they had both been handed up into the carriage, she said, "Perhaps enough time has passed, and Lizzy would like to visit her friend Charlotte in her new home to see how she's getting on."

Mrs. Bennet entered the library and shut the door. "I am sorry to intrude, dear, on your reading, but something has happened." Mr. Bennet looked up, startled by Mrs. Bennet's tone.

"Has someone died?"

"No, Edward, but I fear we will have another broken heart in the household, and to a young girl it can feel like a sort of death. Wickham is engaged to another."

"To another?"

"Yes, he has formed an alliance with a Miss King, a young lady who has come into considerable means."

Mr. Bennet started to pace. "How do you know this?"

"Our source was just a seamstress's gossip. But in a woman's world that is usually reliable."

"Even if it is just a rumor, Lizzy deserves to be told."

Mrs. Bennet agreed but hardly had the heart to crush her daughter's spirit. The decision was made for her when later that evening, a note arrived, brought in by the post and addressed to Miss Elizabeth Bennet. Mrs. Bennet received it and knew immediately that it was from Wickham.

She called for Jane. "Jane, have you told your sister of the seamstress's tale?"

"Not yet, Mama, I was thinking perhaps we should wait; it might not be true."

She nodded. "I have a note that has come for your sister. Take it to her but be close by for comfort. I will go up to her afterwards and propose a visit to Charlotte."

Jane left and slowly made her way upstairs not relishing her messenger's chore.

Mrs. Bennet paced in the library. "I blame this on that hateful Mr. Darcy."

Mr. Bennet inhaled deeply, anxiously puffing on his pipe. "Mr. Darcy? What has he to do with this? Miriam, your hatred for that man is becoming an obsession. How is he at all involved in this?"

"Humph," Mrs. Bennet said. "If you paid half as much attention to my conversation as you do to your paper you would know that Darcy has withheld an inheritance rightly allowed to Mr. Wickham by Mr. Darcy's father. So Wickham is reduced to living in meager circumstances, and forced to marry a wife with adequate means. Wickham has spoken of Mr. Darcy's ill treatment of him to Lizzy."

"If Wickham was seeking a wife of means, continually dining at our table was quite duplicitous of him."

She sighed. "Perhaps he could not help it, for I truly believe he has sincere affection for Lizzy."

Too anxious to wait longer, she left the library and climbed the stairs to Lizzy and Jane's bedchamber, listening for any sobs of distress. When she opened the door she found Lizzy calmly folding up Wickham's note. Jane was seated beside her.

"How are you, Lizzy?"

"Not surprised, Mother."

Relief washed over her at the same time as indignation. "Not surprised? You mean you knew of Mr. Wickham's courtship of Miss King?"

"I mean I am not surprised that he wishes to marry for means. Isn't that what we all are supposed to do? I was supposed to marry Mr. Collins, Jane was supposed to form an alliance with Mr. Bingley. I am sorry for you, Jane, for I do believe there was true affection on both sides. I admit that Wickham's wit suited me, Mother, but I knew I had very little to entice him to walk the bridal path with me. I did have some hope that his circumstances would change, and the lack of a dowry or yearly income would not matter."

Her face was pale, but her gaze seemed at peace. "You do not seem upset, Lizzy."

"No, Mother." She stood and placed the letter on her nightstand. "I am just resigned to the fact that I have no prospects, and I know you needn't remind me that it is a fate I brought on myself."

At this Lizzy did start to tear up, and she sat again. Mrs. Bennet sat beside her. "A change of scenery for a bit would be helpful, perhaps a visit to your friend Charlotte? Would that cheer you? Or do you actually pine for Mr. Collins and resent Charlotte's comfort?"

Lizzy smiled. "No, I do not pine for Mr. Collins, and I would love to see Charlotte."

Mrs. Bennet patted her hand. "I have to admit, Lizzy, I am surprised at your lack of feeling regarding Wickham's engagement, but I am happy for it."

"I think, Mother, I sensed in him some inconsistency of character and a lack of moral fiber."

Mrs. Bennet chuckled. "Well, there is no pleasing you, Lizzy. Mr. Collins' pious consistency and respectability you found dull, and you found Wickham deficient in the very things for which you despised Mr. Collins. However, I agree with you about Wickham. His looks and manner are a little too pleasing. There is something about him I did not totally trust, though he is an engaging rogue."

"But Mama, do you not think a woman's influence would improve him as you thought for Mr. Collin?" teased Lizzy.

"I think perhaps Mr. Wickham's self-interest would be difficult to tame. One senses there is something of an opportunist about him, but, as you say, that may come from necessity," concluded Mrs. Bennet. "So, girls, it is settled; Jane to return to London with the Gardiners when they come to visit and Lizzy to Hunsford. I will tell Lydia the news. I think it's time we get a rest from entertaining any more officers."

Mrs. Bennet stood, feeling contented about Lizzy's state

of mind. As she shut the door behind her, she saw Jane turn to Lizzy. "You don't fool me with your wit," Jane whispered. She opened her arms and Lizzy quietly sobbed.

Down the hall in their bedroom, Kitty was busy trying to fashion Lydia's hair into a crown of ringlets. "Doesn't she look stunning?" Kitty crowed, pleased with her handiwork, as her mother entered.

Mrs. Bennet agreed and complimented her on her creation. "What is the occasion?"

"We thought that perhaps Aunt would give another dinner with Officer Wickham and Officer Denny."

"Girls, I have some sad news," said Mrs. Bennet. Lydia was half listening, gazing at herself in the mirror as Kitty continued to pin more curls into place. "There will be no more visits to Meryton for a while."

"Is our aunt not feeling well?"

"No, my sister is fine."

"Then why?"

Mrs. Bennet sighed and interrupted the next round of petitions. "Girls, I have just learned that Mr. Wickham has become engaged to a Miss King." Lydia's eyes flew open; she began to take short, rapid breaths. Then she stiffened, let out a moan and slumped forward. She started to howl and burst into tears. Kitty threw her arms around her to comfort her. Mrs. Bennet was stunned. "Lydia, what is the meaning of this? I had no idea you cared for him, you were always flirting with so many different officers."

"Only to make him jealous," sobbed Lydia.

"I am so sorry, my dear, I had no idea. I was more

worried about how Lizzy would take it."

Lydia sniffed. "He didn't care for Lizzy."

"How do you know that?" She spoke low and soothingly, stroking Lydia's curls.

"Because whenever he was in conversation with Lizzy, he always looked over at me with a wink and would roll his eyes at her prattle. He even said once, 'Lizzy or Lydia, which one is fairer?' And then he said I was a 'delicious girl', full of life, with an adventurous nature well-suited to be a wife of a regiment officer.' Who is this Miss King?"

Mrs. Bennet, still reeling from Lydia's revelation, said, "She is a girl with an income of six thousand pounds a year."

With that, Lydia started to howl again. Mrs. Bennet's head throbbed, and she left Lydia to Kitty's ministrations.

As the door closed Lydia sobbed, "He would have chosen me if I had a dowry."

"What is all that caterwauling?" Mr. Bennet asked irritably. Pale and shaken, Mrs. Bennet had joined her husband in the library.

"It is Lydia. Her heart is broken."

"Lydia? I thought you were worried about Lizzy."

"Lizzy appears to have taken Wickham's sudden engagement in stride. Lydia, however, has been led to believe that Wickham was going to propose to her."

"Preposterous! She is just near sixteen this month."

"The seamstress had it right calling him 'Wicked' instead of Wickham." Mrs. Bennet sat violently in the chair across from her husband. "He has flirted with both girls for nothing but his own amusement. To trifle with the affections of a young woman of marriageable age is incorrigible, but to trifle with the affections of a young tender-hearted girl is despicable."

"Perhaps it is best that the girls have no dowry to speak of."

"Edward! I don't think so, for if they did, one would be married for sure."

"Consider it, Miriam, if Wickham did choose one, the other would be forever broken hearted and forced to accept him as a brother. Of course, I assume his true interest was Lizzy, and Lydia's hopes were just fanciful thinking."

"I am not so sure. Lydia met Wickham first. He accepted invitations to dine at my sister's, and here, at Lydia's request. Lydia's bold…temperament might have suited him better."

She was being circumspect, for no father wanted to hear this truth: Lydia radiated a sensuality that no amount of proper corsets and gowns could suppress.

Mrs. Bennet remembered her own youthful exuberance. Looking across at her husband, warm in the light from the fire, she thought that maybe she'd been fortunate after all to have outgrown her passion for Red-Coats and settled for her poet instead.

CHAPTER XVI

The Bennet household was a somber one. Mrs. Bennet was making preparations for Jane's journey to London and Lizzy's visit to Charlotte, when a letter arrived from Kent addressed to her. She viewed it with much trepidation, fearing it contained more bad news, that perhaps Charlotte had changed her mind about Lizzy's visit.

When she opened the letter, she let out a small cry of triumph. Lady Catherine de Bourgh had seen the portraits of Mrs. Long's nieces, as well as the charming rendition of the Lucas Lodge hanging over the mantel at the parsonage. She wrote to commission a portrait of her daughter Anne.

Lady Catherine had been apprised of Lizzy's upcoming visit to the Collinses. She suggested that Mrs. Bennet accompany her daughter and stay at Rosings as her guest while the portrait was being done. Mr. Collins had assured her that it would be no inconvenience if Mrs. Bennet preferred to stay with her daughter at the parsonage. However, as Lady Anne had a delicate constitution and tired easily, it would be best if Mrs. Bennet could stay at Rosings.

The most puzzling part of the letter was the discussion of her fee. Lady Catherine noted that she had inquired about the cost of such a portrait from Mrs. Long and was prepared to increase that amount by twenty percent to cover Mrs. Bennet's travel expenses. But the fee mentioned by Mrs. Long was quite a bit more than she had paid.

Slowly Mrs. Bennet comprehended the cause of the increase, and she laughed in delight. Mrs. Long claimed to have paid more than she actually had in order to increase her standing with Lady de Bourgh, and the more-than-lucrative offer would benefit Mrs. Bennet.

She sent her acceptance of the commission immediately. Now the only obstacle to overcome was Mr. Bennet's objection, which, she anticipated would be formidable.

She waited until supper that evening to share Lady Catherine's letter. Jane expressed congratulations and beamed with pride. Lizzy appeared disconcerted by the news; she had not planned on her mother's presence while visiting Charlotte, but Mrs. Bennet assured her she had no interest in staying at the parsonage and would remain at Rosings in a professional capacity. Lydia and Kitty, though happy for their mother's good fortune, loudly exclaimed the unfairness of being left at Longbourn. Mary, sad eyed and solemn, allowed that although she would miss her mother dreadfully, one must be prepared to sacrifice for art's sake.

It was Mr. Bennet's reaction that silenced them all. He stood up from his seat at the table and bellowed, "I forbid it. I will not allow the use of the carriage or horses for the trip to Hunsford, Kent. I'm sorry, Lizzy, if that means you must remain at home too." And with that he retreated to his study and slammed the door shut.

The girls were stunned. All eyes were on their mother, expecting her to break down into hysterics. However, Mrs. Bennet took her husband's reaction in stride. "Lizzy, you needn't worry about postponing your visit with Charlotte. I spoke with Sir Lucas. He was planning a visit to Charlotte and had intended to offer you a seat in his carriage. So your father will not be without a carriage or his horses. Sir William was delighted to hear about my commission from Lady de Bourgh, feeling he has played some part in it as he was my first commission, and she mentioned Lucas Lodge favorably in her letter. He graciously offered a place for me as well."

"Father has forbidden it," said Kitty.

Mrs. Bennet nodded. "Yes, dear, I know, but the remuneration offered for this commission is substantial. It will be of great assistance to us. So, I am asking you, Lydia, Kitty, and Mary"—she gazed at each of the girls in turn—"to help manage the household while I am gone. Be on your best behavior. Do not trouble your father too much, and see to his comfort. Can you do that?"

"Mother, if the remuneration was not as substantial, would you want to go anyway?" asked Lydia.

Mrs. Bennet hesitated. "I would. I suppose I am being selfish."

Lydia, never one to mince words, blurted, "No, Mama, it is Father who is being selfish."

She smiled sadly. "When I return, I promise to take you three on an outing to Brighton. Would you enjoy that? I heard the regiment is posting near there for the summer."

Lydia, no doubt harboring secret thoughts about winning Wickham away from the anemic Miss King, grinned. Kitty was probably thinking of Officer Denny, and Mary would be excited about seeing the sea. They all cheerfully agreed to do their best in their mother's absence.

Mrs. Bennet sought out her husband and found him agitated and pacing in his library. "How can you think of doing this?" he demanded.

"How can I not, Edward?"

"We don't need the money so badly that you can think of traipsing off to Kent, leaving me with three girls to manage."

"Don't think of it as managing; think of it as being a father with some time to enjoy them."

"Enjoy them? How am I to enjoy them with their silly fripperies and gossip? Lydia is headstrong and difficult, Kitty follows her lead, and Mary is constantly spouting sanctimonious drivel."

"Enough, Edward!" Then she modulated her tone. "I am tired of you sneering at your own children and doing nothing to improve them. Lydia would benefit from your guidance. She may argue or laugh at your advice, but at least you would have shown her enough consideration to offer it. Kitty needs counsel on trusting and finding herself, and poor Mary wouldn't fall into that sanctimonious 'drivel,' as you call it, if her father would take the time to talk with her about important ideas, how to live a good life and the consequences of choices. All things a father should be teaching his children."

She stepped forward to take his hand. "I know you mostly fear for your own comfort, my dear. But the girls have promised to be on their best behavior and to see to your needs. Cook will manage the meals. I will assign tasks to each girl: Lydia to oversee the kitchen, Kitty to check the housekeeping accounts, and Mary to keep up with the mending."

"In the evening, instead of retreating to your den, I suggest you choose a book to read aloud, a chapter each night, followed by a discussion. Use that time for the girls to discuss how they are completing their daily tasks, and offer assistance as needed. Get to know them individually. Let them get to know you. Share your love of poetry with them. They will be open to listening to you because of the novel situation of having you to themselves; walk about the property with them, talk with them. Soon all our girls will be gone, and you will regret the missed opportunity of sharing in their growth."

Mrs. Bennet felt quite frustrated with her husband's apathy. She started to determinedly stack up all the books left open and strewn about on the carpet. "This requires you to put forth energy, Edward, for someone other than yourself. I will ask Lady Lucas to look in and allow Mary to occasionally stay at Lucas Lodge to amuse their daughter Maria."

Mr. Bennet's foot toppled the newly created stack. "I have forbidden you to go, Miriam. You are abandoning your family, your duties, to dilly-dally and call yourself an artist. It is unseemly, selfish, and childish. I will not allow you the use of the carriage."

"I have arranged for other means of transport."

"What other means? I will not allow the expense of a carriage for hire."

"Sir William is planning on a visit to his daughter and has graciously offered Lizzy and me a seat in his carriage. He was quite congratulatory about the commission."

"He can afford to be. He is not being abandoned by his wife and left to manage a pack of unruly girls. Is he planning to stay the whole fortnight?"

"No."

"How will you return with no carriage?" he asked triumphantly.

Mrs. Bennet proceeded to gather the fallen books into neat stacks again. "I shall ask Lady de Bourgh to allow the use of her carriage in lieu of a percentage of the travel allowance offered. I will also enlist the aid of my brother, using Lady de Bourgh's carriage only as far as London, and we would return with Jane via his."

"It seems you've thought of everything, my dear. Have you thought about my feelings? How this will reflect upon me? As a minor poet at best, with only two slim volumes to my name, and a struggling gentleman farmer, it will make me appear even more of a failure than I am ready to admit. It will look as if I am sending my wife out for hire." With that, Mr. Bennet sat dejectedly in his chair and hung his head.

Mrs. Bennet felt a stab of pity for him but was not to be dissuaded. She was still smarting from his remark about calling herself an artist. "Edward, I know things have been difficult these past few years. You have tried patience, humor and scorn to deal with my 'bouts of hysteria' as you call them. Though I assure you the pounding headaches, the sensation of extreme heat, insomnia, and as you know, the irritability are quite real. But right now I feel that some of these problems have abated, or if not totally abated, eased somewhat. I feel the most well I have in years. I believe it may have something to do with finally using my talent. Not just dilly-dallying, as you call it, at home with little sketches of this and that. I simply must do this for my own well-being."

"I suppose there is no stopping you," sighed Mr. Bennet.

"Now, do not go into your usual melancholy state, Edward," she admonished. "I see this as an opportunity for some financial gain and perhaps a chance to remember who we are."

"What do you mean?" He looked up, confusion on his face.

"When we married we had decided we were artists, you the poet and I the painter, choosing to live a country life, remember?"

"We were young and naïve then," he countered.

"Yes, and then the children came, and we were overcome by the daily work of raising the girls and managing the estate. Now they are older and we can come back to our original selves."

He shook his head. "My poetry isn't forthcoming. I have been struggling for years in vain."

"Because"—she patted the tower of books—"you shut yourself up in this library like a hermit and depress yourself with others' words. My absence and the need for you to engage more may be just the spark needed."

"What do you mean?"

"Think of it, Edward. You could treat this as a challenge: write an essay each day on the difficulties of a man trying to run a household on his own, managing 'unruly daughters' as you call them. It would certainly provide you with enough material to write about. Some of it could be in verse, some in prose. With your style and wit it is sure to be entertaining. I think it would be quite a success. Edward, every woman would want to read this and some gentlemen as well."

She could see a gleam of interest in her husband's countenance. He arose from his chair and looked at her intently.

"I apologize for my selfishness, Miriam. We have both been lost these many years, you with your affliction, myself wrapped in a cloak of self-preservation and shame. As you gained strength and clarity these past few months, my fear was that you would leave me behind."

"I would never leave you behind, Edward. Besides, dear Edward, if I were no longer Mrs. Bennet, I could not traipse about so freely, entering people's homes to complete my commissions. An unattached woman is open to gossip and scandal."

At this, Mr. Bennet roared with laughter. "I should be offended at being used for such practical purposes, but I am delighted to provide my protection for your reputation." He kissed her passionately, and she returned his embrace.

The girls had retreated to the kitchen, relieving Cook of her duties, fearful of the thunderous argument that was sure to follow. Though they heard their father raise his voice once or twice and their mother speak sharply, they could not make out the gist of the conversation. The quiet that followed was more disconcerting. Just as Lydia announced that she was going to check on Mother, they saw them emerge from the library walking hand in hand towards the meadow. Mary, sneaking a biscuit from the tin, announced, "They seemed to have reconciled."

CHAPTER XVII

Mr. and Mrs. Gardiner came to Longbourn for their visit and took Jane back to London with them as planned. It was decided that Lizzy and Mrs. Bennet would proceed with their travel plans as arranged, in case Mr. Bennet should have need of the carriage for the other girls. As her husband handed her into Sir William's carriage, he murmured, "I shall miss you, Miriam."

She leaned out of the chaise and said with tenderness, "Write me letters about your daily round, but don't send them, use them!"

The journey to Kent should have been peaceful, but

Mrs. Bennet fretted that Lizzy would find herself confronted by remorse for her refusal of Mr. Collins. She hoped desperately that there would be no strain felt between Charlotte and Lizzy. The two girls had always been of like mind, though Charlotte had the easier, more temperate nature. Charlotte could see past Mr. Collins' absurdities; Lizzy, she feared, was a secret, incurable romantic. Mrs. Bennet inwardly sighed. Perhaps Mr. Collins had some gentlemen friends who would suit.

It was decided to go directly to the parsonage first. Mrs. Bennet could refresh herself before meeting Lady de Bourgh. The parsonage was quite picturesque, with roses lining the walkway, a large garden, and a meadow behind. There were several charming walks and lanes that led to Rosings. Charlotte and Mr. Collins awaited their arrival at the end of their brick pathway. The reunion of Charlotte and Lizzy was one of unrestrained joy. Charlotte tucked Lizzy's arm close to her side, and together they walked up the path. Mr. Collins, slightly stiff and respectful, kissed Lizzy on the cheek and addressed her as cousin, offering an arm to Mrs. Bennet.

The cottage was charming and well appointed. Mr. Collins insisted upon a tour, pointing out every amenity with a significant glance directed at Lizzy. Mrs. Bennet winced, fearing Charlotte's reaction to her husband's obvious gloating. She was much relieved when she caught Charlotte giving Lizzy a conspiratorial wink at which Lizzy stifled a chuckle.

After the tour, a light supper was served and Mr. Collins

felt it his duty to give Mrs. Bennet instructions regarding Lady de Bourgh's personage, manners of acceptable address, and behavior towards her Ladyship. He hoped she would be able to execute a reasonable facsimile of dear Lady Anne that would suit her Ladyship. He was quite anxious on this point.

Mrs. Bennet rose to gather her things and smiled stiffly. "I assure you, Mr. Collins, I will, to the best of my ability, fulfill the commission of this portrait and reproduce a true, if not better than, rendering of Lady Anne."

Sir Lucas readied the carriage to transport her to Rosings. Though it was a short walk through the country lane, the carriage was needed for her easel, parchments, paints, cloths, drapes and luggage.

Rosings was a grand house, all stone, marble, dark wood and heavy damask in the old tradition. Mrs. Bennet and Sir Lucas were shown into the drawing room where Lady Catherine sat in a high backed chair near the fire, her daughter Anne reclined on the couch, and a Mrs. Jenkins sat in a small, overstuffed chair next to Lady Anne's reclining head. Introductions were made. Sir Lucas, quite overcome by his surroundings, kept bowing as he spoke. Lady Catherine expressed herself as quite pleased with his daughter Charlotte as a suitable choice for Mr. Collins. She wished him to convey to the Collins household and their guests an invitation to dinner for tomorrow evening promptly at half past six.

By her authoritative tone and deportment it was clear she thought highly of her own importance and superiority to others—*Not unlike her nephew, Mr. Darcy,* thought Mrs. Bennet.

During this exchange Mrs. Bennet had the opportunity to appraise her subject. Lady Anne was small, pale and wan. Her face was almost elfin in appearance. Because of her drawn appearance, her brown eyes appeared to dominate her face. Her chestnut hair was pulled tightly into a bun, with no curl allowed to escape. In contrast, Lady Catherine appeared tall, sharp, and crow like, with small, dark, shrewd eyes, a querulous mouth, and much older than Mrs. Bennet expected. Mrs. Jenkins, Lady Anne's attendant, was a plump, middle-aged woman who busily fussed about rearranging a shawl and fixing a pillow for Lady Anne's comfort and warmth, with an occasional nervous glance towards Lady Catherine. Mrs. Bennet now understood some of Mr. Collins' anxiety.

Lady Catherine indicated she should take the chair near the fire opposite her. "I was quite curious to meet you. I hear you have five daughters."

"That is correct, your Ladyship."

"Married?"

"No, all unmarried."

"Engagements?"

"None presently."

"Yes, I heard about that from Mr. Collins, though he is happy with his bride."

"It appears so."

"You like the new Mrs. Collins?"

"Very much so. She and my daughter are great friends."

"No rancor there over stolen opportunities?"

"They remain close in kinship, your ladyship."

"Mm. I believe your husband's estate is entailed to Mr. Collins, is that correct?"

At Mrs. Bennet's hesitation, Lady Catherine smiled wolfishly. "Come, come, I know all about it. After all, Mr. Collins serves my parish."

Mrs. Bennet forced a tight smile. "Yes, that is how the will was enacted."

"Fortunate for the Collinses, of course, but unfortunate for you. I was fortunate in that Sir Lewis de Bourgh's family did not think it necessary to entail the estate from the female line. Now I understand, with five daughters to support, the necessity of seeking and accepting commissions, though it is an oddity for a woman. I hope my patronage will serve you well."

Mrs. Bennet could not allow this comment to pass without some clarification. "As you may know, I have just embarked upon creating portraits and landscapes primarily because of the persistent personal requests of our friends and family. I was quite flattered to receive your letter of request and to learn that you appreciated my talents. As you saw, I came by carriage with Sir Lucas at no great cost. Your generous offer of a twenty percent increase is not needed. However, once the portrait is done and our visit concluded, might I prevail upon you for the use of one of your carriages? I must travel on with my daughter to visit her elder sister in London."

"That sounds suitable." Lady Catherine glanced toward

her daughter's attendant. "Now, Mrs. Jenkins will show you to your quarters. Breakfast is served at half past eight, luncheon at one, tea at four, and dinner is always half past six."

And with that, Mrs. Bennet understood she was dismissed. Determined to have the last word, she turned towards Lady Anne.

"Goodnight, Lady Anne. Tomorrow you must show me some of your favorite gowns, and we must choose a room you consider having the best light."

Lady Anne appeared startled at being spoken to and murmured a soft-spoken, "Yes, of course."

This is the mouse Mr. Darcy is promised to? She almost looked forward to hearing Lizzy's sharp wit on the subject. For the moment, she wasn't sure whether she pitied Darcy or the girl more.

Mrs. Jenkins kept up a constant twitter as she led Mrs. Bennet to her bedroom. "Lady Anne is very delicate, you know."

"Has she seen a Doctor?"

"Oh, my, yes, several."

"What do they say?"

"They say she is quite a mystery to them. No one can quite pinpoint the cause of her listlessness."

"Has she always been this way?"

"I don't know. They say when her father was alive she

was quite the lively little charmer."

"When did her father pass?"

"Three years ago."

"How old is she?"

"Lady Anne is twenty-one this year."

"My goodness, she looks barely fifteen!"

"Well, she is much too thin, no appetite to speak of."

Mrs. Bennet sighed. As a mother, her thoughts flew to robust Lydia, five years Lady Anne's junior. "Lady Catherine must be quite concerned."

"Oh, she is quite solicitous of her daughter's health, but truth be told I think it suits her."

"How so?"

"Well, Cook says that when Lord Lewis was alive, he doted so on Lady Anne that Lady Catherine often felt put out when not receiving her due. There was a bit of a competition for attention. Now she is quite content to run the whole show."

"I hear she is engaged to Mr. Darcy."

"I don't know about that, Ma'am. I know that was Lady Catherine's intent but considering Lady Anne's health, I doubt she is well enough to be engaged to anyone. Here we are, Ma'am, right next door to me. If you need anything, just ring, and one of the servants will assist you."

The room was plain, with a thin mattress on a small bed with an iron headboard, one tall cupboard and a small bureau with a pitcher and wash basin. There was no mirror. Her luggage had been unpacked and her paints, brushes, easels and cloths set against the wall. It was clear her status in the house was one of hired help. Mrs. Bennet sighed and wondered how Mr. Bennet was getting on.

CHAPTER XVIII

A sumptuous breakfast was served the following morning. Lady Catherine and Mrs. Jenkins ate voraciously, while Lady Anne merely nibbled at her toast. Mrs. Bennet partook gratefully, having had only a light supper the night before.

As soon as Mrs. Bennet proposed the choosing of a gown, it was clear that Lady Catherine intended to control every decision. Mrs. Bennet sorted through several selections, seeking Lady Anne's opinion, but none was forthcoming. She appeared indifferent to the whole undertaking and deferred to her mother in every way.

Mrs. Bennet was partial to something with color, but Lady Catherine favored a more severe grey. Through her artistry and description of various gowns' folds and beading and painting techniques employed, she was able to convince Lady Catherine that she would get her money's worth with a more colorful presentation, as opposed to a flat, simple grey dress that a child could sketch. In the end, a pale yellow summer gown with flecks of green and gold was chosen. Mrs. Bennet particularly liked this one, as with Lady Anne's elfin features and huge eyes, she would appear almost fairylike. However, she was careful to couch her choice in compliments about the exquisiteness of the gown,

The selection of the best room with the proper light was next on the agenda. Immediately, Lady Catherine suggested the main hall with its imposing mantel and illustrious columns of pink marble. Again, Mrs. Bennet prevailed, saying the columns would dwarf the wonderful details of the gown, and that a more intimate setting was needed.

Mrs. Jenkins and Lady Anne looked on in apparent astonishment as Mrs. Bennet deftly guided Lady Catherine toward the decisions Mrs. Bennet wanted. The final setting chosen was Lady Anne's upstairs childhood nursery. There were wonderful wide oval windows, outside of which the green tree branches flowered, almost tapping on the windows, and giving off a feeling of enchantment.

Mrs. Bennet could see a change in Lady Anne's posture as she entered the room; there was a quickness to her step and a small sound of delight as she recognized forgotten childhood playthings. The room was perfect. The smallness of the space, with the spreading out of easels and drapes and placement of the dress form, would leave no room for Lady Catherine to stay and observe the proceedings.

"This room is very small. Are you sure it will do?" asked Lady Catherine.

"Thank you for so much for thinking of it and allowing me to see it. It is perfect. We are out of your way up here. You won't have to bother about a mess and having it cleared away each day as you would if you had chosen one of the larger main rooms. It is most suitable, Lady Catherine, a very wise choice on your part; the light that comes through the windows is just right."

"You're welcome, my dear. Perhaps I shall send one of the servants in to see to a proper airing and dusting."

"Yes, that would be lovely, and if you could also have them send up Lady Anne's dress form. I don't expect my subjects to stand for long periods of time in a heavy gown. It can be very tiring. The dressmaker's form is most useful."

"Considering poor Anne's disposition, it was one of the reasons I considered this commission. Such ingenuity! I must admit," chuckled Lady Catherine, "a male portrait painter would never have thought of it."

"There is just one thing more before we go down to luncheon, as I see it is one o'clock already. As you may know, I have painted mostly relatives and friends. When I paint someone unknown to me, I need to converse with my subject while I paint. It helps me to create a true portrait. So after today, Mrs. Jenkins, would you mind bringing up some luncheon here for both of us on a daily basis, and tea as well?"

Mrs. Jenkins looked to Lady Catherine before responding. Lady Catherine nodded her assent, and Lady Anne looked at Mrs. Bennet in wonder.

CHAPTER XIX

That evening, Sir William, the Collinses and Lizzy dined at Rosings at exactly half past six. Lady Catherine dominated the conversation with inquiries and suggestions to Mr. Collins about the management of the parsonage as well as members of the parish. She interviewed Lizzy at length and seemed shocked to learn that the five Misses Bennets were without a governess and that their education was primarily left to their parents. There was some discussion of Sir Lucas wishing to explore the countryside of Kent the following day, and Mr. Collins and Lady Catherine were both happy to oblige. Mrs. Bennet suggested that perhaps Lady Catherine might wish to have Mrs. Jenkins accompany her as well, as Lady Anne would be spending the afternoon in a portrait session. Mrs. Jenkins started to protest but Lady Catherine cut her off.

"Mrs. Jenkins, you usually accompany Lady Anne on her daily outing in the carriage and as these outings will not be occurring for some time, it is best you accompany me in my duties."

It was decided that Charlotte and Lizzy would remain at the parsonage. Mrs. Bennet could sense that the way she had arranged matters suited her daughter, and for that she was glad. She watched as Lizzy tried to engage Lady Anne in conversation, but with difficulty, as the young woman's voice was so soft it was difficult to hear, and Mrs. Jenkins kept remarking upon every morsel of food taken or not taken in by Lady Anne. While the others were engrossed in discussing the merits of the soil in Kent, Lady Anne chanced to look up at Mrs. Bennet, and Mrs. Bennet winked at her.

The next morning, as she set up her easel the servants helped with the placement of drape cloths, bottles of water and various brushes. She had asked one of the girls to fetch some old-fashioned nursery food of bread and butter sandwiches and jam and lemonade for a mid-morning snack. Then she waited for Lady Anne. At half past ten, she timidly opened the door, looked around the room, and a smile brightened her lips.

"This was an excellent choice and so 'artfully' done."

Mrs. Bennet laughed at her choice of words. The ice was broken.

"I was dreading this whole process, but to be back in my nursery with all my old loved playthings makes it so much easier."

"We have lots of time; why not explore some of your old friends?" While Mrs. Bennet mixed paints and arranged the gown on its dress form, Lady Anne perused the room, opening the cupboards with little exclamations of surprise and joy as she discovered old treasured friends, books, dolls and animals stuffed with bunting.

"Ah, here is Horatio!" exclaimed Lady Anne.

"Tell me about Horatio."

Lady Anne colored a bit and said in a whisper, "You must think me very silly."

Mrs. Bennet replied, also in a whisper, "Not at all, this is what artists do, we play, we imagine, we create."

She patted the window seat for Lady Anne to join her. There she set the nursery sandwiches between them. Lady Anne chuckled and said that the old well-worn stuffed rabbit was her special childhood companion. Mrs. Bennet took Horatio and handled him with care, making playful remarks, as if she were Horatio.

"Oh, no," said Lady Anne and she took him back. "He sounded much more like this." And as they talked and played, Lady Anne, without realizing it, had finished her sandwiches and drunk her lemonade.

Each day, Mrs. Bennet and Lady Anne had their painting sessions. Day by day Lady Anne opened up to Mrs. Bennet. Mrs. Bennet had gotten quite used to being her subjects' confidante, be it Mrs. Long's nieces sharing their secret thoughts and wishes or Caroline Bingley sharing her obsession with and hopes for Mr. Darcy.

Here is another woman whose future is entwined with Mr. Darcy's, and yet Lady Anne never mentions him. As the days passed, she remained soft-spoken, but her personality blossomed with a whimsical sense of fun, a deep appreciation of nature, and a lively mind. She ate her nursery snack every morning, a good deal of the luncheon, and looked forward to the four o'clock tea and biscuits. Mrs. Bennet entertained her with funny stories about her girls, describing their personalities and quirks.

Lizzy and the Collinses dined two nights a week at Rosings, and because Lady Anne was now somewhat familiar with the Bennet household, she was able to comfortably inquire after the well-being of Lizzy's sisters. Mrs. Bennet, on one of her visits to the Parsonage, had asked Charlotte and Lizzy to invite Lady Anne to accompany them on their morning walks. This regular exercise, along with her increased appetite, did much to improve Lady Anne's countenance. She was still small and elfin in her appearance, but now there was a bloom of color to her cheeks.

All this did not escape Lady Catherine's notice. She instructed that Mrs. Bennet attend her privately in her sitting room one morning after breakfast.

"You appear to be quite the tonic for my daughter."

"It's just the result of regular exercise and eating well."

"All the things I have been telling her to do for years, but she just would not comply." Lady Catherine's lips pinched.

Mrs. Bennet nodded as though they were sharing a secret commiseration. "So often young girls do not accept a mother's direction but will take the same advice from another. I have noticed this among my own daughters. I have a sister-in-law whom my two eldest adore. If I make a suggestion, it falls on deaf ears, but that very same suggestion made by her is considered the sagest of advice."

Lady Catherine sniffed. "Well, I am most gratified to see Lady Anne in better spirits. It is just in time."

"Just in time?"

"We will be entertaining two much-looked-forward-to visitors, my nephew Fitzwilliam Darcy and his cousin, my other nephew-by-marriage, Colonel William Fitzwilliam."

At this unwelcome news Mrs. Bennet felt herself grow pale. Her mind flew to the status of the unfinished portrait, which would require at least two more weeks. "When are they expected?"

"I hope to see them by tomorrow in time for tea, or at least we shall dine with them."

"Tomorrow! As you have these extra guests to accommodate, I shall remove myself to the Collinses."

Lady Catherine waved a hand as though it were no concern and said, "Nonsense, you will do no such thing, your presence here impacts no more on the household than Mrs. Jenkins does. Besides"—she sat forward in her chair, reaching for the bell that would summon a servant for whatever she required—"I need you here to bolster Anne up. You may not be aware, but I hope to announce a formal engagement between my nephew and Anne. I believe my nephew was in your part of the county recently. He can hardly be a stranger to you?"

"Of course I am acquainted with him," said Mrs. Bennet carefully.

"And how did you find him, what was your impression?"

"He is very like yourself, Madam."

The answer seemed to please Lady Catherine, and before she could find herself trapped in further dissembling Mrs. Bennet excused herself, murmuring that it was time for Anne's sitting.

CHAPTER XX

Her foremost thought was to warn Lizzy about this impending disaster. Mrs. Bennet slipped out quietly before Lady Anne's visit to the nursery and made for the parsonage. As she walked, she reviewed in her mind her last combative encounter with Mr. Darcy. She forced a deep breath, slowed her walk and considered the situation.

After all, she had the advantage; she was practicing her profession, of which he disapproved. But what did his disapproval matter? His own aunt had commissioned her work and was happy to provide monetary compensation for it. That vindicated her position. Darcy could not very well insult Lady Catherine's judgment. However, he could press her to give up the offer. That would leave an unfinished portrait and no remuneration. Suddenly Mrs. Bennet was grateful to have an attorney for a brother-in-law and that Lady Catherine had put her offer in writing—though she hoped it would not come to that.

She then made a plan: She would try to seat herself at dinner as far from Mr. Darcy as possible, avoiding any direct conversation with him. If Mr. Darcy saw her position in the household as that of assisting his cousin back to health, not challenging his notion of a woman's role in society, not upsetting his idea of the order of things, then she might be able to complete the work. She could easily avoid him while he was at Rosings, take an early breakfast and luncheon and tea in the nursery.

Though that might change, she mused, as Lady Anne would be expected to join the family for meals. But Mrs. Bennet could use the excuse of her work to explain any absence. If she could keep a civil tongue in her head, keep her conversation to a minimum, and excuse herself from their company as much as possible, she thought she might be able to finish the portrait.

So lost in thought was she that she failed to see Lizzy and Charlotte, just setting out for their morning walk, until she was nearly upon them on the path.

"Good morning, Mama, Is something amiss?"

"I haven't much time and must get back to Lady Anne." She clasped Lizzy's hand. "I just came to inform you that Lady Catherine's nephews are coming to stay. Most likely they will be at Rosings in time to dine with us all tomorrow. I thought I should warn you."

She heard her daughter's sharp intake of breath; a spot of color appeared on Lizzy's cheeks.

"Lady Catherine is hoping to encourage an alliance between Darcy and Lady Anne, poor girl. As for myself, I have considered my situation, which is awkward at best." Mrs. Bennet shared her ruminations. "So if I excuse myself from the gathering and am absent from tea or luncheon, please do not concern yourself. My excuses will be the time needed to finish the portrait, which is true, or some pretense of fatigue. I fear that Mr. Darcy may prevail upon his aunt to give up the commission."

"Mama, perhaps you are being overly dramatic. Mr.

Darcy is severe at times in his manner and opinions, but he is civil."

Mrs. Bennet frowned. "I understand the addition of new dinner companions may amuse you, Lizzy, but I can't help but despise the man. I suspect him of somehow influencing Mr. Bingley's withdrawal and causing Jane's unhappiness. Think of your sister."

She arrived back at Rosings still fuming over Lizzy's apparent lack of loyalty. But there was no time to stew, for Lady Anne was waiting for her in the nursery. "I have something to show you," she said shyly. Lady Anne then presented a small sketchbook in which were lovely detailed sketches of the flowers and various plants found on her daily walks.

Mrs. Bennet paged through the sketches. "My dear, these are exquisite."

"I was wondering if I might use some paints to bring them more to life, to represent their actual hue."

"By all means," encouraged Mrs. Bennet. "What hidden talents you have, Lady Anne."

Lady Anne blushed. "I find the concentration required to do these drawings keeps me calm, yet somehow gives me energy."

Mrs. Bennet embraced her warmly. How did her mother not see the absolute charm in this girl? "That is the way it is when you are doing something you love."

"Did Mother tell you that my cousins, Fitzy and Willie, are coming to stay?" She laughed. "It's the effect of being in this nursery. I mean Darcy, whose first name is Fitzwilliam, and William, whose last name is Fitzwilliam. He is the younger son of Lord Fitzwilliam, the brother-in-law married to old Mr. Darcy's sister. So Willie is really only a cousin through the connexion of marriage. Those are the nicknames I called them in childhood."

"When was the last time you saw them?"

"Well, they stayed for a while right after my father died." She grew somber at the mention of his passing. "Then Darcy was here about eight months ago. He was most solicitous."

"You loved your father a great deal?" Mrs. Bennet said gently.

Lady Anne's eyes started to well up with tears. Mrs. Bennet feared that all her careful care of this gentle soul would be undone.

"We shared so much, appreciation of nature, humor; he could draw too."

"You want to honor his memory, don't you?"

"Oh yes," whispered Lady Anne fervently.

"What do you think is the best way to do so?"

"What—what do you mean?"

"Do you think being sad, overcome with constant grief, taking no joy in what he took joy in, is honoring him? Wouldn't he want you to be happy?"

Lady Anne sat quietly on the window seat. Mrs. Bennet picked up her paintbrush, allowing her to process the idea in silence.

"I never thought about it in quite that way," Lady Anne said after a time. "But I see now you are correct. These past few weeks, I have been taking solace in the things he enjoyed, nature, some drawing, a bit of whimsy; it has given me strength, a connection to the things he loved; in a way, a continued connection to him."

It was the revelation the girl needed, and she would need time to process it on her own, later. For now... "I am progressing nicely with the portrait—and no, you may not see it," Mrs. Bennet said. "But I need you to make me something. If you could snap one of those flowering branches from the tree, a thin supple one, and form a circlet of it, tomorrow we will try it with the gown. If it is too fanciful I will not use it, but I'd like to see it."

Lady Anne laughed delightedly. "You mean to make me a fairie queen. Shall I fashion a set of wings as well?" Mrs. Bennet laughed, too, and the melancholy mood dissipated.

"I wonder why Fitzy and Willie are coming for a visit?" Lady Anne pushed open the window sash and leaned forward, testing the longer branches of the tree for a thin one easily snapped.

"Well," said Mrs. Bennet carefully, "as young gentlemen, perhaps they are in pursuit of a wife."

Lady Anne chortled. "Lord, no, not Fitzy, he is much too much like Mother for my taste. But he was very kind when Papa died. He sorted everything out, saw to everything and was a great comfort to Mother. And Willie—I mean Colonel Fitzwilliam; I suppose I should give up these childish names. Colonel William Fitzwilliam's passion is Botany." Branch in hand, she leaned back inside the window and regarded it. "I shall work on this tonight."

She looked significantly at Mrs. Bennet as she retrieved her sketchbook of flowers. And with the supple tree branch in hand, along with various small jars of paints, she flounced out of the room

As Mrs. Bennet gathered her brushes to soak she chuckled. *Why, that little imp, I hope she succeeds.*

CHAPTER XXI

It was nearly the end of tea time when they heard the carriage pull up. Lady Anne posed in the center of the nursery, dressed in the yellow gown flecked with green and gold; around her head was the circlet of green leaves and golden blossoms.

"They're here!" she said. And with that she broke her pose and ran to the top of the stairwell. "Fitzy, Willie, welcome!" Mr. Darcy and Colonel Fitzwilliam looked up from the foyer. Colonel Fitzwilliam gasped. With the wind from the open window blowing the fabric of the gown around her, and the circlet upon her head, Lady Anne looked like a fairy sprite from another world.

"Playing dress up, cousin?" Darcy called up wryly. He indicated her crown.

Lady Anne touched her forehead and laughed. "No, I'm posing for my portrait. Go into the drawing room, there should be some tea left. I'll change and be down shortly."

Mrs. Bennet smiled at her, gesturing encouragement as Lady Anne flew back into the nursery to drop her crown, then flew back out again to change in her room. In the silence, Mrs. Bennet listened to the voices drifting up the stairs.

"She looks completely recovered!" Darcy said.

"Yes," Lady Catherine replied, "getting her portrait done seems to have gotten her back to herself."

"You can't be too careful, Aunt. These artists all have a bit of the scoundrel about them. They often flirt and seduce their subjects."

"Oh, no need to worry on that account," Lady Catherine said smugly. "I engaged a woman artist."

"A woman?" said Darcy, apprehension plain in his voice.

"Yes, from Hertfordshire. Her daughter Elizabeth is great friends with our rector's wife. In fact, the rector is a cousin of theirs. Miss Bennet is lodging with the Collinses, and Mrs. Bennet is staying here at Rosings while she completes the portrait."

For a moment Mrs. Bennet thought they had moved away from the stairs, but then she heard Darcy say: "And you think this is proper? A woman artist?"

"As you said so yourself, one can't be too careful. I think it is the perfect solution. And she has this wonderful technique of using a dress form so one doesn't have to stand for hours in a heavy gown. If I am pleased with Lady Anne's portrait, I am thinking of commissioning one for myself."

♦♦♦

As the dinner hour approached, Mrs. Bennet considered making some excuse, but decided that was the coward's way out. If she could keep herself in check, and inure herself to that man's insufferable arrogance, she might be able to endure until the portrait was finished.

She chose her plainest gown and decided to come down and attach herself to Mrs. Jenkins. She needn't have worried. The seating was arranged almost perfectly, with Lady Catherine at the head, Darcy to her right, then Lady Anne, to her left Colonel Fitzwilliam, then Lizzy, then Mr. Collins, then Charlotte. She endeavored to switch places with Mrs. Jenkins and was able to sit as far away from Mr. Darcy as possible. He would have to crane his neck far forward to get a glimpse of her.

Colonel Fitzwilliam turned out to be a lively conversationalist, keeping both Lizzy and Lady Anne entertained. Darcy was solicitous of his aunt but seemed distracted by the Colonel's attentions to Lizzy and Lady Anne. Mrs. Bennet kept her voice low and responded to Mrs. Jenkins's account of her time with Lady Catherine and all that they had accomplished in the village, with Mr. Collins praising all their efforts.

Only Charlotte thought to ask how the painting was progressing. Mrs. Bennet allowed that she was pleased, her subject was delightful, and she hoped for the portrait to be completed sometime next week.

At the end of the meal the entire company gathered in

the large sitting room that held the piano. Lizzy was prevailed upon to play. The gentlemen gathered round and Colonel Fitzwilliam and Lizzy harmonized nicely on a simple ballad.

If she had not already been privy to the information that Colonel Fitzwilliam was the second son of an earl, which meant not much income of his own, Mrs. Bennet would have had hopes for Lizzy.

As it was, it was clear to her that Lady Anne wanted him, and she surmised that the lady would have him. It was also evident by Lady Catherine's attempts to direct Mr. Darcy's attention towards Lady Anne, that Lady Catherine was oblivious to any possible match for her daughter other than Mr. Darcy.

"Lady Anne, now that she is well, will be able to take up her music lessons." Lady Anne colored at her mother's obvious attempt at redirecting the attention towards her during a pause in the music. Lady Catherine continued, "Miss Bennet, you play well, but perhaps could improve with daily practice. I invite you, of course, to come and practice all you wish on the spinet in the small parlor upstairs near Mrs. Jenkins's and your mother's quarters."

Lady Catherine's tone made it clear she was equating Mrs. Bennet's status with that of Mrs. Jenkins. Even Mr. Darcy appeared startled. Mrs. Bennet rose, and with a great deal of civility replied, "I fear that Lizzy, as perhaps a slightly spoiled Gentleman's daughter, is too used to the easy action of our piano in the music room at home. The spinet you have in the back parlor, though lovely, I'm sure, would impede the mastering of her quick fingering technique. Which, Lizzy, I do implore you upon our return to do exactly as Lady Catherine says and devote more hours of practice at home. And now I must retire, as I have a bit of a headache and wish to be fresh in the morning for you, my dear." She crossed over to Lady Anne, who stood and gave her a kiss on the cheek.

Lizzy stood also. "Mother, wait, I shall accompany you and help you find your headache remedy."

Mrs. Bennet's exit accomplished two things. She took control of the situation, reminded Lady Catherine of her daughter's genteel birth and refocused attention on Lady Anne. Lady Anne's impulsively standing and offering her a kiss rebalanced her status as an equal, yet she remained respectful of Lady Catherine by echoing her words of practice needed.

She left Lady Catherine with the feeling that she was respected yet somehow thwarted.

Standing in her mother's room, Lizzy gave a start. "Mother, this is a servant's quarters!"

"The room is adequate for my needs, and as you can see, I refuse to accept a servant's status."

"Well, you needn't have pointed out my gentle birth. I was a bit embarrassed, but I was glad to see you get the better of that old cat."

"Lizzy, hush!" She sat on the edge of the bed and patted

the thin mattress. Lizzy sat next to her. "I noticed that you and Mr. Darcy have gone back to some of your bantering ways. A word to the wise, Lizzy: the apple doesn't fall far from the tree. He may have been a bit uncomfortable with his aunt's superior airs, but he said nothing to ameliorate her comments."

She put an arm around her daughter and hugged her. "You must go down now and join the others. Colonel Fitzwilliam, I understand, is the second son of an earl and most likely would be in need of a wife with a title and some means."

Lizzy blushed. "The colonel is very amiable, though not at all handsome."

Mrs. Bennet laughed. "There is no pleasing you, Lizzy. First, one has not enough wit and too much piousness, then the other correctly judged by you to have too much of an opportunist's bent and not enough morality, and now this one is not handsome. Go, I can hear the others preparing to leave. If Lady Catherine inquires as to my headache, though I doubt she will, say I am resting comfortably. A true test of Mr. Darcy's nature will be if he inquires it of you, hoping your mother is not too ill. But Mr. Darcy and I have no regard for each other, and he will consider himself above inquiring after someone he considers below his station. Mr. Collins, for all his supercilious ways, will inquire." She kissed Lizzy on the forehead, sent her down to join the others and prepared to retire for the evening. But she hoped Lizzy would take note of what she said and consider it when assessing a man's heart.

Lizzy rejoined the others and prepared to take her leave and it was just as her mother said. As she entered the carriage, Mr. Darcy made a curt bow, and Mr. Collins did enquire after her mother.

◆◆◆

CHAPTER XXII

The whimsical crown of flowers worn by Lady Anne with the trees in the background gave the portrait just the right touch. It changed Lady Anne's elfin appearance into that of a magical, charming, fairy-like beauty. Mrs. Bennet released the lady from further sittings, as she now concentrated on the details of the gown.

Lady Anne was free to attend to her guests, and there were many walks and afternoon picnics with Colonel Fitzwilliam, Darcy, Lizzy and Charlotte. Mr. Collins was often unable to be part of their party, having many rector duties and conferences with Lady Catherine. Mrs. Bennet was glad that Lizzy could have such a long visit with her cherished friend, Charlotte.

It was hard to believe that she had been away from Longbourn for over a fortnight. Though she relished the painter's life, she missed her husband. Mr. Bennet had sent by post his most amusing essays on a father's trials and tribulations running a household and attending three daughters. They were very witty, yet poignant too. In them, he admonished all good gentlemen to become gratefully aware of all that their good ladies do. Next, he wrote of the good news that a small company in London had published his work as a pamphlet of humorous essays. He changed the girls' names and the location of the household for privacy, and signed his authorship as E. B., which only added to the mystery.

He was starting to receive small cheques from the publishing company and based on the initial response, he felt that the royalties would come to provide them with a tidy sum. Primarily ladies were purchasing the pamphlet and mandating that their husbands read it. Mr. Bennet claimed to have heard that many a family had replaced their nightly dry readings from the Bible and were now reading an essay a night.

The publishers had asked for further essays and Mr. Bennet was in the process of writing the trials and tribulations of an unskilled gentleman farmer. He suggested that when Mrs. Bennet returned perhaps collaboration would be feasible; might she consider drawing a few humorous sketches of the gentleman farmer and his poor put-upon animals?

Mrs. Bennet laughed outright at this and was very pleased to read that her husband was in such good humor. She was delighted in the change in him, and, once she visited with her brother in London, and collected Jane, was looking forward to returning home.

♦♦♦

Throughout the course of the following week, Mrs. Bennet occasionally would glance out the window and see Colonel Fitzwilliam in the garden with Lady Anne. On several occasions, she saw her daughter walking with Mr. Darcy. Lizzy did not appear to be enjoying his company, and Mr. Darcy seemed to be walking stiffly but resolutely. Perhaps he was put out that Colonel Fitzwilliam was becoming a rival for Lady Anne. All had dined together twice that week, but Mrs. Bennet kept largely to the nursery and avoided engaging in any conversation with Mr. Darcy for fear of losing her commission.

A gentle knock sounded at the nursery door, and Mrs. Bennet quickly covered the painting, for she wished everyone to see the unveiling at the same time. She looked up to find Charlotte standing there.

"Charlotte, what a pleasant surprise!"

"Am I interrupting your work?"

"Yes, but I was planning to take a break," said Mrs. Bennet cheerfully.

Charlotte paced about the room, picking up nursery things in a distracted manner. Mrs. Bennet waited expectantly. She thought she knew what Charlotte wished to discuss privately, and was grateful and touched that she would come and share the news with her. She assumed an announcement of a new Collins was to be forthcoming.

Charlotte cleared her throat and looked oddly distressed. Mrs. Bennet sought to reassure her.

"Charlotte, dear, do sit down, I am sure it is most welcome news you have, and of course I wish you joy."

Charlotte sat and looked perplexed for a moment. "You wish me joy? Oh, no, that is not my news." She blushed. "Not yet, though it is hoped for, of course. I have come to inform you of my suspicion that Mr. Darcy is extremely partial to Lizzy."

Mrs. Bennet felt her brows rise. "I am sure you are wrong, Charlotte."

"They have been walking together quite a bit."

Mrs. Bennet nodded. "From what I have observed, Lizzy is walking, and Mr. Darcy is being polite by walking with her when they happen to meet."

Charlotte twisted a finger through her red curls, a nervous habit. "He has come twice to the parsonage to visit, alone, and just sits there for these odd, uncomfortable visits. Lizzy is civil, of course. My husband is concerned because he knows that Lady Catherine considers Darcy to be engaged to Lady Anne."

If anything would upset the balance there, it would come not from Lizzy but from Lady Anne. "We shall take our leave in a few days. I am nearly finished with the portrait. Perhaps Mr. Darcy is just bored and feels himself a rival for Lady Anne, for I know her to be partial to Colonel Fitzwilliam."

"Oh dear, that will not make Lady Catherine content."

Mrs. Bennet patted her knee. "It is none of our concern."

Charlotte sighed and said, "I know you are right. We should not concern ourselves, but you must understand that my husband serves at the whim of Lady Catherine."

"I do understand, dear, and I think it best if you counsel your husband to confine his conversation to parsonage matters. If Lady Catherine brings up any concerns, just have him say he would not presume to give an opinion, that only Lady Catherine knows the truth of such matters, and leave it at that. He has provided the compliment she thrives on, yet has protected himself from being drawn into family relationships. No blame can come to him."

Charlotte smiled then, and in that instant she was once again the wry maid who had grown up at Longbourn's table. "Yes, I have seen the way you manage Lady Catherine at dinner. Mark that Mr. Darcy has noticed it too."

"Oh pish-tosh," chortled Mrs. Bennet. "I care nothing for what he thinks." She stood from the seat at her easel. "I know Lizzy will miss you, dear. Go home and use your time well with her."

Charlotte smiled ruefully. "I would like to, but she is out walking with Mr. Darcy."

CHAPTER XXIII

When Lady Anne bounded into the nursery imploring Mrs. Bennet for a peek at the portrait, Mrs. Bennet was firm. "No. Tomorrow after luncheon."

Lady Anne sighed dramatically.

"And how is Colonel Fitzwilliam?" Mrs. Bennet asked.

"Shh, we don't want Mama to hear." She smiled radiantly. "We have been having a lovely time in the garden. I showed him some of my drawings, and he was quite impressed with their accuracy and detail. Speaking as botanist, he thought they were quite professional."

"And how is Mr. Darcy?" After Charlotte's visit, she'd been curious as to whether his walks with Lizzy had been noticed by Lady Catherine, and whether she was putting any pressure on her daughter.

"Fitzy's fine," Lady Anne said, neatly gathering up the dried paint brushes. "Though I heard from Willie that he got his friend out of a scrape just recently."

How unlike Mr. Darcy to put himself out for anyone. "Do tell."

"It seems that his friend was about to make a most imprudent match. So Fitzy whisked him away to London."

Mrs. Bennet had been looking out the window. She kept her back to Lady Anne until she could regain her composure. *Oh my poor Jane, my poor, heartbroken Jane and all because of that horrid man.*

She took a deep breath and managed to choke out,

"What a friend Mr. Darcy is."

"Oh, I know you don't like him. And I don't think he likes you either. He's terribly old-fashioned. I don't think he quite approves of your profession. Though I'm sure when he sees the unveiling, he will be quite impressed. You have been an inspiration to me. I am going to continue with my depiction of flora and fauna. Willie says he would like to include some of my drawings with his treatise."

Mrs. Bennet saw her opening for some revenge against Darcy and a chance to speak her mind. She turned. "Colonel Fitzwilliam is a fine and truly noble gentleman. If he should ask for your hand, even over your mother's objections, accept. He will make you happy. He gives your talent the respect it deserves."

Lady Anne looked demurely down at her hands, "I only hope he asks." And then she looked up with a mischievous grin. "And if he doesn't, I shall ask him!"

"You must encourage him," said Mrs. Bennet. "As he is only a second son of an Earl, he will think you might refuse him."

"I shall encourage him as much as propriety allows and then some. I expect he shall come for a return visit in two months, after he speaks with his father."

"Do write me and let me know," said Mrs. Bennet.

Lady Anne stood and encircled her in an embrace. "Thank you, not just for the painting, but for…for…well, I am alive again."

After Lady Anne left. Mrs. Bennet allowed herself her tears of sorrow for Jane and tears of rage for Darcy.

The unveiling would be tomorrow, and Mrs. Bennet had done all here that she could. It was time to take care of her own daughters now.

With agitation in her heart, she set off on a brisk walk to the parsonage. She needed to see Lizzy, and this terrible, terrible news could not be shared with Charlotte or Mr. Collins.

All were at home, and Mrs. Bennet gave as an excuse her need for exercise, saying she had been feeling cooped up with her painting. At the mention of the unveiling, Mr. Collins fretted about Lady Catherine's reaction—his frequent refrain of late. Mrs. Bennet could not concern herself now with allaying his fears. Lizzy, seeing her mother's discomfort, could only assume she had taken offense at Mr. Collins' comments, and promptly whisked her off on a walk through the parsonage gardens to the meadow.

As they passed the rose garden, Lizzy hooked an arm through hers. "Mama, do not take offense at Mr. Collins. You know what a booby he is, though Charlotte is trying to improve his understanding and countenance daily. She is much more patient than I could be." She laughed.

They were through the garden now and facing the meadow. "Lizzy," Mrs. Bennet said, "you need to know, Mr. Darcy prides himself on preventing a friend's imprudent match quite recently."

"What do you mean?" said Lizzy.

"Lady Anne recounted how Darcy had bragged to Colonel Fitzwilliam about how he whisked a certain friend away to London to prevent what he considered an imprudent match."

"Oh, Mother!" wailed Lizzy.

Mrs. Bennet nodded firmly. "I feel the same. I thought you should know so you don't feel you were the cause, that it wasn't all Caroline Bingley's doing, as I thought, though she may have agreed to not wanting the match. Darcy has a younger sister; perhaps he intends to influence Bingley to marry her. Whatever his intention, he is the cause of your sister's broken heart. Oh!" She stomped a foot in the grass. "I don't know how I can get through luncheon and the unveiling tomorrow. If I were a man I'd challenge him to a duel. I'd like nothing better than to shoot him through the heart as he has wounded my Jane's heart so."

Wounded Lizzy's heart, too, she could see. Far from being relieved that her alienation of Caroline Bingley was not the cause of their flight, Lizzy seemed devastated on her sister's behalf. No doubt she felt queasy that she had extended any courtesy toward that scoundrel Darcy for even a moment. Well, there was nothing to do for the moment. They would get through the unveiling tomorrow as cordially as possible. And then leave for London first thing the following morning, putting the Darcys and their kin as far from the Bennets as possible.

CHAPTER XXIV

Lizzy stood close to her mother and silently squeezed her hand. Sunlight from the nursery window illuminated the covered painting and made the room feel calm and airy despite the group gathered there. Mrs. Bennet stepped forward and removed the linen sheet.

Lady Catherine gasped. She pulled a handkerchief out and started to dab at her eyes; Lady Anne clapped her hands in delight. Colonel Fitzwilliam stood open-mouthed, with his hand held over his heart. Mr. Collins was attending to Lady Catherine, not sure whether her reaction was delight or shock, for the image was quite unconventional. Mr. Darcy seemed unable to remain still; he moved about the room examining the portrait from different perspectives.

Mrs. Jenkins kept exclaiming, "Oh my goodness. Oh my goodness!"

Charlotte whispered, "It is enchanting."

Lizzy was the first to speak aloud. "Mother, you have outdone yourself."

Other than Lady Anne's obvious pleasure, which could be just vanity, and Charlotte's labeling of it 'enchanting,' which could be just kindness, all the other comments and reactions, even Lizzy's, could be interpreted as positive or negative. Mrs. Bennet herself was unsure; she loved the painting as a painting but she realized it was decidedly a radical departure from the usual staid portraits that hung in family galleries.

Lady Catherine stepped forward. "Mrs. Bennet, though the style is rather unconventional, you seem to have captured my daughter's likeness, in truth, I must say her very essence. For in the month that you have been here, she has returned to herself, and if she ever be lost again, all she need do is glance upon this likeness to remind herself. I am most pleased."

Then Lady Catherine did something rather unconventional herself. She turned toward her daughter and held open her arms. Lady Anne walked into her mother's embrace. Mrs. Jenkins started to sniffle. Lady Catherine then reached out to Darcy to include him in this rare family embrace.

He stepped forward and patted Lady Anne's hand and said, "It is a most amazing piece of work. Though I must enquire why she is so surrounded by foliage, why this approach?"

Lady Anne broke the embrace. "Because, dear Fitzy"— she ran around the room pulling out her own floral and botanist drawings for all to see—"Mrs. Bennet understood I am a 'Lady of the Garden,' for it is my passion, as dear Willie knows. What do you think of my portrait, Willie?" she asked mischievously.

"I should like to have it," he blurted out.

Lady Catherine scoffed at him. "No, Willie. We will hang it here at Rosings, though I am not sure where."

Mrs. Bennet thought about that and could see the problem, for she had painted Lady Anne as if she were emerging from the tree, with a bower of flowers at her feet, a flowering wreath encircling her head, flowers emitting from and entwined in her gown. It looked like a fairy book illustration, yet the detail done in oil defined it as a serious portrait.

"Perhaps over a mantel, but not in the main drawing room, for the color and style would clash with that setting, but in the ladies' sitting room, where the afternoon tea is served. What do you think, Lady Catherine?"

"Let us take the painting downstairs and try it," she said.

Colonel Fitzwilliam stepped forward and gingerly removed the portrait from its stand and the whole party proceeded from the nursery to the sitting room.

The room was off the garden and the pale green walls provided the perfect backdrop.

"Darcy," said Lady Catherine, "you must help purchase the frame for the piece; this is the perfect place right above the white mantel. I think, Lady Anne, we should not keep this piece of art solely to ourselves to admire. I shall give a reception, a ladies' tea, at the end of the month. Mrs. Bennet, I hope you will attend. You will receive many commissions after this viewing, I am sure. My endorsement will assure it."

Mrs. Bennet murmured her thanks. "I am most grateful, Lady Catherine, for your patronage. However, I must now leave for London to collect my eldest daughter, Jane"—she added a slight emphasis for certain company—"who is staying with my brother and his wife, and make preparations for us all to return home. We have all spent too much time away from Longbourn."

Mr. Collins bowed slightly to Mrs. Bennet. "Please convey my greetings to Mr. Bennet. I am so pleased that Lady Catherine approves of this rendition of Lady Anne. It is lovely." He bent and kissed her hand.

Colonel Fitzwilliam then stepped forward. "Gazing upon this gives me great joy." He looked at Lady Anne. "Your subject herself also brings me joy."

Mrs. Bennet leaned forward and said in his ear quietly, so none could hear but he, "And I hope I will be able to wish you both joy soon."

Mr. Darcy approached then, and Mrs. Bennet felt herself stiffen much as she saw that Lizzy did. For a moment, he seemed at a loss for words.

"Congratulations on the completion of this astonishing rendition of my dear cousin." He turned, then, and addressed his aunt. "Though I fear, dear Aunt, if you hold this tea, Mrs. Bennet will be inundated with requests of ladies all wanting to be painted in this romantic style, which might be unsuitable for some. And, as Mrs. Bennet has said, it is best she return to Longbourn to see to her first duty, her home and her family."

Charlotte, sensing the rebuke clothed in the compliment, said, "Oh, Mr. Darcy, Mrs. Bennet can paint in many styles. You have, of course, seen Caroline Bingley's traditional portrait and the fine landscape I have over my mantel."

At the mention of Caroline Bingley, Mrs. Bennet's thoughts flew again to Jane. She would not let this pompous, arrogant man demean her family further.

She turned to Lady Catherine. "I cannot stay for the tea, but dear Lady Catherine, let us retire to your private sitting room, complete the transaction of the commission and possibly discuss a small percentage I can remit to you in thanks from each commission received as a result of your support."

Mr. Darcy shook his head at the impertinence of her proposal. That Lady Catherine would lower herself to deal in any way in a commercial transaction was unthinkable.

Much to his surprise, Lady Catherine extended her hand to Mrs. Bennet and said, "An excellent idea, Mrs. Bennet, though I must say we should discuss raising the commission, as I believe, though grateful that I am for what you agreed to for Lady Anne's portrait, it is much too low for future commissions."

CHAPTER XXV

She had completed her packing and all that was left to endure was this evening's dinner. Mrs. Bennet decided to take a brief walk to the parsonage to oversee Lizzy's packing. Her daughter was notoriously tardy in her preparations and often forgot essential clothing items when packing her valises.

As she approached the parsonage, she heard, to her

surprise, Mr. Darcy's voice. She quietly approached near the open window of the room, thinking she would hear more opinions about her artwork. She splayed herself next to the side of the house; the thorny shrubbery, though uncomfortable, helped to keep her well concealed.

To her astonishment, she heard Mr. Darcy offer his hand in marriage to Lizzy. He proceeded to outline all his objections to such a match but admitted to being unable to overcome his feelings for her, despite all his distaste for her family. "At the ball, you mother's ideas of propriety were sadly lacking, especially knowing the proper place a woman should hold in genteel society, not to mention the lackadaisical effort of your poet father to control her, your young sisters and your sister's torturous singing. However, you display a far superior sensibility than your family and your inferior connexions. This superiority gives me hope for a successful union."

Mrs. Bennet had all she could do to restrain herself from bolting into the room and giving him a sound thrashing, either with her tongue or her fists. But she waited, enduring the shrubbery pricking her skin and gnats buzzing around her head. She wished to know Lizzy's reply. Of course she knew she wasn't perfect, and Lizzy often condescended to her about her behavior, her intellect and even her pursuing this profession, but she waited to see where Lizzy's loyalty lay. She hoped it was with her sister who had been so badly used by this supposed gentleman, and to her family, who, for all their faults so severely judged by this proud peacock, loved her well.

After all her scheming for marriages for her daughters, Mrs. Bennet wished with all her heart that Lizzy would refuse him. She could see nothing in this proposal for Lizzy's future other than a gain in materialistic means. She might weep inwardly at the dependence of women, but anything, anything was preferable to a marriage such as this.

Mrs. Bennet drew closer to the open window, for Lizzy's voice was low and measured.

She calmly refused him, saying she was quite surprised and had no wish to encourage him, as she would never consider him suitable. It was clear that Mr. Darcy was taken aback by her response and was affronted that he would be considered unsuitable. From his pose by the mantelpiece, it was evident that he had expected Lizzy to be grateful for his proposal.

Lizzy proceeded to answer each insult in turn. "I am quite perplexed that my mother's use of her artistic talent offends you so. Do be mindful that your own aunt, a woman of impeccable reputation, if not the most overbearing, proud, vain, and selfish woman I have ever met and so like her nephew that if there were no difference of age or sex 'twould be difficult to tell them apart, is intending to make a profit from my mother's artistry. So, in a way, my mother is enhancing your family's fortune. You should be thanking her!

As for my poet father, as you refer to him, he is a wonderful, witty man who has done much to bring about my 'superior sensibility' you so admire. And for my younger sisters, that a young girl's singing and two girls under eighteen dancing at a country Assembly has the capacity to so offend your sensibility makes me fear for the fortitude of your character if faced with any real challenges of life."

She stood. "And truly, what challenges have you faced? You have inherited great wealth, and create nothing yourself. It is well known you are miserly with your father's last wishes, keeping someone you considered a rival for your father's affections—and you know to whom I refer— in poverty, causing him to enter into an engagement where I believe there is little affection."

Lizzy paused and collected herself, no doubt not wanting Darcy to suppose that he was the cause of herself not being engaged to Wickham; she wouldn't want him to have that satisfaction. "But the main reason I am adamantly refusing your suit is that you could think I would ever entertain the thought of joining my life to a man who has caused such heartbreak and unhappiness to my dearest, sweetest, kindest, elder sister. Good day, Mr. Darcy."

Mrs. Bennet exhaled in relief, then let herself feel heartache, once again, for her daughters. She waited until Darcy had left the parsonage with only a strangled, "Good day, Madam" for Lizzy. He hadn't spotted her.

When she entered the sitting room, she found Lizzy sitting and quietly weeping. Lizzy said, "I have given you my answer, Mr. Darcy. Now please leave." She looked up, startled to see her mother there.

"I heard it all, Lizzy," said Mrs. Bennet, and she went to her to comfort her. "It can't have been easy to refuse such a man. He may hold our family in such contempt, but at least he has soundness of judgment regarding your value."

"What is to become of me, Mama? I have just refused my second proposal."

She smiled gently. "If word gets out about this proposal, dear, every gentleman will be curious about why you have refused the great Mr. Darcy and will want to compete for your favor."

"Mother, please say nothing of this. Promise me!"

Mrs. Bennet made the promise but had no intention of keeping it.

They sat there, holding each other, until Charlotte returned from her parish duties. Lizzy claimed a headache and retreated to her room. Mrs. Bennet started to pack her valises; it was just as she had guessed, nothing was ready for tomorrow.

As she packed, Charlotte chatted. "How beautiful Lady Anne looked in that portrait. Lady Catherine has hopes of an engagement soon for Lady Anne and Mr. Darcy, though it does not appear that Mr. Darcy holds Lady Anne in any particular regard. More like an elder brother, it seems to me."

"Yes, so I have observed," said Mrs. Bennet carefully.

"Colonel Fitzwilliam seemed much taken with your portrait," said Charlotte.

Mrs. Bennet smiled. "Charlotte, stop fishing my dear. I cannot brook any confidences given to me by my painted subjects. How engagements are made, asked for, broken, refused, is not for me to say."

Then she looked significantly at Lizzy's closed door. Charlotte comprehended Mrs. Bennet's meaning. She was Lizzy's dearest friend and Lizzy would seek solace in her counsel. It would only be a matter of time before Charlotte, though most discreet by nature, would let slip, either to Mr. Collins or in a letter to her mother, that Darcy had sought Lizzy's hand in marriage. Slowly word would get about.

The packing done, Mrs. Bennet prepared to return to Rosings for the evening dinner, quite curious as to how Mr. Darcy would behave. Lizzy, she knew, would plead a headache and not attend. Mrs. Bennet's plan was to make no show of any knowledge of what had occurred.

CHAPTER XXVI

Lady Catherine was in fine fettle at dinner. She planned aloud the upcoming tea and presentation of Lady Anne's portrait. She sought suggestions from the Collinses regarding who should be invited from the parish. She hoped to host some families from the surrounding areas and some from as far as London. It was clear to Mrs. Bennet that this was more like an informal coming out for Lady Anne, who, because of her prolonged illness, had missed several seasons in London.

Colonel Fitzwilliam was enthusiastic about the upcoming

celebration and Mrs. Bennet could only surmise that he might take that occasion as the opportunity for putting forth his suit. Mr. Darcy was for the most part silent, though occasionally darted furtive looks at Mrs. Bennet. Mrs. Bennet, for her part, did the most she could to encourage Lady Catherine in her plans for the tea, which had now turned into a festive weekend with plans for a simple ball as well.

"A ball! Oh, mother, that would be delightful! Fitzy and Willie, you both must come and put your names upon my dance card immediately," exclaimed Lady Anne.

Colonel Fitzwilliam readily agreed. Darcy appeared distracted, but acquiesced when prodded. "Come on, Fitzy, I know you don't dance often, but you should do so in my honor. It is only fitting. I can't dance every dance with Willie," she teased.

Mrs. Bennet couldn't resist the opportunity. "I did see Mr. Darcy dance. We attended a simple country ball. The young ladies sang, some not terribly well; my own young Mary, who is very shy, did try but has only a light, airy tone, though we were all polite to listen and applauded the singers, not wanting to hurt their feelings."

"Very wise of you to listen so patiently; too much criticism of the young crushes their spirit," said Lady Catherine, and with that she looked over to Lady Anne.

"Yes, so true, Lady Catherine, though those at the ball, not having daughters of their own, would of course harrumph and roll their eyes and judge them harshly." At this, Mr. Darcy colored slightly.

"Who else was at the ball?" Lady Anne asked.

"Charlotte and Mr. Collins also attended. It was before their betrothal."

"And is that when you decided to propose, Mr. Collins?" asked Lady Anne.

"Well, no, not right then and there, but soon after," stuttered Mr. Collins.

Charlotte interposed, "It was a lovely dance and we all enjoyed ourselves. Shall we—"

But Lady Anne was not to be deterred. "And just whom did my cousin deign to dance with?"

Mrs. Bennet saw her opening. "Mr. Darcy danced with my daughter Elizabeth and a lady whose portrait I had just completed."

At the mention of Lizzy's name, Colonel Fitzwilliam had the good manners to enquire about her health and express his sentiments that she would be well soon.

Mrs. Bennet responded. "Thank you for your concern, but it is only a slight headache, most likely caused by the seasonal change of some minor local irritant in the air. I am sure once we are on the road and she has some distance from the irritant, her head will clear."

"Jane is in London staying with the Gardiners, is she not?" Charlotte asked.

"Yes, my brother and his wife are showing her the city life, which I hear she is enjoying."

"Mr. Gardiner in London who resides in Grace Church?" asked Colonel Fitzwilliam.

Mrs. Bennet's brows rose. "He is my brother. Do you

know him?"

"He is a true gentleman, totally trustworthy in commerce, well educated, and Mrs. Gardiner, his wife, is very pleasant and quite knowledgeable about the arts. My elder brother has invested in a commercial venture of his and is most pleased," said Colonel Fitzwilliam.

Mrs. Bennet was incredibly gratified to have her brother's praises sung so well before Darcy, who had so condescendingly referred to Lizzy's inferior connexions in his proposal.

"Please remember me to him when you see him," said the Colonel.

"I'm sure he will be delighted," said Mrs. Bennet.

Lady Anne was intrigued to hear about the portrait of another. "Did the lady like the portrait as much as I like mine?"

"Yes, she did, and she also chose to exhibit the piece. Lady Catherine, I must tell you, from that one night I received three commissions. So your idea of presenting Lady Anne's portrait may be quite successful."

"Lady Anne's portrait is exquisite," said Mr. Collins. "We in the parish will be most grateful for the opportunity to view it during the festive weekend."

"Darcy, did you like the lady's portrait or is mine better?" queried Lady Anne with a humorous glint in her eye.

"As I recall," Mrs. Bennet countered, "Mr. Darcy expressed his disapproval of the portrait, though it was done in the traditional style. I could not fathom what gave him such offence." All eyes were upon Darcy.

Mr. Darcy had gone ashen upon hearing himself referred to as a minor local irritant. But he was not the sort to ignore the challenge Mrs. Bennet had clearly set forth, no matter how clear it now was that his pride had caused him to misjudge their family. He inclined his head slightly towards his cousin.

"Mrs. Bennet's execution in the traditional style of portraiture was not the basis for my objection. My objection was her accepting further commissions and pursuing a profession as a married woman with five daughters to raise."

"Oh what a fusty old fuddy-duddy you are becoming, Fitzy," said Lady Anne. "I hope you won't object to a single young lady's artistry."

"What do you mean?" he said.

"Willie has accepted some of my drawings for his botanical treatise. So, in a sense, that is like a commission and he is giving me full credit for my illustrations."

Lady Catherine was quite astonished. The conversation turned towards Lady Anne's skill as an artist. The dining party finished with their meal and proceeded back to the nursery, where Lady Anne had laid out her drawings.

After a few minutes, Mrs. Bennet excused herself; she had already seen the wonderful illustrations, and she needed the time to prepare for tomorrow's departure. Now, as she closed her valise, there was a knock at her door. Expecting a final and tearful goodbye from Lady Anne, she was surprised to find Mr. Darcy at her threshold.

"I am sorry to disturb you at this late hour," he said.

She watched his eyes travel around the sparsely furnished room and remembered his brief flash of dismay at Lady Catherine's earlier implication that Mrs. Bennet was on par with a governess or household help. *Does he now understand Lizzy's outrage?*

If he allowed that he might have judged the Bennets too harshly, he didn't say so. Instead, he thrust an envelope into Mrs. Bennet's hands. "If you would be so kind as to give this to Elizabeth, Mrs. Bennet."

Mrs. Bennet looked down at the letter. "I will see that she receives it, but understand, sir, I believe her refusal of your suit is permanent. No amount of persuasion will change her mind. And in truth, her father and I would not allow such a match. For we can only foresee a life of unhappiness"—she then indicated her humble room—"and potential servitude if she should join your family through marriage."

He started to speak, but she held up a hand. "My daughter wishes this unfortunate episode to be kept private, and I will respect her wishes. And I am sure you do not wish this to become general knowledge or bandied about as gossip. Of course you are aware that there already exists the gossip that you were quite proud of recently preventing a friend's potential imprudent match."

"I—I have explained that in the letter," he stuttered.

But Mrs. Bennet once again quelled his response. "I merely mention this as it is not my intention to make you appear the fool that you are, sir." And with that, Mrs. Bennet shut her door firmly, leaving Mr. Darcy still standing at its threshold.

CHAPTER XXVII

In the morning there was no sign of Mr. Darcy. Fond farewells were given as Mrs. Bennet entered Lady Catherine's carriage. Lady Anne pressed a small drawing of a rose into her hand. Lady Catherine promised she would write of any potential interest and would try to secure future commissions as a result of the festivities.

Lizzy was waiting at the parsonage. As she settled herself into the carriage, Mrs. Bennet withdrew Darcy's letter.

"I cannot imagine what more this prig has to say, but he entreated me to put this into your hands."

Lizzy quietly read the letter to herself several times before speaking. "It is full of excuses for his behavior. He owns nothing as an error in his character. He apologizes for separating Jane and Bingley but says he did that based on what he observed as Jane's indifference."

"Blaming it on Jane. Can you imagine!" retorted Mrs. Bennet.

"He justifies his treatment of Wickham based on Wickham's wasting his inheritance on several ventures that he did not complete. Mr. Darcy says he twice provided a substantial living for Wickham. The most upsetting piece, and Mother, if I share this, I do feel it should not be told to anyone, as it is clear Mr. Darcy trusts me to be circumspect regarding this. It appears Wickham attempted to lure Mr. Darcy's younger sister, who was just fifteen at the time, into an elopement as an attempt to secure his fortune."

"That is shocking," agreed Mrs. Bennet. "As we are aware of Wickham's recent engagement to Miss King, and suspect his motives to be purely mercenary, that could be true. However, Mr. Darcy has a tendency to judge harshly. His perceptions of Wickham's intentions could just have been a brother's alarm at Wickham's ability to flirt and charm. We must not bandy this about. It would do no good to our reputation, as our family entertained Wickham often. It would reflect badly on us. Say nothing about this, Lizzy."

"Yes, Mother, that is what I was admonishing you to do before I told you." Lizzy sighed in exasperation. "I wish not only to protect our family's reputation but also to protect Mr. Darcy's confidences."

"Then you do care for him?"

"I think he is a man who is limited by his pride and some prejudices regarding what he deems proper, but I admire his intellect and discern underneath a man who wishes to do right."

"To do right? To do right?" repeated Mrs. Bennet. "Must I remind you that this is the man who is the cause of your sister's unhappiness?"

But Lizzy refused to say another word. For the rest of the journey Mrs. Bennet's thoughts were of Jane, of seeing her brother and of deciding how long to remain in London. If Bingley was in London, perhaps he would hear about Mr. Darcy's proposal and decide to renew his suit to Jane.

If news about Mr. Darcy's proposal got about, it might improve Lizzy's chances also. She would have a frank talk with her sister-in-law; Mrs. Gardiner was well connected as a patroness of the arts and moved in slightly higher circles than the Bennets. She could be the conduit for society at large to learn that Elizabeth Bennet had refused the heir to Pemberley. There would be much curiosity about the Bennet girls and perhaps many invitations to teas and balls.

She must send a letter to her husband, knowing he would be disappointed at the delay of her return to Longbourn and that he surely longed to be relieved of his solo duty to their three younger girls. But it was essential to stay in London and strike while the iron was hot. She hoped he would understand.

The reunion with Jane was filled with hugs, laughter, and tears. For all that they had been separated a month; it may as well have been a year.

Her two daughters promptly took themselves off to spend a few long hours in conversation together, and Mrs. Bennet could only surmise that Lizzy was sharing the secret of the surprise proposal. Mrs. Bennet's brother was away on business overnight, so the four women, Mrs. Gardiner, Mrs. Bennet, Lizzy, and Jane, could dine in complete privacy with no male presence.

Mrs. Gardiner inquired as to the time spent at Rosings, and Mrs. Bennet regaled them with a fine impression of Lady Catherine at her most imperious and the small, devious ways in which Mrs. Bennet was able to thwart her. She remembered then to convey Colonel Fitzwilliam's sentiments; Mrs. Gardiner was surprised at the connexion but then remembered that he was also cousin to Lady Anne, as was Mr. Darcy.

"Gossip has it that Mr. Darcy is engaged to Anne, though her health has been rumored to be weak."

At that, Mrs. Bennet glanced over at Lizzy, venturing, "I doubt that will happen. I say watch the other horse in the race."

"You mean the Colonel, but he is a few more years her senior," said Mrs. Gardiner.

"I believe their temperaments suit," was all Mrs. Bennet would say, "but let us wait and see."

Lizzy looked around the room and saw no servants lingering about. Jane giggled slightly. Mrs. Bennet was biting her cheek.

Finally, Mrs. Gardiner remonstrated with them all. "It is clear you are all privy to some amusing information. Are we not all sisters in womanhood together, bothered not by the propriety required of ladies when a male is present? For heaven's sake, tell all!"

Jane was the first to speak, the words rushing from her in one breath. "Mr. Darcy proposed to Lizzy."

"What?" exclaimed Mrs. Gardiner. Jane repeated her statement. Mrs. Gardiner turned. "Lizzy, is this true?" Lizzy nodded. Mrs. Gardiner was about to wish her joy when Mrs. Bennet spoke up.

"She refused him."

"Refused him? Refused Fitzwilliam Darcy, the Master of Pemberley, worth over ten thousand pounds? Granted, he is a bit stiff in his manner, but I assure you his reputation as a gentleman of fine standing is well known. Why was he refused? I can barely believe it."

Mrs. Bennet shot a warning glance at both girls. She did not want Darcy's objections to her family to be known, nor did she want her sister-in-law to be hurt by Darcy's referral to the Gardiners as lowly connexions in trade. "His pride."

Lizzy echoed her words, as did Jane. "Yes, his pride."

Lizzy did one better. "You know he is very like his aunt, Lady Catherine, and you saw a remarkably accurate impression of her rendered by Mama. Can you imagine I would be happy being wedded to that?" And Lizzy used her humor and cutting wit to entertain them throughout dessert.

Just as Mrs. Bennet hoped, the news traveled quickly through London society. Mrs. Gardiner visited her dressmaker the next morning and couldn't resist boasting of her niece's refusal. Mrs. Bennet took great pains over the girls' appearance for the next public emergence of the Bennet sisters at the opera. Several lorgnettes were trained more on them than on the singers below. At the reception afterwards, Jane and Lizzy found themselves inundated with invitations to picnics, teas and balls. This was better than if they'd done a formal season! Mrs. Bennet was thoroughly pleased.

CHAPTER XXVIII

Caroline Bingley came to call with the excuse that she had heard her favorite artist was in town. Mrs. Bennet received her, luckily on a day when the girls were out.

Miss Bingley mentioned she had heard of another extraordinary portrait executed by Mrs. Bennet. "I understand Lady Anne has been transformed through your artistry."

"She is a lovely young woman. It was easy to paint her," said Mrs. Bennet as she proffered some tea. Caroline Bingley promptly burst into tears.

Mrs. Bennet was taken aback, but secretly she felt vindicated, for she had not forgotten Caroline's part in separating her brother from Jane. "Why, Miss Bingley, what is the matter?"

"Oh, Miriam, please, may I call you Miriam again, and you call me Caroline? Can we resume the intimacy we had while I was your subject in portraiture?" sobbed Caroline.

"Of course," said Mrs. Bennet. She patted the girl's hand.

"I have done a dreadful thing and all for the want of affection from a man who does not love me."

"Mr. Darcy," Mrs. Bennet said quietly.

Caroline Bingley blushed and kept her eyes downcast. "I…I helped Darcy convince my brother to leave Netherfield. I told him that living in the country with country relations was not in his best interest. It was fueled by my jealousy, for I could discern Darcy's partiality for your daughter Lizzy. Darcy also persuaded my brother that Jane was amiable towards Charles but did not appear to return Charles' depth of feeling. I knew how wrong it was, for any woman could see that Jane, despite her gentle, shy nature, was in love with my brother. Now my brother sees Jane here in London, surrounded by potential suitors, and he is mad with grief. He will not speak with me. He tried to engage Jane's attention again at a picnic this past week. Jane was cordial but distant. She acted as if he were just a mere acquaintance."

Good for Jane. Mrs. Bennet permitted herself a wry smile.

"And now there is a rumor about that Darcy actually proposed to your second daughter and that she refused him! Darcy is here in London now, and he goes about in a fog. He spies Miss Bennet at functions, and though they go to great lengths to avoid having to speak to each other, it is clear they are very aware of each other's presence.

"Colonel Fitzwilliam told me about the exquisite portrait of Lady Anne. I know Darcy was there and saw it; he claimed to be much taken with it. I assume he will become betrothed to Lady Anne, as that is what was expected. My only hope was hearing how sickly Lady Anne was, but now that she is much restored to a robust health..." Caroline lowered her face into her hands. "In seeking love, I have lost my brother's good opinion and have been undone by a man's indifference to me." She started to weep.

Mrs. Bennet was not made of stone. Caroline's plight did touch her.

"It seems we have Mr. Darcy to blame as the cause of all this unhappiness. He goes about with your brother and your family, and as you develop a friendship, he raises your expectations. He passes severe judgment on a respectable family and the propriety of a woman wanting to be something other than a wife, and then thwarts his friend from obtaining one. I will make your mind easy on two accounts. Yes, Lizzy has refused him."

Caroline looked up and gasped. Mrs. Bennet realized that she'd been hoping the rumor was not true. "And I believe if he seeks Lady Anne's hand, she will refuse him also."

"How do you know that? Why will she refuse him?"

"That, I am not at liberty to say. I will tell you this. I observed the interaction of Mr. Darcy and Lady Anne during my time at Lady Catherine's, and their relationship appeared to be that of an elder brother to younger sister."

"Like Charles' relationship with Georgianna."

Mrs. Bennet's eyes widened. "I had wondered if Mr. Darcy, in addition to his objections to our family, had hopes of an engagement between Mr. Bingley and his sister. In fact, I have represented that to Jane as the probable reason for Mr. Bingley's withdrawal of his affection."

"No, Charles has always viewed Georgianna like a younger sister—nothing more."

"Caroline, what is the true purpose of your call?"

"I am here to plead on my brother's behalf. Ask Jane to open her heart again and receive my brother. And now that I know Darcy has actually proposed to your Lizzy, I can be certain there is no hope for me."

"But she has refused him, my dear," said Mrs. Bennet gently.

"I do have some pride," sniffed Caroline. "I do not want to be second choice. And watching him, it is clear he is looking for the opportunity to ask again."

"He can ask all he wants. She will always refuse him. My husband and I would not allow the match."

Caroline looked alarmed, and not unaware of the irony that now it may be the Bingleys deemed unacceptable by the Bennets. "I hope you do not hold the same opinion of my brother."

Mrs. Bennet sighed. "I was disappointed that your brother could be so easily persuaded to withdraw his affection and abandon Jane."

"Let me assure you. His affection has never been withdrawn, and in truth, he has been pining ever since we left Netherfield. We went abroad for a short period, and now that we have returned here to London, he is quite desperate."

"I am sure Jane still has feelings for him, though she is

wary. Tell your brother he may call, but he will have to earn his place in my daughter's affection again. If he does propose, Jane is free to accept him. My husband and I will make no objection. For, in truth, we liked your brother for his easy manner."

That Mr. Bingley had not relinquished his love of Jane endeared him to her more. Mrs. Bennet was elated. She would have Jane married and near her at Netherfield as originally planned after all!

CHAPTER XXIX

Bingley did come to call and Jane received him with a gentle yet reserved manner. She and Lizzy were invited to several teas, picnics and dinners orchestrated by Caroline Bingley, where her brother could pursue his suit. This matched perfectly with Mrs. Bennet's plan, though she remained apprehensive since Darcy was an occasional guest of the party.

Darcy's presence was not as constant as before. Good manners would not allow the Bingleys to snub him completely; but it did appear there was a cooling of the friendship between Darcy and Bingley, most likely based on his interference regarding Jane, and to spare Caroline Bingley's feelings.

The Bennets meanwhile had become very popular. Mrs. Bennet was sought out for her consideration of possible future commissions; she was so busy that Lady Catherine's patronage was proving unnecessary. And there was much talk, amongst the ladies young and old, about the identity of E. B., the humorous essayist. Everyone, it seemed, was reading the essays about the trials of a father coping with three daughters at home. All were touched by his loving tribute to his wife and his new understanding of the difficulties of running a household.

At after-dinner parlor gatherings, many gentlemen scoffed at the essays and declared themselves totally competent to take over their wives' duties. They professed that they didn't understand what the fuss was about. The ladies challenged them to do so. But when the challenge was presented, there was much blustering about business that needed to be seen to and how it was best not to disturb the natural order of things. Lively discussions abounded, and Mrs. Bennet smiled to herself every time a new E.B. essay was read and discussed.

But she missed her husband. His most recent letter informed her that he had allowed Lydia and Kitty to accompany Colonel and Mrs. Foster to Bath, where the colonel's regiment was now stationed. He remembered that Mrs. Bennet had promised the girls a trip to the sea when she returned. As she was delayed, he thought it only fair that the girls be allowed to enjoy a visit to Bath. And in truth he needed more concentrated time to finish his next round of humorous essays for his publisher. Mary had remained behind and was quite helpful, reading each essay carefully and correcting any mishaps in spelling or sentence structure. They were having a fine time together.

Mrs. Bennet sighed. What Mr. Bennet said was quite true. She had promised the girls a trip to the sea, and this did seem to be the perfect solution. Yet Mrs. Foster, being a young new bride herself, might not be an adequate chaperone for the girls. However, Colonel Foster was a pleasant man and most likely would shield the girls from any danger. She was aware of the flirtation between officer Denny and Kitty, and she did not object to the young officer; in a few years' time, it may be a suitable arrangement for Kitty.

Lydia's main temptation had been removed with Wickham's recent engagement to Miss. King. Mrs. Bennet toyed with the idea of passing along to Colonel Foster the information gleaned from Darcy's letter about Wickham's character. But seeing that he was soon to be wedded, she could not see the advantage of sharing that knowledge. *Besides,* she mulled, *it may not be true.* Considering Wickham's looks and charm, it could be that Mr. Darcy's sister had tried to entrap Wickham.

We only know Darcy's side of the story anyway, she thought, and his judgment had been wrong before regarding Jane and the respectability of the Bennet family. Pride and arrogance clouded his judgment. She resolved to be cheerful about the opportunity for Lydia and Kitty to be at Bath. She congratulated her husband on his great anonymous success in London's drawing rooms and wrote she was in accord with the girls' trip to Bath and looked forward to the publication of *The Gentleman Farmer.*

The following day, Mrs. Bennet was out, consulting on a commission, when Mr. Darcy visited the Gardiners with Bingley. Mrs. Gardiner later confessed that she had taken pity on him, for she could see he still had strong feelings for her niece.

Jane and Bingley fell deep into conversation, while Mr. Darcy, knowing Mr. Gardiner's great love of fishing, extended an invitation to him to fish at the lake in Pemberley. He expressed his desire that the Bennets and Gardiners would make a day of it to walk the grounds of Pemberley. He himself would be away on business for most of the day, but hoped they would take advantage of his offer. His sister would be very glad to receive them. Mr. Bingley enthusiastically endorsed the outing and at the conclusion of their visit, Mrs. Gardiner agreed to the plan and the date was set

Upon Mrs. Bennet's return, Mrs. Bennet's sister-in-law, gossiped that Lizzy had blushed, and seemed to find this new contrite Mr. Darcy quite compelling. She hoped her sister-in-law would acquiesce and agree to the plan.

Mrs. Bennet did not protest. She also was curious to see

Pemberley, and when she heard that their host would not actually be available the day of the visit, it made her more determined to go. She could see the beauty of Pemberley, which was always talked about, and she could meet this Georgianna to ascertain if she was a vixen who entrapped Wickham or a victim of a rogue's charms.

CHAPTER XXX

It was decided that they should make the short journey in two carriages. The ladies would go earlier for a tour and tea, and Mr. Gardiner would come after with his fishing paraphernalia and stay later. If he was successful in his fishing expedition, he would present part of his catch to the cook of the house and journey home with the rest of his catch. The ladies had no desire to share a carriage with fish for companions.

The housekeeper met them at the door. She was a talkative woman and expounded upon the greatness of her master as she gave them a general house tour. When Mrs. Bennet was surprised that Miss Darcy did not immediately come and greet them, the housekeeper allowed that Miss Darcy was quite shy. As they approached the drawing room, sounds of exquisite piano playing reached their ears.

"That is Miss Darcy. She expresses herself best with

music. Tea is laid out in the drawing room." And with that the housekeeper withdrew. Miss Darcy stopped her playing, turned and slowly rose.

She was fair and quite pretty. She moved awkwardly towards them and shyly took Lizzy's hand. "Wel-Wel-Wel-co-co-Welcome."

Mrs. Bennet ascertained at once that this was no vixen. She thought Darcy cruel to put his sister in the position of having to entertain them. Lizzy immediately thanked her for having them. Mrs. Gardiner remarked on what a lovely tea was set. Jane helped her pour. They all became quite talkative to fill in the gaps of poor Miss Darcy's halting speech. Mrs. Bennet, with a mother's heart, finally asked Miss Darcy if she would resume her magnificent playing. Miss Darcy beamed and returned to the piano.

As she played, she started to hum. "Why don't you sing, my dear?" Lizzy shot a glance at her mother, surprised at her cruelty, but Miss Darcy started to grin and sang her answer.

"I sing well," she sang.

Mrs. Bennet then started to sing her questions and Miss Darcy answered, singing fluidly. Soon the little tea party was singing away in a lively conversation. Mr. Darcy, having returned early from his business, stood unobserved at the doorway, watching the scene with tears in his eyes.

They were singing about events, fashion, and Miss Darcy seemed just about to reveal, in her melodious voice, her awareness of her brother's feelings towards Lizzy, when Mr. Darcy interrupted. "I have returned early from business," he said gruffly. Then, much to Mrs. Bennet's surprise, he cleared his throat and in a deep baritone sang, "Thank you, Georgianna, for entertaining our guests. Let us give them a tour of the grounds."

She sang back, "Of course and you are welcome. Take Miss Elizabeth's hand; I will accompany Miss Jane, Mrs. Bennet and Mrs. Gardiner."

As the party went strolling through Pemberley woods, Mr. Darcy murmured his gratitude to Lizzy for making his sister comfortable.

"But it was not me, Mr. Darcy, it was my mother. I thought my mother was being unkind but once your sister started to sing, we realized that she could do so with ease and we all joined in, singing our conversation."

"How did your mother know that Georgianna's difficulty with speech would not also give her difficulty in singing?"

"Georgianna sang that very question to my mother. Mother sang back that she had a dear childhood friend who had the same problem. She remembered that her friend had daily singing lessons. The friend never faltered in speech while singing, and eventually, with many lessons was able to speak fluidly."

Mr. Darcy at that point resolved to make amends to Mrs. Bennet. He was at a loss as to how he would accomplish this.

CHAPTER XXXI

Pemberley's beauty was enthralling. The house itself, with large, well-appointed rooms with handsome furnishings, had an understated elegance so different from the gaudy furnishings at Rosings.

As she walked with Mrs. Gardiner, Jane and Georgianna, Mrs. Bennet could not help regretting that Lizzy had given up the chance to be mistress of this place. The rolling green knolls, charming woods, river, valley and meadow were all breathtaking. And Mr. Darcy's rare display of tenderness towards his sister had touched her.

Perhaps she had misjudged him. He was proud and arrogant but perhaps that arrogance was a cloak of insecurity. He was quite young to manage such an estate as this—his father had died when he was only twenty. The responsibility was enormous.

As they strolled about, taking in the beauty of the grounds, Mrs. Gardiner remarked to her sister-in-law, "See how the young couple stroll together so amiably." At that moment, some response from Lizzy caused Darcy to throw his head back and laugh.

Georgianna started to giggle. "In truth, dear ladies," she sang softly, "I have never seen my brother so relaxed. He is usually tense and overburdened with the cares and responsibilities of Pemberley, and forgets to enjoy its beauty."

If Darcy wished to pursue Lizzy again, she would encourage her to consider it. Was she swayed by the wealth and ease that would be offered to her daughter? *What other way may a woman survive?* If he pleased Lizzy, and had no further objections to the Bennets' low connexions, she should not prevent it. But if Mr. Darcy still had serious intentions about Lizzy, he must find a way to apologize for his previous rudeness and cruel misjudgments.

Mrs. Bennet realized she could not express a total change of heart without appearing entirely mercenary. And so she offered only a remark about the beauty of Pemberley and Darcy's able shouldering of such a large responsibility. Mr. Darcy seemed gratified by her acknowledgment, but the real tell was in Lizzy's expression. Her daughter's eyes danced with delight.

The party returned to the house to find Mr. Gardiner anxiously pacing upon the stone portico. Mr. Darcy called to him, "You are a little late, Mr. Gardiner, but we may be able to catch a few before sunset."

Mr. Gardiner merely shook his head and continued his pacing. It was clear that he was quite distressed.

When the party reached him, he spoke with some urgency. "Mr. Darcy, is there somewhere private I can speak with my sister?" Mrs. Gardiner, Lizzy and Jane were quite alarmed. "What is it, Uncle? What is wrong?

"Dear, you look so distressed. Tell us what has happened."

But Mr. Gardiner refused them. "No, I must speak with Miriam in private." Darcy nodded. He led them to the library.

"James, what is it?" asked Mrs. Bennet, once Mr. Darcy had left them and closed the door. She could only think that some harm had come to Edward, an accident, perhaps, on the farm. He was always trying to do things beyond his physical strength and— "What's happened to Edward?"

"Nothing has happened to Edward, and the devil take him for all I care!"

"James, what are you saying, what has happened?"

His face flushed red with rage. "Lydia has run off with an officer. It seems Edward allowed the girls to go to Bath with a Mrs. Foster, an empty-headed little thing, as their chaperone. Lydia met up with an officer she claims to love, and they have supposedly gone to Gretna Greene. I say 'supposedly' because, according to Kitty's officer friend, a Lieutenant Denny, the officer has no intention of marrying her. He is a known gambler and is running from his debts. Why he took Lydia with him is a mystery."

Miriam collapsed into a nearby chair as she spat out the name. "Wickham."

"Yes!" answered James in surprise. "And how are you acquainted with this rogue?"

"Wickham was part of the militia at Meryton. We had entertained him frequently in our home. He was well known as a charming gentleman of wit and intelligence. He appeared to have an interest in Lizzy. However, he often teased and flirted with Lydia. I did not think it to be of any consequence, as it became known he was interested in finding a wife of means. In fact, he was engaged to a Miss

King, who recently came into an inheritance of six thousand pounds a year."

"According to Colonel Foster, Miss King's relations have whisked her off to Ireland. I must say in Colonel Foster's defense, he is searching for Wickham now, trying to recover them before any damage is done. Your husband has ridden to Bath and is stopping at any inns along the way to inquire of their whereabouts."

"Do not castigate Edward. I gave my permission for the girls to go to Bath. I thought that since Wickham was betrothed, there would be no danger to Lydia's reputation. She is a flirt and revels in any officer's attention, as all young girls do. But I fear I misjudged the depth of her feelings toward Wickham. Poor Lydia."

"Poor Lydia? How can you say poor Lydia? She has caused a scandal and will bring shame upon all her family and connexions! Most likely she has ruined any chances of respectable matrimonial prospects for Jane and Lizzy." Mr. Gardiner pounded his fist into his palm. "She is a selfish, stupid girl."

Mrs. Bennet stood, smoothing her skirts. "James, I realize that you are worried that any scandal or impropriety will reflect on your good name, hence your business—"

"Miriam, I didn't mean…"

"But I say 'poor Lydia' because she is a young, impressionable girl who is following her heart. She is in love with Wickham. He may have some partiality towards her, but he will be swayed to save her reputation only by mercenary persuasion. Otherwise he will make physical sport of her and abandon her. And I say 'poor Lydia,' for if we can persuade him through monetary means to become her husband, she will be married to a man who has little regard for her and most likely will abandon her anyway, emotionally if not physically. I now ask, as your sister, that you join us in making the monetary offer to ensure a marriage takes place."

"Of course I will," said James gruffly, "how could you think I would not?"

She nodded. "As I have been receiving several commissions of late, I believe I can contribute a goodly sum. Edward also has recently come into some funds from his publisher. We were going to start small dowries for the girls, but that will have to wait."

"I'm willing to make a substantial contribution, Miriam, but the problem is, we don't know where they are."

Mrs. Bennet sat down and with a resigned sigh said, "Please ask Mr. Darcy to come in."

"Darcy? But isn't that to whom you would want to present a modicum of respectability regarding your family? Think! He is close friends with Charles Bingley, whom I'm given to understand may propose to Jane. Any whiff of this scandal will put an end to any engagement."

"Mr. Darcy has dealt with Wickham before on a similar matter."

"By Jove! And how do you know that?"

"James, please just call in Mr. Darcy. And let Lizzy and Jane know that their father is all right. We can explain everything to them on the way home."

♦♦♦

CHAPTER XXXII

Darcy entered and stiffly took a seat by Mrs. Bennet. A sob escaped her lips. "I fear a red fox has invaded my hen house and stolen one of my chicks. I know you have experience with this sly fox. He must be found immediately."

Darcy sprang to his feet. "Wickham again!" His eyes thundered. "Which chick?"

"Lydia," sighed Mrs. Bennet. Darcy pursed his lips and looked down at the floor.

"Oh, I know you think her a brash and forward girl, but inwardly she is not so very different from shy Georgianna, both young with tender hearts. Lydia has been in love with Wickham from the outset. But it seemed to be only a childish crush and, with his recent engagement to Miss King, I thought it prudent for me to keep to myself the information you gave regarding his conduct towards Georgianna. If I had warned the Fosters or my husband, this might have been prevented." *May the Lord forgive me for this subtle form of extortion, but I fear I cannot just rely on his affection for Lizzy to spur him to action.*

Darcy took her hand in his. "I am grateful for your discretion regarding my sister and implore you to not divulge it to anyone. I may be able to offer some assistance in locating him."

"What I don't understand is what he thought to gain? He knows our circumstances. She has no dowry to speak of, no property. I am at a loss as to his motives. I can only assume he means to take advantage of her young heart and ruin her." Mrs. Bennet could no longer keep her composure and started to weep.

Mr. Darcy's voice was gentle. "He is a desperate man. Miss King's fortune had been whisked away. I am sure his gambling debts have finally caught up with him."

"He surely didn't expect our family to be able to excuse his debts and offer a living," cried Mrs. Bennet.

"Mrs. Bennet, you have become a person of some renown. Fashionable young ladies and titled gentry have been commissioning their portraits for several months now. And your husband, I believe, has been publishing some very entertaining and lucrative essays as E. B."

At the mention of the essays Mrs. Bennet became even more distressed.

"Mr. Darcy, I implore you to be discreet just as I have been about Georgianna's temptation by Wickham. I concede the correctness of your opinion that a woman's place is only in the home, not gadding about trying to earn income. If I had been with my daughters at Bath, I could have thwarted Wickham. However, if you share your suspicions about E B's identity, we will only be held up for more ridicule and disgrace."

Mrs. Bennet was overcome by the humiliation of all that lay ahead. She sighed in deep despair.

"We shall return to Longbourn immediately. My hope is to spare Jane. I, of course, will understand if you advise your friend again that an alliance with the Bennet family would be most unsuitable. As I, unfortunately, must agree." She started to weep again.

"I will not do anything to dissuade Bingley from becoming engaged to Jane. And I shall not reveal E.B.'s identity, though I fear some do suspect. As for Lydia's situation, take heart, Mrs. Bennet, it may still be repaired."

Mrs. Bennet stood and paced the room in agitation. "If my husband finds them, he will challenge Wickham to a duel. With Wickham being younger and a soldier skilled in fire-arms, I foresee a dreadful outcome for Mr. Bennet."

"I doubt your husband will find them. Wickham is too wily to leave a trail at any local inn. Return with your brother to London. When your husband arrives, convince him to return with you. I have an idea where Mr. Wickham may be found. Discuss with your husband and your brother any financial arrangement that could be offered the happy couple."

"I have already discussed the need for monetary assistance with Mr. Gardiner."

"Excellent," said Mr. Darcy. "Now you must act as if you are a happy mother-in-law."

Mrs. Bennet stopped pacing and turned to face him. "A happy mother-in-law?" she said incredulously. "How could that be?"

"You entertained Wickham often at your table, did you not? Had him as a frequent guest to parties and picnics?"

"Yes."

"Well, then, you should express no surprise that he married one of your daughters, and you must act joyful about the outcome," Mr. Darcy said firmly.

"But they may not be married," whispered Mrs. Bennet.

"I assure you, Mrs. Bennet, that you will have a married daughter returned to you."

"Mr. Darcy, I fear I have misjudged you." She leaned forward and touched his arm lightly. "It is as Lizzy said, that you are a person wishing to do what is right and true."

"She said that?"

"Yes, and I must say she is a wonderful judge of character. She had the good sense to see through Mr. Wickham, even before your letter."

"Was Wickham pursuing her, too?" asked Darcy vehemently.

"Wickham would seat himself betwixt Lizzy and Lydia. Lizzy was amused by his banter but deflected any serious suit. Poor Lydia was beguiled by his charm and must have believed his attention to her was true affection." She sighed. "Thank you, Mr. Darcy, for all you will attempt to do on our behalf. I don't know how I can repay you."

Mr. Darcy hesitated. "Mrs. Bennet, I have seen the way you helped my cousin. Perhaps you would consider creating a portrait of Georgianna, and, in the process, perhaps, assist her with her shyness and to overcome her speech difficulties. She seemed most comfortable with you. I have been a poor substitute for a mother," he said gruffly.

"I have seen that your sister adores you. She lights up

when you enter the room and delights in your attempt at easing her communication with singing. You are to be commended for your protection and care of her."

"Let us settle all this first for Lydia. She will return to your household with Wickham as her husband. In the meantime, go back home to Longbourn," commanded Mr. Darcy. "Perhaps in a fortnight when things settle down, I and Georgianna shall return to Netherfield with the Bingleys to enjoy the summer months in the country."

CHAPTER XXXIII

They sped in the Gardiners' carriage from Pemberley to London. "We are to persuade him that it is best to return to Longbourn and let Mr. Gardiner and Mr. Darcy search for Wickham."

"Why?" asked Mrs. Gardiner. "Why would Mr. Darcy involve himself?"

Mrs. Bennet replied carefully. "He has some knowledge of Wickham. Wickham did grow up in his home." Mrs. Bennet looked meaningfully at Lizzy.

Mrs. Gardiner misinterpreted Mrs. Bennet's meaningful glance and whispered, "But of course, he is in love with Lizzy and means to win her. He will bring all his influence to bear, and I am sure will make it right."

Jane and Lizzy, seeing the carriage from home under the Gardiner's port-cochere, hastened into the parlor and ran to their waiting father and embraced him. Mr. and Mrs. Gardiner instructed the cook to lay out a cold supper while Mr. Gardiner poured himself and Mr. Bennet a dram of whiskey. Mrs. Bennet entered the parlor slowly. She nodded to the girls and the Gardiners and asked for some privacy. All went towards the dining room.

Mrs. Gardiner turned. "Supper will be laid out soon; you both must eat something." Mrs. Bennet closed the sliding wooden doors and turned towards her husband. She went over to the small table and poured herself a dram.

"Miriam!" said Edward, clearly shocked at her taking the spirits.

"Edward," sighed Mrs. Bennet as she raised her glass in a mock toast.

"I am sorry, Miriam."

"I am sorry, too. Though what we have to be sorry about I am not sure."

"Well," said Edward gruffly, "I allowed her to go to Bath."

"Yes, and I was not there to supervise her outing as promised. Edward, you feel guilty because you took the opportunity to concentrate on your writing. I feel guilty because I took the opportunity to chaperone our older daughters and pursue my painting. You know who does not feel guilt or shame? Lydia, our brash, outspoken daughter. No amount of careful guardianship, paternal constraints, cautious advice, or stern warnings would have changed the outcome. She got what she wanted. She wanted Wickham, and now she has him; poor, silly, passionate fool that she is."

"She is just sixteen, too young to know her own mind. I must find them and call him out."

"Edward, if you find them and call Wickham out to duel, she will not go with you, and you may end up getting yourself killed."

"Well, what do you propose I do?"

She outlined the plan. "This sum, hopefully, will induce Mr. Wickham to do his duty. Mr. Darcy is in the process of locating him and with my brother will offer the dowry."

"Darcy? What has Mr. Darcy to do with this?"

"We were touring his estate when James gave me the news."

"Be that as it may, Miriam, why you would choose to share this scandal with him is beyond comprehension!"

Miriam took another dram and enlightened her husband about all that had occurred since their stay at Lady de Bourgh's. "And he has personal experience with Wickham, as Wickham tried the very same thing with Darcy's younger sister. He knows how to ferret him out. He assures me that Lydia will return to our household as a married woman. He advises us to return home and receive the couple with all forms of happy congratulations."

"Is he mad?"

"No, quite sensible really. Think about it, Edward. We have entertained Wickham often in our home; that he marries one of our daughters would be expected. If we act joyful about the elopement, there is no scandal. Darcy will see to it that the marriage is certified. His standing up for Wickham may make tongues wag but in another direction. I see his objective clearly. It will appear that Wickham and Darcy have reconciled. Then Darcy will be free to pursue his suit towards Lizzy, and we will appear as one lucky family to have two daughters soon to be possibly engaged and one married."

"I don't know if I can pretend joy." Mr. Bennet sat down angrily, folding his arms across his chest.

"Think of Lydia then." Mrs. Bennet, her voice thick with tears, raised her empty glass. "Her life will not be happy. Let us allow her this short honeymoon."

CHAPTER XXXIV

And so it came to pass that Lydia and Wickham had their marriage certified. Mr. Darcy stood for Wickham and Mrs. Gardiner for Lydia. And Mrs. Bennet gossiped to her neighbors that she wasn't thrilled that they chose to go to Gretna Greene, but only because it deprived her of the joy of shopping for proper wedding clothes and planning the parties and wedding feast the young couple so deserved. As a happy mother-in-law, it would give her great pleasure to host the couple; upon Lydia and Wickham's return, Lydia was given a new set of wedding and traveling clothes, and a celebratory feast was held in the church hall with all of Longbourn's families in attendance.

Their mother's oppressively high spirits and Lydia's crowing about the first to be married appalled Jane and Lizzy. Lizzy, with Jane at her side for support, confronted her mother.

"Mama, you must stop this ridiculous farce. It is an embarrassment. Papa, at least, has shown the good sense to respond with composed resignation to this horrid match."

"Where is your sense of decorum?" Jane added, blushing.

"Where is your compassion for your sister?" countered Mrs. Bennet. "What should we express to our neighbors? Shame that Lydia was seduced and almost abandoned, so there will be a taint forever upon our family and all hopes dashed for any proper engagements for any of you?"

Mrs. Bennet folded her arms across her chest and jutted her chin forward. "You think I am not aching inside for Lydia's poor future with such a rogue? Thank goodness his manners are always so pleasing, and he is impudent enough to play his part as the smitten bridegroom. I have put out that your sullen attitudes towards Lydia and Wickham are just the result of two older sisters' anxiety about still being unmarried.

"As for your father's reserve, I have attributed that to his sadness at the loss of his youngest daughter. Lydia is accompanying Wickham to the North in a few weeks where he has been given a new commission in the army under

General Potter."

Mrs. Bennet looped an arm through each of the girl's arms. "Poor Lydia has not the ability of your discerning minds. She wears her heart on her sleeve, and I assure you within a month's time, it will be broken. Show some sisterly support. Give her, her moment of glory, wish her joy, and let her know her family loves her. And for goodness' sake, stop assuming I am an idiot. I know exactly what I am doing, and I am doing it for you and the good of the family. I am doing precisely what Mr. Darcy instructed me to do."

"Mr. Darcy!" cried Lizzy.

"Yes, you pea-brain, Mr. Darcy was the one who suggested we carry this off as a joyous, acceptable marriage. It saves our family from scandalous gossip and allows him to continue the connexion with our family."

"Continued connexion?" stuttered Lizzy.

Mrs. Bennet sighed in exasperation. "Darcy and Bingley are returning next month to Netherfield. Darcy is bringing Georgianna and I am to paint her. You, Jane, hopefully will finally secure an engagement from Charles Bingley, and you, Lizzy; well, your fate is up to you. Though I agree with your estimation of Mr. Darcy's true character; he always tries to do the right thing."

Jane and Lizzy were astounded by their mother's ability at pretense. That she was so convincing in her presentation of false feelings made them wonder about her true nature. In private, the sisters reflected upon the changes in their mother's sensibility.

"Was she always thus?" inquired Jane.

Thinking back to their childhood, they remembered a pretty woman, laughing and teasing them, playing silly games, singing them to sleep. They remembered fine holiday dinners with their mother still in apron running back and forth to the kitchen. They remembered sitting in the parlor as she schooled them on their letters, reading and simple arithmetic, bouncing one infant upon her knee and rocking another one to sleep. They remembered the poultices applied to a heavy chest in the middle of the night. They also recalled that after the birth of Lydia, their mother was quite ill.

"Where was father in all this?" asked Lizzy.

"Managing the farm and doing the accounts, I suppose," said Jane.

But they both remembered seeing their mother by candlelight wearily tabulating expenses, Father shouting at her. Lizzy started to weep as she recalled how her mother accepted the servant's quarters at Lady Catherine de Bourgh's in order to fulfill the commission. Commissions earned that would help support the family and perhaps provide a dowry for them. Lizzy now understood her mother's motivation for promoting a match with Mr. Collins and the engagement to Bingley. She did not want her daughters to struggle as she did.

CHAPTER XXXV

Lydia was like an overexcited, distracted child throughout most of the week's festivities, but Mrs. Bennet was finally able to get her fifth daughter alone. She proposed a final mother-daughter walk to the meadow, knowing that she could not have an honest, forthright talk about Wickham because her daughter was too blinded by her infatuation with her dear "Wickie" to heed any warnings. So she decided to try and appeal to Lydia's vanity, "one married woman to another," and hoped that her instruction would be followed.

"Lydia, as you are now a married woman—"

"Yes, Mama, I am just like you!" she interrupted.

"Yes, we are both married women. May I offer you, as a new bride, some advice?"

Lydia blushed. "Oh Mama, I doubt I am in need of that."

Mrs. Bennet soldiered on. "Lydia, you want to enjoy your time with Wickham, don't you?"

"Yes, Mama."

"Wickham likes parties, and dancing and riding."

"Yes, he does, and so do I."

"Precisely!" said Mrs. Bennet.

"Precisely what?" queried Lydia.

"In order to continue to enjoy your time as newlyweds, you must avoid any extra responsibilities."

"Extra responsibilities?"

"Children," said Mrs. Bennet.

"Oh, but I would want Wickie's children. They would be so beautiful." Lydia plucked a fuzzy dandelion and blew away the wisps.

"Yes, they would, but if you have them right away, then you are left at home with a baby, not able to attend the parties and dances as a young officer's wife."

"Oh." Lydia frowned.

"Mark your calendar the day you start to bleed, then ten days from that date, for nine days, avoid intimacy with Wickham."

"Why?" whispered Lydia.

"Because my dear, during that time is when most babies are conceived. Now it is not foolproof." Here, Mrs. Bennet thought of Mary and smiled to herself. "But it does work most of the time."

"Every month?" Lydia pouted.

"Yes, every month."

"But what if Wickie becomes impatient?"

"Think of other ways to entertain him," responded Mrs. Bennet dryly.

Lydia gaped at her mother. Then she threw her head back and laughed. "What a conversation from one married woman to another."

Mrs. Bennet hugged her daughter fiercely. She had given Lydia longer parameters than usual, making allowances for her daughter's impulsive nature. She did not want to see Lydia abandoned with children to care for on her own. She had no illusions as to the longevity of this marriage. She wished only that she could protect her from the heartbreak that was sure to come.

"My dear one, you are my particular favorite, and I will be quite bereft without you. So do not hesitate at any time to return home to see your mother who loves you so."

CHAPTER XXXVI

The loss of Lydia left Mrs. Bennet feeling quite low. "This is the consequence of marrying off a daughter," Mr. Bennet teased. "You now must feel more satisfied that the other four remain single."

"Certainly not!" retorted Mrs. Bennet. "Lydia does not leave me because she is married, but because Wickham's regiment is so far off. And I fear that she may return to us within the year, a bitter young woman."

And so when Officer Denny came to call on Kitty, Mr. and Mrs. Bennet were in attendance in the parlor for each of his visits, and their second-youngest daughter was assiduously chaperoned by both of her older sisters when walking in to town. Kitty felt the loss of Lydia most severely, and Jane and Lizzy tried to assuage her sorrow with increased sisterly attention.

Officer Denny however, turned out to be more solid in

his character than Wickham. Before making ready to leave with his regiment, he came to call on Mr. and Mrs. Bennet and expressed his intention of being worthy to marry Kitty someday. He proffered Kitty a small gold promise ring, with a pledge to write daily. Mr. Bennet allowed that Kitty was very young, and he would not consent to any formal engagement for two years.

Officer Denny agreed to wait. He was only three years older than Kitty but had seemed steadfast in his devotion to her throughout the tumult of the past year. And in truth, he had been her only dancing, walking, and picnicking partner for a full year. She never flirted with the other officers like Lydia had. Mr. Bennet shook his hand, Mrs. Bennet offered hers, and Kitty wore her promise ring proudly, serene in the knowledge she was loved and would be formally engaged in two years' time.

"Well, well, so Mr. Bingley returns. I will say, Miriam, that your life with five girls is never dull."

Mrs. Bennet heard the slight longing in her sister's words. She'd come to Longbourn for a short visit and brought some welcome news: She had heard that the housekeeper at Netherfield was instructed to make the place ready for her Master.

Mrs. Olivia Philips had married their father's law clerk and thus the family home had been deeded to her and her husband. After their father's death, Miriam had lived with her sister and brother-in-law. Though it was her family home too, she'd felt in the way of the newly married couple. She recalled their relief when Edward Bennet finally proposed. A small income had been settled upon her at her marriage, with her elder siblings feeling that their duty was done.

She replied carefully. "Yes, I have been blessed with these girls, and I am no stranger to the worry of providing financial support and hoping for a good match, as you must have had for me."

Mrs. Philips blushed, knowing, as she must, that both she and her brother lived a life with less financial strain than their sister's. Yet Mrs. Bennet wondered if her sister secretly envied her chaotic life and the recent development of her respected ability as a painter. She was not a mother and perhaps felt she had no special talents to offer.

Mrs. Bennet rushed to reassure her sister. "My dear, as you know, you are invaluable to my girls. In fact, I was going to ask for a bit of help with them. As you may know, a dowry was settled on Wickham, and James helped with that. When it is time for the others to be wed, I may need some contribution from you for their dowries."

The balance of power in a sisterly relationship is a precarious one, thought Mrs. Bennet. With her request for support, Olivia was restored to her place as the elder, wiser, more rational one. Mrs. Philips readily agreed to be the girls' benefactor, no doubt happy to be of some use, knowing the girls would be grateful to so generous an aunt. Perhaps she was also secretly pleased that her younger sister still needed her despite her newfound artistic talents.

With the imminent arrival of the Bingleys and Darcys at Netherfield, Mrs. Bennet wondered how that balance of power played out amongst her own girls. She could see that each had carved out an identity within the family: Jane the gracious beauty, Lizzy the keen wit, Lydia impulsive and generous-hearted, Kitty emotional and moody, and Mary trying to be the learned scholar.

How she wished each girl could be defined by expressing a special talent. She was grateful to have found her artistic self again. It emboldened her to meet life's challenges and gave her some comfort that she could provide monetary support for herself and her family. Beyond making good marriages, this is what she wished for her girls.

CHAPTER XXXVII

Mrs. Bennet was busy in the small shed where she kept her painting supplies, preparing her brushes and gathering her materials in anticipation of Georgianna Darcy's arrival, when she heard the wheels of a carriage approach. *Surely that couldn't be Bingley and Darcy so soon.* She hurried out of the shed, brushing the dust from her apron, and came face to face with Lady Catherine de Bourgh peering out of the carriage window at her.

Lady Catherine looked at Mrs. Bennet's disheveled state and harrumphed. "Mrs. Bennet, I have come to see you and your daughter."

Though flustered, she attempted to be gracious. "What a lovely surprise, Lady Catherine. I will return to the house and arrange for some tea."

"Never mind all that," said Lady Catherine. "Brush the dust off of you and get in," she commanded. She opened the carriage door.

Mrs. Bennet seated herself next to Lady Catherine and inquired about Lady Anne. "I am not here to discuss Lady Anne, though she displeases me greatly." From Lady Catherine's response, Mrs. Bennet inferred that Lady Anne had chosen Colonel Fitzwilliam, and she smiled.

Lady Catherine caught the smile. "I see that you approve of her choice, perhaps even encouraged it to further your own ends."

Mrs. Bennet sat straighter in shock. "What are you talking about?"

"I am talking about how you and your daughter schemed to entrap my nephew," hissed Lady Catherine.

"Excuse me?"

"Don't play the innocent with me. I have it on very good authority that Darcy actually proposed to that chit of a girl."

It was all she could do to prevent herself from shoving this dreadful woman out of the carriage. "That chit of a girl, my lovely daughter Elizabeth, refused him. Surely you have heard that."

"Probably just a ruse on her part to keep him dangling

after her. If she said yes right away, he might have gotten bored with her already. I know that my nephew is preparing to stay for a time at Netherfield. I want to make sure that your daughter does not become engaged to him. I am well aware of the hasty marriage your younger daughter has made, and I want no connexion with the Bennet family."

Mrs. Bennet thought about Mr. Collins and realized he was the most likely source of Lady Catherine's information. She'd received their regrets to the invitation to Lydia's wedding accompanied by a letter from Mr. Collins filled with sanctimonious lecturing about marriage.

Lizzy must have confided in Charlotte, who must have discussed it with her husband. Mrs. Bennet did not believe Darcy would have divulged Wickham and Lydia's situation to his aunt.

"I demand an audience with your daughter," said Lady Catherine.

Her first instinct was to protect Lizzy from this gorgon, but considering the girl's indiscretion with Charlotte, she decided to let Lizzy deal with the consequences. "No need to alight from the carriage, Lady Catherine, considering your advanced age. I will send Elizabeth out to you directly."

She watched from the window as Lizzy entered the carriage. When she exited, Lizzy's cheeks were flushed but her head held high as she entered the house. "Oh, Mother, she wanted me to give her a guarantee that I would not accept Mr. Darcy!"

"And did you give her that guarantee?"

"I did not. Mother, she said awful things about our

family and Lydia. If Mr. Darcy does ask again, which is doubtful, and if I did accept him, I fear she would try to ruin us."

"So now, in order to help our family you must reject a proposal." She sighed and said gently, "You were unwilling to accept Mr. Collins' proposal to save us."

"Mother, I am so sorry," sobbed Lizzy.

"Actually, Lizzy, I find the whole situation amusing. However, what I don't find amusing is your telling tales about Lydia outside the family to Charlotte. Did you not think that eventually she would share this with her husband, who in turn shared it with Lady Catherine? I worked very hard to save Lydia's reputation.

"You must now deny that any impropriety occurred and say it was your romantic imagination that got carried away, and perhaps you were suffering from a bit of envy, as you were once considered the object of Wickham's affection. I am sorry to ask you to do this, but you must write Charlotte and say something to that effect. Something like you have examined your conscience, and realized that you were maligning your sister's reputation unfairly. If it works, expect a letter from Mr. Collins counseling you on sisterly love and duty. Will you do this, Lizzy, to repair some of the damage you caused?"

Lizzy sighed. "I will do it."

Mrs. Bennet softened and pulled her into a hug. "If Mr. Darcy asks, and you decide he is the one for you, accept him. If that old cat puts out any vicious gossip about our family, I will counter that it is just her spite and anger over her daughter not receiving a proposal from Mr. Darcy and accepting Colonel Fitzwilliam instead, whose income is substantially less. My brother's wife is exceedingly adept at placing the right phrases upon gossiping tongues."

Lizzy nodded against her mother's chest. "She was the source of the gossip in London about Mr. Darcy's proposal, wasn't she?"

"It served us well. You and your sister were the toast of London. Mr. Bingley resumed his pursuit of Jane and Mr. Darcy was taken down a peg, which I believe did him no harm. Now I am exhausted. I am going in for a lie-down and you need to compose that letter to Charlotte."

CHAPTER XXXVIII

When Mr. Bingley arrived at Netherfield he immediately called upon Jane and paid his respects to the Bennet family. He had some wonderful news to share regarding his sister. "Caroline has joined the titled ranks," he exclaimed.

"How did this come about?" Mrs. Bennet was quite concerned about Caroline's depth of feelings and Mr. Darcy's deliberate obtuseness regarding her affection for him. If Jane were to marry Bingley and Lizzy accepted Darcy, Caroline's presence would be awkward. She feared that the friendship between Bingley and Darcy would have to be severed. It had cooled somewhat in London. She noted that Mr. Bingley came alone to Netherfield.

"Well, Caroline went abroad for part of the season. She felt she needed a change of air." At this, Bingley looked a bit uncomfortable, but continued his affect brightening as he retold the tale.

"It seems while abroad, she ran in to Lord Worthing on holiday with his daughter. As you may know, Lord Worthing lost his wife several years ago. He was having quite a time of it trying to go to the shops with young Amelia. Watching them struggle over what was fashionable, what was correct, Caroline took pity on them. You all must admit she has exquisite taste."

The Bennet girls nodded in agreement.

"Lady Amelia was delighted with her purchases, and Lord Worthing was grateful to Caroline for rescuing him. From that time on they were a merry trio. Caroline became quite attached to Amelia, writing that she liked the girl very much, and enjoyed the feeling of being needed. I believe Lord Worthing came to rely on Caroline greatly.

"The charming end of this story is that Amelia took Caroline's hand and her father's while walking between them, joined them together, stomped her foot and said, 'You must marry.' Lord Worthing agreed and with a wink said he always granted his daughter's wishes and proposed there right on the spot! The nuptials took place in a lovely church in a small village in Italy. With my sister still on her honeymoon, I fear she will not be able to make the trip to Netherfield. Darcy will be coming with Georgianna and his housekeeper. So I won't be rambling about on my lonesome."

The girls expressed their delight over Caroline's marriage. Jane said she would write to her immediately to offer her joy.

Mrs. Bennet smiled and took Mr. Bingley's hand. "I got to know Caroline quite well during our painting sessions. She is capable of great passion and devotion. Lord Worthing and young Lady Amelia are truly blessed."

Mr. Bingley was invited to join them for the evening meal. He then joined them every night until Darcy's arrival and was already being treated as part of the family. He made a formal offer of marriage to Jane within a week of being at Netherfield, and she happily accepted.

At luncheon, Bingley dropped in and announced Darcy was soon to arrive so unfortunately he could not join them today. Mrs. Bennet saw Lizzy blush and fidget nervously with her napkin.

Mrs. Bennet turned to Kitty and explained. "There is a young lady accompanying them, Mr. Darcy's younger sister, Georgianna. Mr. Darcy asked that I do her portrait."

"How old is Georgianna?" asked Kitty. Mrs. Bennet knew that Kitty, since Lydia's departure, had been lonely. Her elder sisters were so bonded and though they tried to include her, she felt an outsider, and Mary was too cerebral for equal companionship.

Mrs. Bennet smiled at her daughter. "She is exactly your age."

"What is she like? Is she like Mr. Darcy, very proud and

arrogant?"

"She is not at all like Mr. Darcy; she is very, very timid but has great musical gifts. She plays the piano like an angel."

"Oh," said Kitty. "Someone so accomplished may not be in need of my friendship."

"Miss Darcy is very shy and has slight difficulty with her speech."

Kitty looked up. "Difficulty?"

"Yes, she stammers and because of it avoids social situations."

"Oh, that's awful," said Kitty as her eyes became moist.

"However," continued Mrs. Bennet, "she is able to overcome her stammer in song."

"In song?" said Kitty, looking quite confused

"Yes, if we converse with her, singing our words, she converses, singing clearly her responses with no stammer."

"How odd, but that still would be socially isolating in general company."

"Exactly, Kitty, and that is why I want you to accompany me to our painting sessions, befriend Miss Darcy, and help her to overcome her stammer."

"Me? How can I do that?"

"By being her friend, being patient, and slowly we will work on slower speech with her, but she must have a trusted friend to practice with. Will you do this?"

"Of course, but what if she doesn't like me?"

"Georgianna will take to you, I am sure. You are open and expressive with your emotions where she is not. It will be a good balance. Keep in mind this is a girl whose mother died young. She has had mainly the company of governesses and housekeepers. I think she will take great comfort from you girls. She has already met Lizzy and Jane, but I think she is in need of a special friend, and I am hoping that it will be you, my dear Kitty."

Kitty's bosom swelled with pride, and she looked forward to making a new friend.

Shortly thereafter, Mr. Darcy arrived with his housekeeper and Georgianna. Mrs. Bennet paid a call at Netherfield with Kitty in tow. The housekeeper answered the door.

"I'm afraid Mr. Darcy and Mr. Bingley are out hunting for a bit."

"No matter, it is really Georgianna we have come to call on," said Mrs. Bennet cheerfully.

"For that I'm grateful, Ma'am," whispered the housekeeper. "Poor thing keeps too much to herself."

She showed Mrs. Bennet and Kitty to the music room. Georgianna was at the piano practicing her scales. The young woman rose from the piano and rushed to greet Mrs. Bennet, but when she saw Kitty she hung back shyly. Mrs. Bennet proceeded to introduce her daughter in the slightly sing-song style used at their last meeting.

Kitty warbled a meek, "How do you do?" and Georgianna relaxed and laughed. The rest of the visit was conducted in that singing style. Mrs. Bennet fixed a time to start Georgianna's portrait, and Georgianna promised to give Kitty piano lessons. As they were finishing up the arrangements, Mr. Darcy entered.

Kitty sat at the piano. Georgianna was teaching her a simple scale.

"Mrs. Bennet, how good of you to call," Darcy said.

"I wanted to set the times with Georgianna for her portrait." Mrs. Bennet stood. "And you have turned down two of my dinner invitations."

"Yes… well, Georgianna was shy about coming."

"She needn't be. She has met Lizzy and Jane and now Kitty. I hope you don't mind that Georgianna has offered Kitty piano lessons."

Mr. Darcy looked over at his sister to see her giggling with Kitty as she helped her with her fingering. Mrs. Bennet saw the smile of affection that bloomed on his face.

After a moment, Mrs. Bennet spoke quietly. "Mr. Darcy, I am not unaware of the great service you did our family in securing Wickham's billet and most likely offering him additional monetary inducement to do his duty. What my brother and I offered could not have been what swayed him. Please allow me to offer this portrait of Georgianna as a gift of thanks."

Darcy smiled at her; she might even describe the smile as sheepish. "After all our arguments about respecting your work as a professional artist even though you are a woman, it shames me to now take it as a gift," he said.

A backhanded compliment if ever there was one. "Mr. Darcy, think of it as helping my career. If you display the portrait at Pemberley, those who visit may inquire about the artist."

He bowed. "As you wish, Madam; the portrait of my

cousin Lady Anne has caused quite a stir, and I am sure you must have heard that Lady Anne has married Colonel Fitzwilliam."

"Yes, Lady Catherine came to visit to inform me of the fact. She was quite enraged."

"Enraged?" said Mr. Darcy with surprise. "But Colonel Fitzwilliam is a fine gentleman. Why is Aunt Catherine upset about their marriage, and why would she bother to come all this way to speak to you about it?"

"She accused me of engineering the whole thing."

"But that's preposterous."

"Yes, but she could not be persuaded otherwise. In truth, I did know of Lady Anne's partiality towards Colonel Fitzwilliam and did nothing to dissuade her."

Was Darcy truly unaware of his aunt's plans? Perhaps he had also been oblivious to poor Caroline Bingley's feelings for him. *How typically male of him to consider only what concerns or interests him.* "Your aunt had plans for you and Lady Anne to marry."

"Nonsense!" He frowned. "I am like a brother to Lady Anne."

"That may be, but Lady Catherine was quite upset and demanded a private audience with Lizzy." Now she could see the light of comprehension come into his eyes.

His color was heightened as he asked, "What was said?"

"I do not know the exact content of their conversation. Suffice it to say Lizzy was quite upset after the interview. Unfortunately, Lady Catherine had heard of your offer to Lizzy. I believe she wanted an assurance from Lizzy that she would not accept you."

"Did she give it?" he asked in a strangled voice.

Mrs. Bennet had no intention of relieving his anxiety. "I do not know. You must ask her yourself."

The housekeeper arrived with a tray of lemonade. She drank hers quickly. Mr. Darcy set his glass down distractedly and moved to stare out the window.

"Come, Kitty," she said, "We must be off." She gave Georgianna a warm smile and watched the girls hug. "We will return on Thursday to start our portrait and piano sessions."

CHAPTER XXXIX

There was no question that she would paint Georgianna at the piano, where the young woman was in her element. This pose required her to be seated and did not concentrate one's attention so much on the fineness of her gown as on the position of her hands and shoulders and the tilt of her head. No dressmaker's form would make the process easier.

During their breaks, Georgianna continued to instruct Kitty on the piano. As she became more comfortable in Kitty's presence, the sing-song speech to overcome her stammer became just a slower speech with breaths taken at appropriate intervals. Kitty was delighted with her new friend and the accomplishment of some rudimentary piano skills.

Mrs. Bennet extended a dinner invitation to Georgianna. As Kitty would be at her side and the girls had already come for a visit or two, she accepted. Mr. Darcy had also been to the Bennet household on several occasions for afternoon tea, rejoicing in Bingley and Jane's happiness. Lizzy was courteous and friendly on these occasions, but seemed to avoid being left alone with him.

Mrs. Bennet could only watch. She saw the sadness in her daughter and knew that Lizzy feared that he would ask her to reconsider his proposal; if she weakened and accepted, would Lady Catherine make good on her threat and cause the ruination of the Bennet family? She wished to assuage her daughter's worries, but Lizzy was headstrong and must make the decision in her own time.

The first dinner with Georgianna engendered a delightful time all around. And the second did as well. This time, Mrs. Bennet added the Lucas family to the table. Georgianna again attended and, though a bit nonplussed to meet new people, acquitted herself quite well. Darcy, watching all, gave Mrs. Bennet a grateful nod.

A few days later, she encouraged the girls to go for a walk in Meryton for a look in the shops and a visit with their aunt. Kitty watched over Georgianna with tenderness and made sure the outing was a success. They returned in high spirits.

"Aunt says that a party should be given to announce Jane's engagement," said Kitty.

Jane started to protest, but Bingley seized upon the idea. "Yes, let's have a party. Should it be a ball?"

Jane blushed and laid a hand on his arm. "Perhaps not so formal."

Georgianna was looking nervously at Kitty. Kitty squeezed her hand and whispered, "It will be all right, and you shall do what you do best."

"What is that?" whispered Georgianna.

"Why, play the piano of course!"

"I know!" Bingley said. "We should have a buffet, a concert by Georgianna and then a bit of dancing and cards."

All were in agreement except Lizzy and Darcy. The objection to the arrangements united them in a common goal. Mrs. Bennet saw from the bay window Darcy and Lizzy deep in conversation in the garden.

As they approached, she let out a little squeal of delight, and sought out Mr. Bennet. "Mr. Bennet, prepare yourself, I believe Mr. Darcy will be asking for an audience with you!"

"Me! What would he want with me?"

Mrs. Bennet sighed. Were all men so oblivious? If she had said something in reference to a chapter he was writing, he would be all attention. As long as it referenced himself and his interests, he was responsive. He was good enough when he'd had to be left alone with the girls, but as soon as Mrs. Bennet returned, all was left for her to manage. *It is that way with most men. Consider Mr. Darcy's total oblivion to Lady Catherine's plans and to poor Caroline Bingley's affection.* She wondered if, after the courtship period, Bingley would remain so social and attentive to Jane's needs. Marriage was no bed of happiness once the bloom wore off. Children helped for a little while. But what other recourse did women have to gain financial security, respectability, and status, other than through a man?

She looked at her husband. His head was bent over his writing desk, absorbed in his work. She did not begrudge him that. She knew the joy of total immersion into her painting.

What she disliked was his obstinate inability to deal with anything else. His expectations of her were to keep the household running, meals on the table, manage the accounts, and tend to the girls' needs, while she could only allow herself to steal away a few hours a week to paint. When she returned from a tiring session of trying to capture Georgianna's likeness at the piano, he had made no effort to settle the account with the butcher or even pay the servants' wages. All was left for her to manage.

As she watched Lizzy and Darcy walk up the path, she was tempted to dissuade them from their purpose. She thought about having a talk with Jane as well.

But much to her surprise, it wasn't Mr. Bennet they intended to see. Darcy and Lizzy sought an audience with her. *How odd,* she thought as she entered the drawing room with them. Darcy closed the door.

Lizzy began. "Mama, I would like you to ask Jane and

Charles to reconsider this engagement party."

"Whatever for? They are engaged."

"Yes, but a public celebration just now would not be seemly."

Mrs. Bennet looked from one to the other. "The Bennet family has nothing to be ashamed of, and if we act like we are ashamed it will be the worse for our reputation. A celebration of your sister's engagement is appropriate."

Mr. Darcy then spoke up. "I am most happy for Charles and Jane. Do not misunderstand me, but I, too, wish that there were to be no public celebration. I do not believe my dear sister Georgianna is up to it."

"Mr. Darcy, you are a devoted brother, I know. But you cannot keep Georgianna in a gilded cage. There would be no safer celebration than this one for her to further test her social skills. I have had her to dinner, adding more guests each time. She has gone about to the shops with Kitty. At the party she will be giving a concert. She is most herself when playing the piano. She will be given a chance to shine. Has she expressed to you that she does not want to attend the event or perform in the concert?"

"Well, no. However, she has told me she is very nervous."

"That is to be expected. I have a plan for that. I am almost finished with her portrait. Once it is complete, Kitty and I plan to set up the concert room and have the girls, your housekeeper, you, and Charles come and listen to the selections. I have asked Kitty to dress your sister as she will be dressed for the party. We will have a rehearsal. Then, on the night of the ball, Kitty will introduce the program.

When Georgianna is introduced to people, she can keep her conversation to a minimum at first with 'How-do-you-dos' and, of course, 'Thank-yous,' as people compliment her on her playing. She will be dancing, and there is usually little conversation one is capable of when dancing a lively reel. Kitty has taught her some of our local reels. Her partners will be a smattering of local boys from local families. This celebration is actually the perfect opportunity for her to try out her newfound social ability. Consider it a prelude to presenting her for her season in London."

Mr. Darcy paled.

"Mr. Darcy," said Mrs. Bennet softly, "you will have to do that soon."

Darcy put his head in his hands. Mrs. Bennet took that as her cue. She exited the room but left the door slightly ajar.

"Oh Lord, she's right, Elizabeth, I shall never be able to do that."

"Of course you will."

"I could do it if I had someone at my side who cared for me and cared for my sister."

Through the open door, Mrs. Bennet saw him go down on bended knee. *Oh, was there ever anything as heart-trippingly romantic as a proposal?* Mr. Darcy offered his apologies for his previous proposal and pleaded with Lizzy to consider this one from the heart. Mrs. Bennet held her breath, then heard Lizzy's tearful acceptance.

She was glad for them and didn't doubt Mr. Darcy's

sincerity, but as the excitement of the moment passed, she couldn't help wondering if Mr. Darcy's realization of his impending responsibilities for Georgianna's London season was not the precipitating factor in his ardent proposal. He had been at Netherfield for a month's time and had other opportunities to present his suit. Lizzy would of course take charge of Georgianna, and then Darcy would be free to hunt, run his estate, buy livestock, and continue his self-interest.

Mrs. Bennet sighed and went to prepare her husband to meet with Mr. Darcy.

CHAPTER XL

"Well, Miriam, it seems you have another daughter engaged. One wed, two engaged and one promised. You must be pleased."

Mrs. Bennet smiled at her husband as he found her in the parlor. She should feel pleased, shouldn't she? Yet she wondered why she didn't. "We shall announce Lizzy's engagement at Jane's party. The nice thing is, we will be able to just have one wedding celebration for both. Considering our finances, we are most fortunate."

"Don't you think Bingley will want to have it at Netherfield?"

"No, that won't do. We must shoulder this responsibility for our girls. A simple country wedding, first at the church, with field flowers, then we will have tables brought outside here in the meadow. We will supply fresh fruits, meats, wine, and fiddlers for some lively dancing. To save on the curate's fee, I am thinking of asking Mr. Collins to officiate. He is family."

"Well, it seems you have it all worked out," harrumphed Mr. Bennet.

"Do you want to do something differently?" Mrs. Bennet asked sweetly. "I mean, other than trying to stick Bingley or Darcy with the expenses. Need I remind you that Darcy has helped in too many ways to mention with Lydia's situation?"

"Miriam, can you for once keep your indiscreet comments to yourself?"

"If I can't speak my mind with you, dear husband, then there is no sense in being together."

"Now look here, Miriam. I have been patient as you gad about painting portraits and engaging in all your marriage schemes for our girls. We have been feeding Bingley almost every night and now Darcy and his sister occasionally. I am just pointing out a reality. That it would be nice to be relieved of taking on more debt to give a wedding. Not to mention the clothes you will have made for each girl. How are we going to handle all of this?"

"Your pamphlets are selling well, and, after the engagement party, I hope to secure more commissions from Georgianna's painting."

However, Mrs. Bennet was finding Georgianna's portrait more taxing than usual. It was all the dark-grained wood of the piano she was struggling with, trying to demonstrate the wood's texture. But she didn't share her concerns about the success of the painting with her husband; he never inquired about her work and she didn't want him to use it as another excuse to be cheap about the wedding.

She'd seen the alarm, though, on his face when she made the comment about not being together. The loss of her companionship to him likely meant that he would have to manage things alone. Planning all these engagements and weddings had the opposite effect on her, and she reassessed her situation as she watched each girl enter the yoke of marriage.

She found herself occasionally daydreaming about living alone.

Mary was still at home, of course. But she was formulating a plan about Mary too. Opportunities for young ladies were slowly evolving. Mary may have options that were not available for her sisters.

While in London, Mrs. Bennet had learned of a new way of educating young ladies. Nannies and governesses were giving way to private schools. She had not shared her research into these matters with her husband, for she knew she would only meet with opposition.

Mr. Bennet, grumbling to himself, was walking toward the parlor door.

"Edward, as your gentleman farmer booklet is selling so well, have you considered writing another?"

"About farming?" He turned.

"No, not farming. How about something more true to your current situation?"

"What? Having a wife gadding about painting up a storm and constantly feeding my daughters' fiancés?"

"Now, now, Edward, think. Here is a father amid wedding plans for two daughters; what chaos, what situations ripe for wry wit about society, marriage, love and the tender feelings of a father walking his girls down the aisle, the concerns of a father as he hears the potential fiancé's presentation before he gives consent. Everyone would read it, Edward."

He shook his head and folded his arms across his chest. "I am not sure I like drawing from so close to our reality, Miriam; it offers too much exposure. We are the only family hereabouts due to give a double wedding."

"Disguise it then as two separate weddings."

He liked the idea but hesitated. "I feel guilty about you having to seek commissions, though I know you enjoy the work. I can see that it can be tiring, standing at the easel for long periods, racing to complete the portrait."

He had found her up late at night trying to complete some touches by candlelight. He was a poet by nature, and she wondered if with his sensitivities he might not sense that she was distracted and distant. Not just with settling the girls, but some deeper discontent.

"The idea for the book is a good one, but I think it would be even more popular if it had your illustrations in it. You know, what the gowns look like, a father's concerned face, the wedding bouquet. These book sketches would be easier than working on full portraits. I will ask my editor if we can have an advance. Perhaps this can cover the costs of the wedding, and you needn't accept another difficult commission unless you wanted to."

Mrs. Bennet was surprised—more so that he had noticed that she was tired and having difficulty with this portrait. Of course, he made no offer to manage any household details to relieve her daily burden. But the offer of another artistic collaboration pleased her. She had enjoyed doing some of the animal sketches for his last book.

Can he really be concerned about losing me as a companion? She looked up and saw her husband watching her hopefully. What would she actually do with her freedom if not married to him?

Here they were, two people in the middle years of their life, knowing no other. She clasped her husband's outstretched hand. "It is a wonderful idea, Edward. You handle the prose and I the paint."

Mr. Bennet brought his wife's hand to his lips and kissed it, and in the silence they shared was acknowledgment that amid the bustle of engagements and wedding plans, no love was as passionate as that which had passed the test of time.

CHAPTER XLI

Kitty and Georgianna returned from the dressmaker happy with their choices for the Netherfield party. Jane and Lizzy delivered invitations to all the county families. Mr. Darcy had secretly invited his cousins the de Bourghs to hear Georgianna play. He kept it as a surprise, for he did not want Georgianna to become nervous, knowing her notoriously critical aunt would be in attendance at the party. Caroline Bingley and Lord Worthing were still abroad, but had sent word that they planned to return for the wedding.

The dress rehearsal was a success. And at the end of it, Mrs. Bennet unveiled the portrait.

Georgianna gasped in delight.

Darcy was stunned. "This is no portrait," he said.

"Mama, it's beautiful!" exclaimed Jane.

Lizzy, her sharpest critic, clasped her arm. "Mama, Mr. Darcy is right. This is no portrait. This is a painting; it would be a disservice to display it over any mantelpiece, no matter how grand. It belongs in a museum or a gallery."

"Thank you, Lizzy." She accepted the compliment without her usual self-deprecation. She knew that this piece went beyond her portraits of ladies in their fancy gowns. She had started on this path with her representation of Lady Anne. This piece had taken all her skill, with the perspective of the room, the instrument, the player's hands and face expressing the movement and emotion of the music.

Mr. Bennet was moved. He whispered, "Miriam, I fear our talk of future illustrations pales against this."

"Not to worry, Edward, after this I need the restful work of the sketches."

"Mama, why not send this to a museum if Mr. Darcy and Georgianna will allow?" asked Kitty.

Mrs. Bennet sighed. "It would never be accepted."

"Why not?" said Jane.

"Because," interjected Mary, "it is painted by a woman."

"I know," said Lizzy, "just sign it with your initials!"

"No, Lizzy, I will not sign it with my initials. Those that would judge this unfit because a woman's hand held the brush are unfit judges."

And with that Mrs. Bennet dipped her brush and completed her signature.

As the girls were dressing for the party, Mrs. Bennet took a moment to be alone with Lizzy and Jane to wish them both joy. "Are you planning to announce your engagement tonight?"

"I think not, Mama. It is a party to celebrate Jane, and to enjoy Georgianna's concert. I think that will be enough excitement in one evening."

"Well, it is up to the two of you, but I do want to talk to you both about the weddings. I hope you do not mind, dear, but your father and I discussed it and if it is all right with you and Jane, we would like to do a double wedding at the church and one party."

"Perhaps we could have my wedding at Pemberley?" said Lizzy.

"No, that won't do dear. You should cross Pemberley's threshold only as a bride." There was an embarrassed silence, for all were thinking of Lydia.

"This is the last time I will have you girls at home. We would like to give the wedding party here in our meadow, a lovely country wedding, with all your friends as attendants, the last gathering before you go away to your respective fine houses and married lives."

The girls started to tear up. They hugged their mother and agreed to her plan.

"Now, no tears," admonished Mrs. Bennet, "your faces will be stained."

Lizzy looked lovely in her amber gown with gold ribbon laced throughout her chestnut curls. Jane was in blue, as it was Bingley's favorite, and it suited her well. Mrs. Bennet went to check on the others.

Kitty looked a dream in pale yellow with embroidered daisies at the bodice and hem and one secured in her curls. Georgianna was flushed but looked lovely in a pale pink gown that shimmered when she moved. Her blond curls were swept up in ringlets with a lacy pink ribbon woven in. Mary had chosen an emerald green gown. She wore a lovely matching ribbon around her neck with a gold locket.

Mrs. Bennet had chosen to have Lizzy's elegant pewter dress altered to suit her. Mr. Bennet, for once, was dressed and ready to depart.

It was decided to have two receiving lines to facilitate the guests' entrance, Mr. and Mrs. Bennet on one side with Lizzy, Mary, and Kitty. Charles, Jane, Darcy and Georgianna on the other. Mrs. Bennet was in the process of welcoming her sister, when she heard Georgianna gasp with surprise. She turned to see Lady Anne in Georgianna's embrace, with Colonel Fitzwilliam behind her and behind him, a most unfortunate sight: Lady Catherine.

As the guests proceeded to enter the buffet, Lady Anne and her party crossed over to speak with Mrs. Bennet.

"Have you heard the news about our marriage?" she asked shyly.

"I have and I wish you much joy." It was apparent that Lady Anne was unaware of her aunt's visit and threats. But Lady Catherine had no plans to back down. She turned and addressed Mrs. Bennet, clearly snubbing Lizzy.

"Darcy asked us to come to support Georgianna's concert. As I understand it, today is also a celebration of you having succeeded in marrying off another daughter. I have a letter from Mr. Collins to your second-eldest."

She reached into her silken bag and placed it in Mrs. Bennet's hand. "I have assisted him with several quotes from the scriptures, outlining the importance of truthfulness and avoiding coveting thy neighbor's goods. Darcy!"

Lady Catherine put her hand out and with a grimace her nephew took it and escorted his aunt to the buffet.

Mrs. Bennet was looking down at the letter when her husband approached. "What was that all about?" he asked.

Mrs. Bennet sighed. "Just the vile complexities of women and society. Come, let us enjoy the buffet."

After the buffet and champagne were thoroughly depleted, the guests moved on to the concert room. The painting of Georgianna had been set up for viewing in the anterior room, with a card explaining that it had been inspired by Georgianna's gift for music, visible to all as the guests filed past. Lord Lucas immediately made an offer of purchase. He was quite proud of his initial support of Mrs. Bennet's artistry and felt it his right as he was her first patron. Darcy, of course, responded that it was not for sale.

Lady Anne grasped Mrs. Bennet's arm and whispered, "I was thrilled with my exquisite portrait, but it is clear since then you have gone beyond. As a fledgling artist myself, I have not your talent, but I have the understanding. This is not a mere portrait, this is Art."

Mrs. Bennet graciously replied, "It was inspired by Georgianna's gift for music." And with that, the guests moved into the concert room.

Kitty announced the program prettily. Georgianna entered the room, her pale gown shimmering as she moved to seat herself. Darcy was standing at the back of the room, his back stiff with tension. Georgianna looked out over the audience. Kitty gave an encouraging nod, Georgianna took a deep breath, closed her eyes, and began to play.

All her pent-up emotions, her inability to communicate freely, were channeled into her music. Here was passion, playfulness, sympathy, despair, and joy. At the end of the performance, women were weeping and the men were shouting, "Brava!"

Georgianna stood and bowed and spoke hesitantly. "Thank you... for listening."

Darcy leapt upon the platform, his eyes moist, and stood near his sister. He raised a glass as he spoke.

"I am so proud. A year ago, you knew me as a man filled with pride, pride for all the wrong reasons. Tonight I stand here once again a very proud man: proud of my sister's extraordinary musical gift, proud of my friendship with Charles Bingley, proud to celebrate his betrothal, and now I am most proud to announce that Miss Elizabeth Bennet has consented to be my wife."

Lizzy, with a look of surprise, joined him on the platform, and the guests responded with cheers and applause.

Lady Catherine flushed red with fury. She probably felt that Mrs. Bennet had out-foxed her in the attainment of Darcy. Mrs. Bennet smiled to herself. Lady Catherine would now have a blood connexion to Mr. Collins. And he might presume himself to be on equal terms with her.

As Lady Catherine turned and made a hasty exit, she hissed in Mrs. Bennet's ear, "I'll ruin you."

CHAPTER XLII

The newly engaged couples were allowed to return to the Bennet house in one carriage without a chaperone. Mr. and Mrs. Bennet, with Kitty and Mary, followed. As Darcy and Charles took their leave of the Bennet household, Mrs. Bennet took the opportunity to say, "Mr. Darcy, I could not help noticing that Lady Catherine left in some haste. I hope she is not ill."

Darcy reddened. "No, Ma'am, she was not ill. I fear the surprise announcement of our engagement was the cause. I should have spoken with her privately."

"Mr. Darcy, please allow me to say that I fear no amount of private explanation would have changed her reaction. In fact, both of you young couples must prepare yourselves for similar reactions in certain sections of society."

"Surely not!" said Bingley.

"Charles, though it pains me to remind you, think of your sister's and your friend's original alarm regarding your affection for Jane."

"But that was all a misunderstanding. All is well now," said Bingley brightly.

Mrs. Bennet sighed. "I urge you all to consider that there will be snubs from society. Jane, it may not be as difficult for you, as you are to reside close by in Netherfield where local society loves you. But for you, Lizzy, at Pemberley..."

"I won't allow it," said Darcy determinedly.

"You can't do much to stop it. Your aunt's behavior tonight is an indication of how things may proceed. Go slowly. Socialize at first with those closest to you, with intimate evenings at Pemberley. Perhaps Georgianna will assist with another concert or two. She will need a chaperone for her season in London. I believe you will need the assistance of Lady Anne, as well as Lizzy, for Georgianna to have a successful season."

"But why?" sputtered Darcy.

"Georgianna will need invitations to various teas, picnics, balls, and house parties. Lady Anne's title and social standing will assure that she will receive them."

Darcy sat down slowly, shaking his head. "Who makes these things so complicated?"

"It isn't us men," said Bingley.

Mr. Bennet concurred. "I can hardly drag myself to all the folderol Miriam wants me to attend."

"Why are women so mean?" moaned Bingley, half teasing.

"A woman's very survival in this society is dependent upon a man. So the desperation of attaining stability, respectability, through marriage is tantamount to survival. It makes for a vicious competitive cycle. One I personally have no desire to be part of."

All looked at Mary in amazement. Mrs. Bennet could see that her serious, somber, thoughtful girl had by far the most astute understanding.

Mr. Darcy was frowning, and now he cautioned the Bennets. "I fear Mary must be reading that Wollstonecraft woman."

Lizzy, not hearing the censure in Darcy's voice, said to Mary, "Surely that cycle can be broken?"

"Yes, perhaps one day," challenged Mrs. Bennet, "when a woman is allowed to support herself through her own means, not through inheritance or marriage."

Lizzy laughed. "Oh Mama, you are talking about your art again."

Mrs. Bennet did not share in her laughter. It wasn't the first time Lizzy had denigrated her mother's talents and ambitions. She was not sure why. Perhaps her daughter saw her aspirations as competition, or truly judged them as foolish.

"I am also talking about Georgianna's music," said Mrs. Bennet quietly.

Here Darcy paled. "It is only her passion, Mrs. Bennet, not her profession."

"Exactly," said Mrs. Bennet. "Now examine your response, Sir! Why could it not also be her profession?" She turned to both her daughters. "Make no mistake. I am thrilled for you both, for it does seem love is the motivating factor, but think now, if you had not these fine husbands-to-be, what would your future be? If you were not to become wives, what else could you be?"

Mr. Bennet cleared his throat, no doubt fearing she had become too combative in her remarks. "It has been a jolly evening. It is getting late. We have a wedding to plan. Let us all get some rest."

The gentlemen departed. As Mary was ascending the

stairs, she turned to her older sisters. "I do have Mrs. Wollstonecraft's writings. Mother bought them. You can read them if you like."

As Mr. Bennet was preparing for bed, he turned to his wife. "I don't understand you, Miriam. Why provoke the girls and their young men? Isn't this what you wanted, the girls both married and comfortably settled? If you stir things up this way, you may put off the gentlemen, or the girls will start to think the life of a spinster is attractive."

"I know, I know," sighed Mrs. Bennet. She turned towards her husband and delicately put a hand on his shoulder. Mr. Bennet reached over to grab his pince-nez from the night table, settled them upon his nose and opened his book to where he had laid his ribbon to mark his place. It seemed that there were consequences for speaking one's mind about independence for women. Mrs. Bennet quietly turned on her side, smarting from the unspoken rejection.

CHAPTER XLIII

The next few weeks were a flurry of activity. Mrs. Bennet ordered fruits and meats for the wedding feast. Mr. Bennet hunted for pheasants with some of the locals. Mrs. Johns, the cook, baked the wedding cake as her gift to the family. Poor Mrs. Robbs, the seamstress, made a dozen trips to get the measurements right. Each girl's dress was unique. Jane's dress was all tiers of lacy ruffles, a frothy concoction that rested upon her creamy shoulders. Lizzy, loving understated elegance, had her dress made with simple flowing lines, a high lace collar, and mutton silk sleeves with tight lace from elbow to wrist.

The seamstress, having known the girls growing up, decided to also make her work a wedding gift. Mrs. Bennet was quite touched by Mrs. Johns' and Mrs. Robbs' offers, and as she accompanied them to the gate, she made a most unorthodox suggestion.

"Dear Mrs. Johns and Mrs. Robbs, we hope you and your husbands will be able to attend the meadow reception as well as the service."

The two women were speechless. Mrs. Robb ventured nervously, "Nice of you to invite us, Ma'am, but don't think it's quite the correct thing, don't you know."

"But why isn't it correct? You have both offered these wonderful wedding gifts, without which we could not celebrate, and you have seen my girls grow from babyhood.

I believe it is quite correct. Are you saying you wouldn't enjoy seeing the girls in your creation, Mrs. Robbs? And wouldn't you, Mrs. Johns, like a taste of your fine cake?"

The two women looked at her in amazement, then started to laugh. "Well, seeing you put it like that, yes, we'll come, though we can't answer for the menfolk."

"Aren't Mr. Johns and Mr. Robbs helping with Mr. Bennet's pheasant hunt?"

"Yes, they are, Ma'am."

"Well, then, surely they will want to take part in the feast?"

As Mrs. Bennet walked back into the house she made a mental note to invite Georgianna's housekeeper too.

One week before the wedding, Lydia arrived home. She hugged her mother with an intensity that even for Lydia was surprising. Wickham had not accompanied her. Lydia gave the excuse that he was on duty with his regiment, but when she was alone with her mother she sobbed out the truth.

"He is never home, and when he does come home he is reeking of drink and usually in a foul mood. If I approach him, I must be wary, for he strikes out in his drunken stupor. He is mean and bitter and takes no joy in anything. He complains of being stripped of his rightful inheritance and place in life and being saddled with me. Oh, Mother, I don't know what to do. I try to make him happy. I even joined him in his drinking and gambling, thinking that would bond us, but in truth it made me ill. He has changed so. He is no longer the Apollo he was. I have sold my engagement band and most of my trousseau to pay off his gambling debts and to put food on the table."

The misery of her marriage was evident. Lydia was too thin. She did not look well, and there was a fading yellow bruise on her upper arm. All her exuberant healthy glow seemed extinguished. "You will stay here with us for a while," Mrs. Bennet said. "Kitty so misses you. And after the wedding there will be so much packing and helping your sisters settle that I can simply not spare you to return to your husband. That is what we tell the neighbors if they ask why you are staying on."

"How long can that last?" sobbed Lydia. "I will have to return eventually."

"No, you won't, my dear," Mrs. Bennet said fiercely as she touched Lydia's bruised arm. "Perhaps your mother may fall ill and need the attentions of her daughter. Or if fortune smiles upon us, perhaps Wickham may drink himself to death."

"Mother! I did love him."

"No, Lydia, you were infatuated with him and no amount of good advice could change your mind." Mrs. Bennet sighed. "Welcome home, my love."

Mrs. Johns, the cook, had come into the parlor with tea. She gave a knowing look to Mrs. Bennet and set about fussing over Lydia. "Come into the kitchen right now! I sent you away a fine healthy girl, now you're skin and bones. You may think it is the fashion, but I don't agree. You need a pudding and some meat."

Lydia laughed and turned to her mother. "It's good to be home."

Mrs. Bennet watched them leave, then gave herself a moment to indulge the grief she felt over a mother's wish to spare her child pain. She would need to speak with Mr. Bennet about Lydia's situation, for it must be handled carefully, but it could wait. Now was the time for celebrating the promise of marriage. There would be plenty of time for reality later.

At Netherfield, Mrs. Bennet, Elizabeth, and Jane consulted with Bingley and Darcy over the guest lists. Mr. Darcy offered that he was sure his cousin Anne and Colonel Fitzwilliam would attend, though his aunt had already sent her regrets. Charles knew both his sisters and their husbands would attend, along with assorted cousins. Lord Worthing expressed concern about having his daughter attend, but Mrs. Bennet assured Charles that his daughter would feel most comfortable; after all, Mary was the same age. Mrs. Bennet decided now was the appropriate time to bring up the invitations sent out to the country folk. "Mrs. Johns has made the wedding cake as her gift, and Mrs. Robbs has sewn their gowns. They are so looking forward to seeing the girls and joining in the celebration."

There was a moment of awkward silence. Finally Jane spoke up. "Mother, you know I adore them both, but won't they feel uncomfortable at the gathering?"

"Oh, I don't think so. Their husbands, who helped your father with the quail hunt, will attend to them and as it turns out, they also know the musicians we have engaged for the reception. In fact, Jeremiah Johns is the main fiddler. I do so wish this wedding to be a celebration for all the county families. Remember Charlotte Lucas's wedding? It was such a drab affair. Your father has already cut and dried the planks for the dance floor to be set in the meadow."

"Mother, just how many have you invited?" asked Lizzy

"With the mix of local gentry, our relatives, country families, and London visitors we should number about sixty."

"Sixty people, Mother, really!"

"Well, think about it. It is a double wedding therefore, double the attendance."

Charles Bingley started to laugh, "I think it is marvelous. Shouldn't we consider having it at Netherfield, though?"

"That is very kind of you, but we'll have long tables for the food and enough chairs and seats for all. Girls, for the rest of your lives you will be hosting formal dinner parties or balls. This is the last time you will have to enjoy a fiddle and dance a country reel in our meadow with the sun upon your face."

Georgianna clapped her hands. "It sounds charming. I am so looking forward to it."

Darcy smiled at her indulgently—the perfect opening. "I am so glad you think so," Mrs. Bennet said. "So with the entire county celebrating this double wedding, I was hoping that Mrs. Wilkes, your housekeeper, could attend. It would be a shame to leave her all alone here."

Darcy cleared his throat, his thoughts evident on his face; it was all very well and good for Mrs. Bennet to cross class lines in her own household, but he would be the master in his own house. "I believe Mrs. Wilkes, after seeing to managing our various guests that morning, is planning on a day off."

"Yes, so I heard from Mrs. Robbs. Because, you see, usually on her day off she takes tea with Mrs. Robbs. Mrs. Robbs, our seamstress, will be attending the wedding. I thought Mrs. Wilkes would enjoy being included as well."

"That is the perfect solution!" exclaimed Georgianna.

"I am so glad you think so, dear." Mrs. Bennet fumbled around in her net bag and produced an invitation addressed to Mrs. Wilkes. "Would you see that she gets this?"

Darcy grimaced when he realized he'd been outmaneuvered. Mrs. Bennet was not unaware that Darcy was disgruntled about his housekeeper attending his wedding. Lizzy smiled tightly, seeming embarrassed once again by her mother's behavior. Mrs. Bennet continued to smile. If he refused he would seem arrogant. *Darcy is a good man, but a terrible snob. I hope Lizzy will be happy. Perhaps with her pert ways she can soften him a bit.*

CHAPTER XLIV

Mr. Bennet had more than enough material for his book on wedding preparations and mishaps. There was always a flurry of debate regarding attendants' gowns, color and style, proper flowers for the church versus the reception, church music to be chosen versus dancing reels for the meadow. It was exhausting. He was almost at the concluding chapter. Here, he allowed his emotions to seep in, talking about a father's worries and concerns, his sadness at a daughter leaving the safe bosom of her family.

Mrs. Bennet read the final draft. She laughed uproariously at the satirical depiction of the mother of the bride, the chronicling of all the little skirmishes over the style, and sometimes the substance, of the wedding. She was quite moved by the final chapter. She settled the manuscript in her lap.

"Mr. Bennet, you have outdone yourself!"

"Do you really think so, Miriam?"

"I do, my dear. I may take issue with you as a lackadaisical householder, but as a writer, my dear, you are perfection. The last chapter is most moving and will touch all who read it. It will help married women understand their husbands as fathers. And give insight to the daughters of a father's feeling."

Mr. Bennet flushed with pride. She could see that her husband was pleased by her opinion, and she was gratified that it mattered to him. Having opened the discussion about the final chapter, she thought it best now to apprise him of Lydia's situation.

"My dear, that last chapter, as I said, is so poignantly true. What a good father you are to our girls. You are there when they need you. I was going to wait until the wedding was over, but I think you should know about our dear Lydia's current situation."

"You mean that her husband is a rotter and a drunk, and she is back to stay?"

Mrs. Bennet choked. "How did you know?"

"Miriam, I live here. I overhear the whisperings, the weeping. How bad is it actually?"

"Well, she has some fading bruises on both arms."

"Enough said. She must stay here. More scandal." He sighed.

"Not necessarily. I can put out that she is needed to help her sisters with the packing and settling of new households, and perhaps I could become slightly ill so she would have to stay and attend her mother for a while."

"You mean to play sick? What would that accomplish? It would only delay the inevitable."

"It might buy us some time away from scandalous tongues so that Wickham could come to his senses and reform."

"Hah!" said Mr. Bennet. "Not likely."

"Well, let's get through the wedding," sighed Mrs. Bennet. "Meanwhile my dear, I suggest you send this wonderful book and my drawings off to your publisher immediately."

"You mean, beat the scandal," said Mr. Bennet wryly.

The day of the wedding dawned sunny and bright. Mr. Collins and Charlotte were staying with Sir Lucas. Mr. Bingley's sisters and their husbands and offspring were at Netherfield along with various cousins. Lady Anne and Colonel Fitzwilliam were also at Netherfield. The Bennet household was full with Mr. and Mrs. Gardiner, Mr. and Mrs. Philips, and all five daughters. Mrs. Johns was helping with the breakfast and overseeing the reception tables.

Mrs. Bennet took a moment with each girl. As she placed the wreath of flowers upon Jane's head, she whispered, "Be happy, my dear, for if you are happy then your husband is happy."

To Lizzy, as she adjusted her necklace, she whispered, "Be true to yourself always." Both girls shook their heads in amazement.

"Mother, what odd advice to give a bride. Isn't a wife's duty to make her husband happy?" said Jane.

"And should I not be more true to my husband than myself?" countered Lizzy.

"Jane, if you make your husband happy at the expense of your happiness, you will come to resent your husband. Lizzy, if you are not true to yourself, and adopt your husband's thoughts and opinions, you will come to resent your husband. That is my advice—that and to have fun before the children come."

At the mention of children, Lizzy said, "Lydia is married a year and not with child. She said you gave her some special instruction." Mrs. Bennet went on to describe the same method she'd outlined for Lydia. The girls blushed.

"Mother," asked Lizzy archly, "did you intend to have five children?"

"Well, Lizzy," Mrs. Bennet said with a laugh, "no method is foolproof!"

The Church was filled with a mix of local gentry, Londoners, and country families. Each bridal attendant looked resplendent in soft lavender; the dresses were the same, with only the sash varying in color. Lydia's dress had long sleeves tapered to the wrist, similar to Lizzy's wedding sleeves. It marked her as Matron of Honor, but in truth the sleeves served the purpose of hiding her fading bruises. Kitty, Georgianna and Mary were a picture. Each girl carried a small bouquet of lilacs and lily of the valley.

Officer Denny had been chosen as one of the ushers and looked fine in his uniform. Colonel Fitzwilliam was acting Best Man for Darcy, and Darcy was acting Best Man for Charles.

Mrs. Johns had outdone herself on all of the girls' gowns, but Mrs. Bennet was a picture in understated elegance. The material was a fine silk in a light peach color. The color electrified her already very blue eyes.

As Lady Anne was ushered to her seat by Officer Denny, she remarked to Caroline Bingley, "Mrs. Bennet is a remarkably pretty woman. When she was painting my portrait, I did not notice."

"Yes," agreed Caroline, "while she is painting you, one is most self-conscious about one's self; she draws you out and gets you to talk about yourself. So I understand you not noticing her beauty. Pretty or not, Mrs. Bennet is a formidable woman."

"Do you not like her?" asked Lady Anne.

"I have come to have a deep respect for her. Did you know I had to plead with her to allow Charles to woo Jane?"

"I know that Lizzy rejected my cousin at first and that Mrs. Bennet was glad she did."

If Caroline felt a slight pang of jealousy to learn that Lizzy had been so sought after by Darcy that he'd risked rejection twice, she did not show it. Instead, she looked over to her husband, Lord Worthing, who returned her gaze with such love. She was now a woman well loved, and was satisfied.

With Lizzy on his right arm and Jane on his left, Mr. Bennet proceeded slowly down the aisle. All heads turned to view the bridal procession. Mr. Bennet slid into his proper place next to Mrs. Bennet. As the question was asked, "Who gives these women in marriage?" he stood with moist eyes and a quavering voice and responded, "I do."

Mrs. Bennet squeezed his hand in support. As Mr. Collins read out the vows, each couple responded. She saw Officer Denny mouthing the vows to Kitty, with Kitty mouthing them back. Lydia was taking in all the ritual, the flowers, the clothing, what a proper wedding was, and tenderly rubbed her arms where her bruises were. She was crying silently.

Mrs. Bennet dabbed at her eyes as the vows were spoken, but she also felt immense relief. The road to this matrimonial end had been a difficult one, but she was delighted for her eldest girls. She could see that Kitty intended on following her older sisters in their matrimonial state soon. She was looking into a proper school for Mary. Mary had a thirst for academics and perhaps would excel as a teacher.

Looking at Lydia, she sighed. Lydia, with her wild bold boisterous nature, always one step ahead of trouble, was, if a mother was allowed to have favorites, her favorite. Lydia was all emotion and heart. She was the one helping out the poorer families, making jokes as she dispensed extra clothing or food, able to mix well with the country folk. Jane and Lizzy also helped, but one could sense them just doing their duty.

Lydia had a natural warmth. Lydia was also the one more attuned to her mother's needs. Lydia was the one who remembered her birthday, made sweet little gifts for her. When Mrs. Bennet was feeling poorly, Lydia was the one with a soothing cloth, encouraging her to sketch. Lydia would stay with her. What to do about Wickham was another matter.

◆◆◆

CHAPTER XLV

The formal ceremony over, the guests returned to their carriages and headed for the Bennets's meadow at Longbourn. Mrs. Robbs had instructed her two daughters to prepare the reception. They had laid the tables with the linen cloths, strewn the tables with wild flowers, and set out all the food and drink.

The meadow reception was a great success. The quails were done to perfection, the ale and wine flowed freely, and the musicians played reel after reel. Georgianna was dancing and laughing. Mr. Bennet took Mrs. Bennet for a twirl. Lady Caroline and Lord Worthing were dancing. A line was formed on either side with each couple dancing the gauntlet. Even Darcy danced and did a form of a jig that amused everyone.

"Lor I never thought I'd live to see the day that my master did a jig," laughed Mrs. Wilkes. Mrs. Wilkes, in her simple grey dress and frilly cap, clapping her hands in time with the music, was clearly enjoying herself. She was grateful to be included. Mrs. Bennet had gone out of her way to make her feel comfortable, introducing her to the local families.

Mrs. Bennet squeezed her hand warmly. "I am so glad you came, and I hope you will watch over my daughter."

"I take your meaning, Mum, and I will do my best. I can shield her from some of them toffs, and I'll put her wise."

Everyone was having a good time. The country families would start a reel, teaching the Londoners the local steps. Then the Londoners would request a society dance, teaching the country the city ways. All were laughing at each attempt, and soon every guest was dancing— country folk paired with city folk and the fiddlers were in a wild frenzy.

Hours later, as the sun set, casting a warm orange glow on the meadow, Mr. Bennet gave the signal, and the musicians slowed their pace to gentle country ballads and aires. As the celebration wound down and the guests prepared to depart, the wedding couples came to say goodbye.

"Mother, you were so right, the meadow reception and with everyone attending it was wonderful," said Jane.

"I think we should have a meadow dance every fortnight!" said Bingley. "This was so much more fun than an ordinary ball at Netherfield."

"Mother, you know how I love to dance," said Lizzy breathlessly. "I don't think I ever danced so much in my entire life. And my new husband does a jig that I will demand of him whenever I remember his first refusal of me as his dancing partner!"

Darcy reddened, but responded good naturedly, "Am I

never to be forgiven?"

"Never," said Lizzy playfully.

Mrs. Bennet laughed. "Before you depart for Pemberley, I hope you all will join us tomorrow for one last luncheon. We have so much food from the wedding."

They all agreed to return to Longbourn tomorrow.

Mr. Collins and Charlotte thanked them for the celebration. "A most unconventional gathering," noted Mr. Collins, casting an eye at Mrs. Robbs and her husband, now helping to carry food in from the tables.

Charlotte shushed him. "It was so nice to see all the families of the county."

Mr. Collins cleared his throat. "Mr. and Mrs. Bennet, I would like to stop by tomorrow sometime, after breakfast. There is something of import we must discuss."

Mrs. Bennet did not really want to include him in her last luncheon with her whole family, but considering Lizzy and Charlotte's friendship, she graciously extended the invitation. "The newlyweds are joining us at luncheon; we would love to have you."

Mr. Collins cleared his throat again and looked down at his shoes. Charlotte was biting her lip and looked on the verge of tears. "I think it best if we meet privately," he said. "Is ten o'clock tomorrow morning too early?"

Mr. Bennet grunted. "Not at all."

Later that night, propped up in bed and reviewing the day's events, Mrs. Bennet sighed. "The day went really well. I was right to have all the families."

"Yes, dear," said Mr. Bennet, "but it was a great

expense."

"Oh, Edward, stop it! The quails came from our woods, the fruits from the local orchards, the dresses were a gift, the cake was a gift and Mr. Collins officiated free of charge."

"There was the expense of the wine and ale, the bread and cheese and the musicians, Miriam."

"Speaking of Mr. Collins, what a bother to have to see him tomorrow morning." Mrs. Bennet yawned. "Whatever can he want?"

Mr. Bennet did not answer as his wife started to drift off to sleep. Let her sleep, he thought, for tomorrow will come soon enough, and he had a dark foreboding that what it would bring would not be good news.

CHAPTER XLVI

Mr. Bennet came down the stairs as Mrs. Bennet was setting aside coffee and warm muffins in expectation of the Collinses' morning visit. He was quite formally dressed.

"Edward, surely Mr. Collins doesn't require you to wear a neckpiece and coat. He is, after all, a relative."

But there was no time for debate. She could see through the window that Mr. Collins and Charlotte were coming through the gate. Mrs. Bennet waved them in, wishing to get this part of the morning over with.

"Hello, dear Charlotte, so good to see you again. Dear Mr. Collins, you did such a lovely job officiating the double ceremonies."

Mr. Collins thanked her and then they all sat as Mrs. Bennet poured out the coffee and served the muffins. Mrs. Bennet noted Charlotte refused the muffin.

"Are you ill, my dear?"

"No Ma'am, just a bit queasy."

"A bit queasy this morning?" Then she laughed, clapped her hands together and hugged Charlotte. "Edward, shake Mr. Collins' hand, for I believe I know the purpose of this meeting. I wish you much joy, Charlotte, in your motherhood, and may you have an easy expectancy, my dear."

Charlotte blushed. Mr. Collins admitted that Charlotte was with child and that they were very pleased.

"Why call a special meeting? Lizzy will be ecstatic for you, my dear. Did you not want the girls to know yet? Why tell just us privately?"

Mr. Collins cleared his throat. "I need to enact the entail."

Mrs. Bennet was stunned. "What? Why?"

Mr. Bennet merely asked, "When?"

"Mr. Collins, can't you wait? Kitty and Mary are still home, and Lydia," she faltered, "may need her family home."

"I am sorry, Mrs. Bennet, but I cannot wait. Lady Catherine de Bourgh has given us thirty days' notice to quit the parish."

"But why?" cried Mrs. Bennet.

"It seems she was unhappy with Mr. Darcy's recent marriage and wants no connexion with the Bennets or their relations," said Charlotte gently.

Now Mrs. Bennet could see the reality of Lady Catherine's threat to ruin her.

"But, surely, you can find another parish, Mr. Collins, or Charlotte, during your time of expectancy, might it be wiser to reside with your mother."

"Though Charlotte loves her family, she would not wish to reside in the same household. After officiating at your weddings, I met with the parish vicar. He has asked me to stay on as his assistant, with the eventual plan of assuming his duties full-time. Longbourn suits our needs, for Charlotte to be close to her family, and for me to take this new position. I feel I cannot refuse it, considering I will soon have to support a family."

Mrs. Bennet started to weep.

Mr. Bennet rose and ended the interview. "We will vacate by the thirtieth day from today."

He did not shake Mr. Collins' hand.

Mr. Collins drew some documents from his vest.

Mr. Bennet said, "I will look these over before signature and take them over to Sir Lucas. Are you planning on staying for a few days?"

"We are," said Mr. Collins.

"What are we going to do, Edward? This is too much to bear."

"We will store our belongings, and possibly move in with relatives for a short time. Dry your eyes, we have a luncheon to prepare. I think it best we not share this news at the luncheon," cautioned Mr. Bennet.

Mrs. Bennet set out her finest china, crystal and linens. If this was to be her last time entertaining her whole family in her home she wanted it to be special.

"Mother, you have outdone yourself!" exclaimed Lydia when she and Kitty came down the stairs.

"It does look lovely, doesn't it?"

Lydia, hearing the thickness in her mother's voice, turned and saw her mother's misty eyes.

"Now, Mother, be brave. You will see Lizzy when you visit your brother in London. Pemberley is not too far off, and Jane is still nearby at Netherfield. Perhaps Kitty should wait to tell you her news."

"News, what news?" For she could think only of the news she had soon to sadly impart.

Kitty turned to Lydia. "I told you I want to wait until luncheon, and wait I shall."

At the moment there was a knock upon the door, and the newlyweds entered. Jane and Charles looked radiant. Darcy looked smugly contented, and Lizzy looked almost demure. Mrs. Bennet led everyone to the table. She sought Mr. Bennet, but he was not nearby.

Mary went in search of her father and returned with the news. "He is in his study with Officer Denny. He says he will be out shortly and to set another place." Kitty jumped up and secured the extra china and crystal and set a place next to her.

Mr. Bennet entered with Officer Denny. "I know it is a year earlier than what we agreed to, but Officer Denny has received a new commission, so it appears we have another wedding to hold, Mrs. Bennet!"

The newlyweds shouted their congratulations; Mr. Bennet offered a toast. Kitty beamed. Officer Denny, standing by her side, took her hand.

Mrs. Bennet burst into tears. She excused herself and went into the kitchen.

"I think this is too much for Mama," said Lydia.

"She still has me," said Mary.

Mr. Bennet, aware of the true cause of his wife's tears, tried to make light of the situation. "Perhaps the thought of putting on another wedding just overwhelmed her."

He excused himself and joined Mrs. Bennet at the sink, where she was trying to compose herself.

"Miriam, this is good news for Kitty. I know it is a bit earlier than we expected, but Officer Denny is a man of character and truly cares for her. I will be sad to lose her, but considering our situation…"

Mrs. Bennet burst into tears again.

Mr. Bennet held her and comforted her. "We'll manage."

"Oh, Edward, I am glad for Kitty."

"I told them you were overwhelmed at the thought of putting on another wedding."

Mrs. Bennet smiled. "True enough."

"Well, let's go back in and tell them that it was the thought of all your girls growing and going," said Mr. Bennet. "Let's not ruin this happy occasion for them."

She dried her eyes and entered the dining room on her husband's arm. "Forgive me, girls, new husbands and Officer Denny. You must allow for a mother's heart."

"Ma'am, as I am to be part of the family soon, I think you can call me by my given name."

"Why, of course! What is it?" laughed Mrs. Bennet.

"Robert, Ma'am, who loves your daughter very much, and Ma'am, don't feel obligated to put on another shindig like yesterday. Kitty and I have discussed it, and there is a lovely chapel where my regiment is stationed. I always wanted a military wedding. Kitty will look lovely walking under the crossed swords."

CHAPTER XLVII

Another toast was offered to the newly engaged couple. Mrs. Bennet glanced around her table. She felt grateful that three of daughters would have settled lives. She watched Lydia play the happy sister, and her heart ached for her. Mary, with her bookish ways, was polite to her new brothers-in-law, and congratulated Kitty, but somehow seemed removed from it all.

Mrs. Bennet had written last week to the Abbey school, a serious boarding school for young ladies, modern in its ideas that education and the life of an academic might be possible for women. Now, with their losing their home, Mr. Bennet might acquiesce in allowing Mary to further her studies at the Abbey.

Mrs. Bennet sighed and got up to start clearing away the dishes.

Jane and Lizzy protested. "Mother, this may be the last time we have to do our kitchen chores. Let us clear."

"All right," said Mrs. Bennet, "but Mrs. Johns has come to help with the washing up. Go in and give her thanks for that wonderful cake and for helping to feed you all these years."

The men gathered in the parlor for cigars and politics. Mrs. Bennet sat alone at the table, feet up on a chair, savoring her tea. When the last plate and glass were cleared, Lizzy kissed the top of her head; an odd show of affection from her daughter.

"Lizzy, I am neither your child nor a household pet to be kissed on the top of the head," she said irritably.

"I am a married woman, now, Mama, you cannot scold me."

Mrs. Bennet rose to her feet. "I suppose that's true, but come show your mother your affection properly."

They embraced, then Lizzy exclaimed, "Oh, I must go over to the Lucases and see Charlotte before I go."

"I believe they have already left," Mrs. Bennet said with alarm. She did not want Lizzy to speak with Charlotte.

"Nonsense! Charlotte and I made a plan before either of us left, to sneak away into the garden that separates our properties and have a tête-à-tête like old times."

She watched Lizzy slip through the hedge. *Well, sooner or later all will have to know. I did well enough through luncheon. Edward can't blame me for blurting out anything in my distress.*

She took a sip of her tea, which had grown quite cold.

Lizzy stormed back into the parlor. She called for Jane, Lydia, Kitty and Mary. But as soon as she spotted Darcy she flew at her new husband, pummeling his chest. "How dare she! How dare she! You must stop her! She is wicked!"

Lizzy started sobbing. Darcy, at a loss as to the cause of this explosion, held his wife's balled-up fists in his hand.

"What has happened? Who is wicked?" The girls, busy packing up Jane's things upstairs, heard the commotion, ran down the stairs and into the parlor, breathless.

Mr. Bennet spoke sharply to Lizzy. "Be quiet. This has nothing to do with your husband."

"I have just been with Charlotte, and she informs me that she and her husband are to take possession of Longbourn in thirty days. Lady Catherine de Bourgh has given Mr. Collins notice from her parish. It seems this is her response to our marriage."

Darcy was flummoxed. "How can he take Longbourn?"

Mr. Bennet sighed. "Unfortunately, the estate is under entail to him. Lizzy, the estate would have been entailed away from us some day."

"I thought Charlotte was my friend," wailed Lizzy.

"She is your friend, Lizzy," Mrs. Bennet said, "but she and Mr. Collins will be without a home soon, and Charlotte is with child. I am sure she married Mr. Collins knowing about the entail. Charlotte is no fool, though you thought her one for marrying Mr. Collins. The property is valuable, and it adjoins the Lucases. The eventual joining of Longbourn to the Lucas estate will be most advantageous to that family."

Mrs. Bennet did not mean to sound bitter, but she was so upset she could not help herself from pointing out the repercussions of a match that had been so spurned and laughed at by Lizzy.

Bingley, seeing his wife pale at the news, said graciously, "You must all come and live at Netherfield. Our home is your home." Jane looked up at her husband with gratitude. Never had he seemed more her hero.

Lizzy looked to her husband, whose response to this crisis she found wanting.

"Perhaps I could speak with my aunt, get her to see reason," said Darcy.

Mrs. Bennet responded first to her most generous son-in-law. "Dear Charles. What a lovely offer, but I am afraid we shall have to decline."

"But Mother, what else is there to do?" said Jane.

"Jane, Charles, you are just starting your life together and having your in-laws underfoot is not ideal. However, I would prevail upon you to allow us to store our furnishings."

"Of course, dear Madam, anything," said Charles.

"Unfortunately, Mr. Darcy, I do not think your aunt can be persuaded to reconsider. But thank you for the offer."

Here Lizzy reddened with shame, for Darcy's plan offered no comfort.

Mrs. Bennet thought it was a good thing for Lizzy to see her husband's selfishness now. She would always be grateful to Darcy for helping Lydia become respectable, but she knew that it was his own interest in protecting Georgianna from gossip that had most motivated him.

Robert Denny proved his worthiness by saying, "Mr. and Mrs. Bennet, when you make the trip for the wedding, I am sure the regiment has access to some temporary housing, and I know Kitty would like to have her family close by."

"Dear boy." Mrs. Bennet embraced him. "I am quite touched by your offer, but you newlyweds should also be on your own."

Mr. Bennet finally spoke. "Mrs. Bennet and I will discuss what to do. I have a mind to make some arrangements to be in London, as I must meet with my publisher soon. Perhaps it is just as well you are all aware of the situation. Mrs. Bennet can take some time with the girls today, helping them to pack, and each can choose something to take with them to remember their home at Longbourn."

The little party dispersed in a much more somber mood than before. Officer Denny prepared to return to his regiment; the wedding was to take place in two weeks. Darcy and Bingley returned to Netherfield. Darcy would return to Longbourn in a week's time to take Jane back to Netherfield and then continue on with his bride to Pemberley.

♦♦♦

CHAPTER XLVIII

Mrs. Bennet divided her china and crystal so that each girl might have a set. Lydia wrapped the blue and white china in clean rags and nestled it carefully in a box. She waved the next plate in her sister's face and smirked, "I'm putting this in Jane's box. I doubt you'll be using any of this at Pemberley.

Lizzy took exception to her sister's tone. "And why not?"

"Well, his high-and-mighty self might not like this country pattern. Don't see you setting it at his table."

Lizzy tried to snatch the plate from Lydia's hand. "You are incorrigible," hissed Lizzy. "You caused this family much pain and embarrassment, and my husband helped legitimize your marriage."

"Your husband was the cause of my husband's downfall," screeched Lydia as she tussled to retrieve the plate.

Mrs. Bennet stood up from her task, grabbed the plate from both of them and shouted, "Enough!"

Jane was in the corner quietly weeping. Kitty wrung her hands, happy about her upcoming marriage but sad to leave and to lose her home.

Mary, in her dry manner, said, "Mother, I think it is time to discuss everyone's true situation."

Mrs. Bennet eyed her warily and made a decision. "You are right. Everyone sit. Stop packing and wrapping." When they were settled, she said, "Lydia, you must hear some hard truths about your husband. Mr. Darcy was instrumental in convincing Wickham to legitimatize your arrangement. I am most unhappy that you were heedless of the consequences of your actions to the family, but feel the current situation you are in is punishment enough."

Lydia pouted. "Why would Mr. Darcy put himself out for me?"

Kitty put her hand gently on her sister's and said, "It was to protect Georgianna, and I think because he was in love with Lizzy."

"What has Georgianna got to do with it?"

Kitty, in the most delicate terms she could muster, described Wickham's attempted seduction of Georgianna.

"How do you know this?"

"Because Georgianna has confided it to me."

Lizzy, now calmer, said, "I can see that Wickham has fed you stories about Darcy's past injustices to him and, in truth, when I first met Wickham and he related those same stories to me, I believed him too."

"To the untrained observer," Jane said, "Darcy is all stiff and proud and does not present himself as a person of a generous nature, whereas Wickham, with his engaging manner and glib tongue, wins the hearts of many."

Lydia looked into the faces of her concerned sisters and started to cry.

"But what am I to do? I have done what Mother asked and played the cheerful sister, taking part in your weddings, seeing the fine matches you have made. I am happy for you, Kitty, but I wish I had never met Wickham."

"Lydia, my dear, Wickham was an experienced seducer, and you have a tender heart. You are going to stay with your father and me, as we need you now to help with the arrangement of a new household."

"You are to stand up for me at our military wedding. If it is not too difficult for you," said Kitty. "For we have been like twins, and I wouldn't feel right if you were not there for me. You who have jollied me out of my moods and helped me gain confidence. Wickham is not posted there, so that should not present a problem."

Lydia hugged Kitty gratefully. "Yes, I will be there."

"It is odd, he has not come looking for you or demanded your return," said Mary thoughtfully.

"It isn't really, if you understood, Mary."

"Oh I understand. I know he's a rogue. Watching all of you, through your courtships and marriages, I want no part of it."

"Really?" teased Jane.

"Your husband is besotted with you and that is very nice, but I would find that irritating after a while. And yours," she said to Lizzy, "I would find quite intimidating. He is very dogmatic and has opinions about a woman's place that I would find quite stifling. Kitty's officer is quite sweet, but the social obligation of officer wives' teas and luncheons might prove draining."

The girls all guffawed and hooted at Mary's opinions. Secretly, Mrs. Bennet thought they were incredibly accurate.

"And what, Miss, will you do if you do not plan to marry?" teased Kitty.

Here Mrs. Bennet intervened. "Mary is going to attend the Abbey school just outside of London."

"What!" they all said in unison.

Mary turned to her mother in amazement. "Is it true?"

"Yes, my dear, your father and I have discussed it. I submitted the application before the weddings. They sent their acceptance a few days ago. It is a boarding school. Mary, you don't have to go if you don't want to."

Mary, with her direct, practical nature, said, "But, Mother, considering our situation, it is the perfect solution! And I will be able to do what I love, continue my studies and perhaps become a teacher there!" She paused. "But how are we to afford it?"

Mrs. Bennet decided candor was best. "This school is a new concept and they wish it to be a success and are seeking to have serious students. Your application was viewed most favorably, and they have made some monetary concessions regarding the cost of your board. In exchange, they have asked me to conduct their drawing and painting classes once a week."

Mary threw her arms around her mother's waist and in a

most unusual display of affection said, "I shall always be grateful, Mother!" The girls were astonished. Lizzy looked quite envious.

"All right, girls, let's continue to pack up. We are going to reside temporarily at your uncle's in London. The Gardiners are going on a trip to the Orient in search of exotic goods to sell. They'll be away for at least six months. Your father and I will help oversee the shipments at the warehouse. Lydia will help with the management of the household and oversee the receipts from the sale of goods at your uncle's establishment. So you see, Lydia, I will need you, as I must be away at the Abbey school twice a week."

Lydia dried her tears, for she could see that residing in London was much preferable to living in the country at Longbourn.

Jane said, laughing, "How unfair! So I am the one who remains in the country."

"And I shall be wandering among the shrubbery at Pemberley," sighed Lizzy.

"Nonsense, Jane. Charles has a house in town, and Lizzy, London is not too far away. You can both come for a visit. I expect, Lizzy, that you will be quite busy with Georgianna and the season."

"Won't you visit us, Mother?" asked Lizzy.

She could foresee much contentiousness about Mary's attendance at the Abbey. The more distance the Bennet family kept from the Darcys the better. "You'll be in London, and we shall see each other then. And when Jane comes to town, we will all get together. We will plan a time when Mary is on holiday."

She felt a sudden rush of tears at the backs of her eyes, and she blinked quickly. "Now, back to the china. It is nice to have a bit of your past home to take with you. When you give a tea, Kitty, or host a small luncheon, Lizzy, or put on a Sunday breakfast for visitors, Jane, or Mary, when you have dessert and tea after a book discussion or just to savor a cup of tea in private, I hope you all get a chance to put it to some use that you find gratifying."

CHAPTER XLIX

At week's end, Jane and Lizzy had packed all they needed, each taking the quilt and pillow from their beds, along with various knick-knacks and china. Lizzy was allowed to take a few treasured books from her father's study. Kitty had her trunk packed and was taking the sideboard, dining table and chairs, one of the front parlor settees, and various pots and pans from the kitchen, as she was moving to unfurnished quarters. The rest of the beds, sofas, tables, paintings and the library would be dismantled and stored at Netherfield.

Darcy came to collect Lizzy and Jane. Mrs. Bennet had tea set in the parlor and met privately with Lizzy and Darcy. Darcy started to apologize again for the tumult his relation was causing, but Mrs. Bennet stopped him.

"No need, Mr. Darcy. It can't be helped. But I am cautioning you both. You must isolate yourselves from your aunt's influence immediately. Otherwise you will find yourselves ostracized. I suggest you ask Lady Anne and Colonel Fitzwilliam to join you at Pemberley, and have Lady Anne help with Georgianna's coming out season in London. Lady Anne's patronage will automatically extend to Lizzy. Then Lady Catherine's influence will be restricted to her housekeeper and her parish at Rosings."

"We also will dine with Lord Worthing and Caroline, which will help," said Darcy.

"I suggest you wait until Jane and Charles are in town and can attend the dinner."

"Why?" Darcy shifted impatiently. "This all seems so silly."

Mrs. Bennet met his eye. "Caroline does not particularly like Lizzy. You will need Charles and Jane as a buffer. She may have softened her stance towards Lizzy now that she is married and busy mothering, but it is best for all the Bingleys and the Darcys to dine together. Lizzy, for a time you will have to do what I do when people snub or condescend to me, pretend you don't notice, continue on in your conversation, or notice someone beckoning to you and remove yourself politely."

Lizzy blushed, thinking of the many times she had condescended to her mother, now knowing her mother had been fully aware.

"I hear Miss Mary Bennet is planning to attend the

Abbey school," said Darcy.

"Yes, she is quite excited about the chance to pursue her studies," Mrs. Bennet said, hearing the lilt of a challenge in his voice. This was the exact argument she'd hoped to avoid.

"I was quite surprised to hear that Lord Worthing's daughter is also planning to attend," said Darcy.

Mrs. Bennet raised her brows. "How wonderful! Mary will have a chum. They got on quite well at the wedding."

"Yes, well, I am not sure just how wonderful it is, all this schooling and academics. To what purpose?"

Mrs. Bennet just smiled. "Let us speak about this again when you have daughters."

Jane came downstairs then, followed by her father, who was carrying several valises. The girls bid tearful goodbyes. Mr. Bennet, quite overcome with emotion, gripped his wife's hand as he watched the carriage depart through the gate. As he looked about the house in its various state of packing, he lamented, "Two gone, one about to leave, the other to a boarding school, no more home, such loss, such loss."

Mrs. Bennet said nothing. She and Mr. Bennet were opposite in nature, he the pessimist and she the optimist. She took a deep breath. *Such freedom! And a new adventure.*

Kitty's military wedding was charming. Officer Denny's full regiment attended in the chapel. He looked handsome in his uniform. Kitty was radiant in a gown of simplicity and grace. As they said their vows to each other, under the arch of the gleaming swords, Mrs. Bennet found herself quite overcome with emotion.

She was still weeping as the bridal party exited the chapel. Georgianna and Lizzy had come for the ceremony as well as Jane and Charles. Lizzy could not help making a joke. "Mother, you are so overcome, yet I recall nary a tear was shed for Jane or me."

Mrs. Bennet tried to smile through her tears. "I cannot understand it myself, girls."

Mr. Bennet interceded. "I believe no tears were shed at your wedding, Lizzy, because your poor mother did not have time! She organized the whole thing, sent out the invitations, oversaw all the preparations, tended to the guests at the reception"—and here, Mr. Bennet lowered his voice—"as well as keeping Lydia's spirits up. She was quite distracted from her emotions. Here she can just relax and allow her motherly feelings to surface. I believe the tears of joy and melancholy are for all of you."

Mrs. Bennet was astonished to realize that he was right. Officer Denny and Kitty had planned the simple ceremony and the wedding breakfast; she'd had little to do. "Thank you Edward, I think you have discerned it correctly." She dried her eyes. "Girls, your father's ability to see to the heart of the matter is a rare gift."

Mrs. Bennet took her husband's arm and proceeded up the walk towards the wedding breakfast. Lydia stood at the door, beckoning all of them to enter.

Lizzy, who'd been expecting her father to join in poking fun at her mother, said to Jane, "Since when is he her champion?"

"Since we are all gone and he realizes mother's value. Do not vie for his affection and try to make mother look ridiculous." Jane squeezed her sister's hand to soften her words. "That is an old, petulant game, Lizzy, and father no longer wants to play."

CHAPTER L

The Bennets settled easily in London. Having seen the Gardiners off after much instruction from her brother regarding the administration of the warehouse, the various duties of tracking and sending of goods purchased and sold, Mrs. Bennet was glad to finally wave her brother goodbye from the dock.

"Well, Edward, welcome to London. I know you will be meeting with your publisher, but I must insist you help me attend to all the duties James has outlined. I cannot handle it all myself. I will be at Mary's school at least two days a week."

Mr. Bennet chuckled. "I assure you, Miriam, I will shoulder the burden. I am ever so grateful to your brother for this respite from our troubles. While our labor in his absence repays him for his kindness, keep in mind that we must find a permanent home in just under six months. Let us be off to settle Mary in her school next."

The Abbey was a lovely school housed on lush green grounds and in beautiful gray stone edifices. The girl's dormitory was simple, but furnished well. Each girl brought with her her bedding and some small pieces of furniture or art to remind her of home. Six simple frocks and sturdy shoes were supplied by the school. Mrs. Bennet was quite surprised that this simple wardrobe was provided.

As she toured the facility with the headmistress she said, "Surely the girls can afford to have their own clothing?"

Miss Elders, a seasoned, comfortable-looking, middle-aged woman, replied, "We have many fine young ladies here who can afford the most luxurious dresses, with fine lace and beading and a well-turned shoe. But we do not wish them to wear their own clothing. We want all the girls to concentrate on their studies and to form friendships based on character. The simple frocks even the field, so to speak. Our girls do come from different walks of life. We seek to remove the definitions of privilege or poverty."

Mrs. Bennet, reflecting on Mary's status compared to that of Lord Worthing's daughter, considered that the practice made much sense.

Miss Elders, as if reading her mind, continued, "Some are very highborn, others from well-endowed families, and some with no family at all. Of course the girls learn which is which, but in the course of the day it matters not. They bond and learn together based on a natural intellectual affinity."

Mrs. Bennet sighed. "I wish this school were in existence earlier. My second-born would have loved it. She is quick of wit, a great reader, and has a lively mind."

"Perhaps she can still come. We do have students older than Mary. And we are always looking for teachers."

"Regretfully, no, I cannot see that she would be able to do that, considering her recent marriage. Though her new sister-in-law is a gifted pianist and might be persuaded to give a private concert for the girls."

"That would be wonderful," said Miss Elders. They had reached a small, round, stone building with ivy growing in the crevices. "Here is the art studio. I hope that you find it sufficient."

Indeed, who would not? The studio had three large, arched windows, letting in the natural light, and enough space to handle separate easels for a class of ten. There was a long table in the back that held an over-abundance of art supplies. Inwardly, she rejoiced, for here was a place she could work. The Gardiners' apartments, though charming, had no extra room that she could use as a studio.

Mary came bounding up to her, her father not far behind. "Oh, Mother, I love it! Amelia, Lord Worthing's daughter, is going to be my suitemate. The library is amazing. So much bigger than ours at home, and I think I want to learn French!"

Mrs. Bennet laughed, pleased by Mary's exuberance, for at home she was a much more taciturn child. She could see that in this environment, out from the shadow of her sisters, she would bloom. "So you won't miss me very much?"

Mary, with her usual honesty, said, "At night I might become a bit homesick, but knowing that you will be here on a weekly basis will make it more bearable. I might even take your class!"

Mr. and Mrs. Bennet traveled home in thoughtful silence. Finally Mr. Bennet spoke. "What about Lydia?"

Mrs. Bennet sighed. "I am hoping to keep her busy with the management of the household and my brother's establishment, but Lydia's natural restlessness may become a problem. I shall take her with me when I give the art lesson at the Abbey; she can be my assistant. I fear leaving her without constant supervision and distraction will result in some other ill-fated partnership. Have you heard anything regarding Wickham's whereabouts?"

Mr. Bennet made a low rumble in his throat. "He has deserted his regiment. I have made inquires amongst the gambling set here in London. None have seen him."

They returned to find Lydia working industriously setting up the household. For all her flightiness, Lydia liked to deal in practical matters: where to shop, what to cook, what to order. She might do very well organizing shipments from the warehouse with her father and helping with the art class.

This could be a new and fresh start for her. If only Mrs. Bennet could shake off the fear that Wickham would soon turn up like a bad penny, and ruin it all.

CHAPTER LI

By the time the London season arrived, the Bennets had settled in to a routine. Lydia and her father tallied the shipments to and from the warehouse. Mrs. Bennet set up the goods for sale in Mr. Gardiner's establishment and oversaw all the receipts. She traveled to the Abbey school twice a week to give art lessons, and she was pleased with her pupils. Lydia proved a capable assistant, and Mary even joined the class. She did not display the talent for art like the others, but she learned enough about perspective and light and shadow to be an educated viewer of great works.

Lizzy, Georgianna, and Lady Anne took up residence in town, and their first order was a visit to the Bennets. Mrs. Bennet thought her daughter looked well, and was pleased to hear that Lady Anne would remain with the Darcys in London for the season.

Lydia watched Georgianna with a look of envy. "Just think of all the lovely balls you will be attending. Have you had many gowns made up?"

Georgianna sighed. "Actually, I wish this was over with.

I'd much rather be playing my music. There is no piano in the townhouse, and my fingers shall become less limber every day."

Mrs. Bennet surveyed both girls. Here was her Lydia, her life in limbo, feeling like a pariah, ruined by a scoundrel, aching for society. And here was Georgianna, lucky to have escaped that same scoundrel. He had left his mark, with her slight hesitancy of speech and lack of confidence and an aversion towards society.

"Georgianna, do you think you would like to use the piano at the Abbey? I go there twice a week to teach art to the students, and they would be thrilled if you would play for them."

Lizzy gave a bit of a start, no doubt concerned about what her husband would think of his sister visiting this so-called female institute of learning that merited his scorn. "Mama, I think Georgianna will be too busy with her social obligations this month."

Lady Anne, seeing her cousin's crestfallen countenance, offered a compromise. "Why don't we all visit the Abbey for just one day? I would like to see your art class, Mrs. Bennet, and Georgianna could practice on the piano. We could make a special picnic of it, for I hear the grounds are beautiful, and I am curious myself to see it. Lizzy, we needn't mention it to Fitzy."

Georgianna was thrilled, and Lydia was happy to have someone nearer her own age to have an outing with, for her social life had been limited to her parents and school children.

Lizzy acquiesced, but like her husband, seemed wary of any plan her mother might suggest. Mrs. Bennet suspected her worst fear about the influence of Pemberley was coming to pass.

Lizzy came to the Bennet apartments for a quiet family dinner. The dinner was anything but quiet.

"Lydia," Lizzy lectured at the first opportunity, "do not be so forward and press a friendship upon Georgianna she may not wish."

Lydia rolled her eyes and grimaced. "That poor girl, cooped up with the likes of you and your stuffy husband. She needs a bit of fun!"

Lizzy wagged a finger in her sister's face. "That is exactly what I am worried about. Your idea of fun has already almost brought this family to ruin."

Lydia slapped the hand away. "And your priggish selfishness is the reason we have no family home."

"Girls! Enough!"

Lizzy had always been quite judgmental about Lydia's behavior and manners; Lydia in turn felt rebellious in her sister's presence. Mrs. Bennet's head ached trying to keep the peace. She longed for her other daughters, realizing that Jane and Kitty always provided the balance and balm between these two. Mrs. Bennet felt sympathy with Lydia as she herself had also borne the brunt of Lizzy's censure in the past. However, she understood Lizzy's anxiety that her sister's behavior not damage Lizzy's acceptance into society, which was precarious at best.

"Girls! Let us have a truce. Lizzy, you wish for your sister's happiness, do you not? And Lydia, you wish for Lizzy's happiness, correct?"

Both grudgingly grumbled a reply.

"So let us compromise," Mrs. Bennet said. "Lizzy, let Lydia enjoy the outing with Georgianna. Perhaps they could have an occasional tea or a day of shopping together, for she is quite lonely with only her old parents for company. And Lydia, you must be on your best behavior, watch your speech and manner, for your sister has married into a highborn family, and his titled aunt is determined to ruin her socially. One false step, and your sister could be permanently ostracized from society."

Lydia's heart, always big and forgiving, started to weep. "Oh Lizzy, I am so sorry. I did not understand the stress you were under."

And Lizzy, seeing Lydia's tears, understanding her sister's hurt and disappointment and need for companionship, replied, "I shall try to be a better sister to you. We will go on more outings together and with Georgianna too."

Just as the sisters embraced, Mr. Bennet arrived late to dinner. He was greeted with a chorus of weepy females.

"What's this? What's this?"

Mrs. Bennet smiled through her tears. "Nothing, my dear, just sisters making amends."

He cleared his throat. "Well, I have some good news that

will bring a smile or two. The publisher has enthusiastically received my recent humorous book and they loved your illustrations, Miriam. I asked for a bit more money because of the illustrations and they agreed. They are set to release it within a month."

Mrs. Bennet let out a yelp of joy. Lydia laughed. "Will this make us all famous?"

Mr. Bennet admonished his family. "You know the rules, and, Lydia, this is very important. I write these books and pamphlets anonymously. That's what keeps people interested. You cannot ever admit you know the author, even if people think it might be me."

"Congratulations, Father." Lizzy seemed the least enthused. "But did you disguise our characters? If you mention a double wedding, people in Longbourn will be sure to recognize it, and news travels fast."

If Mr. Bennet felt deflated by his daughter's implicit chide, he hid it well. "I did not mention a double wedding. I do mention a wedding and incorporate some humorous details that would be common to all wedding plans and a father's feelings about losing his daughter to marriage. Also a father and husband's frustration at all the female frippery and folderol involved. Now, mind you, and I mean you especially, Lydia, if you are at a party or a tea and some excerpts are read aloud as happened with my other novellas, you are not to claim any familiarity with it at all."

"Well, that will be easy, because I haven't read it yet!"

"We will read a copy of it when it is released and not before," said Mrs. Bennet with mock severity. She smiled to herself, for she wondered how Lizzy would react to her father's stinging wit when it was more than just her mother being parodied.

CHAPTER LII

Mary, overjoyed to see both her sisters, joined them as Miss Elders gave the visitors a tour of the Abbey school. Georgianna squealed with delight when she saw the piano. She immediately sat down to run her fingers over the keys, but blushed and stood up, apologizing to Miss Elders for her impulsive behavior. The headmistress assured her that the piano was just waiting to be played. Lady Anne wanted to see the art room, and Mary wanted to show Lizzy and Lydia her bedroom suite, so they left Georgianna at the piano.

Lady Anne was enchanted with the art class and joined in to draw the still life Mrs. Bennet had set upon the table in the center of the room. Watching her draw with such fervor inspired the students, for Mrs. Bennet had never encountered so many hands raised at once, volunteering to present their work at the class's end.

As the students gathered their belongings, they could hear lovely music wafting through the closed door of the piano room. They all slowly crept in and sat silently on the floor. Georgianna had her eyes closed, playing with her usual virtuosity. When the final movement was over, the students rose to their feet, applauding and stamping their feet.

Mrs. Elders went to the front of the room. "Brava Miss Darcy, Brava! Girls, this is Miss Darcy. Doesn't she play wonderfully?" The girls broke into applause again. "Perhaps, if we ask nicely, Miss Darcy will come again and play."

The girls started to plead, "Please! Miss Darcy, please!" Georgianna blushed but laughed and nodded.

One student raised her hand. "Miss Darcy, could you teach me how to play?" Others joined in with their requests.

Mrs. Elders turned to Georgianna. "It seems you are quite a hit with our young students. Might you consider coming once a week to help our students learn the piano? We could pay you a small stipend."

Georgianna blushed deeper. "I would love to, and no stipend is necessary if you will allow me to come and practice when I want. We have no piano in our London townhouse."

Lizzy, standing at the back of the room, looked over to her mother. Mrs. Bennet smiled in return, quite pleased with how the day had gone.

But on the carriage ride home, Lizzy turned to Lady Anne. "How are we going to tell Darcy about Georgianna playing there? He doesn't even know we went, and I am sure he won't approve."

"Did you like the school, Georgianna?" Mrs. Bennet

asked.

"Oh, my, yes!" she said.

"And Lady Anne, what did you think?"

"The school needs patronage, and we should organize a special evening. Lord Worthing's daughter attends, and I noticed several other titled young ladies on their roster. Lizzy, you must speak to Fitzy." Her green eyes lit up. "If we all are united in our support of this endeavor, he can't object. I know my husband will support it, and we should bring Lady Caroline into this. Jane and Charles are due for a visit, and they should join us as well. Lizzy"—Lady Anne leaned across the carriage and clasped her hand—"as Caroline is now married to Lord Worthing, having a mutual project to work on together would be most beneficial for you socially."

Lizzy frowned deeply; something in her seemed ready to erupt. She turned to her mother and said viciously, "Mother, you have put me in an impossible situation! You constantly have to meddle and manipulate."

"Lizzy!" Lady Anne's and Georgianna's expressions were quite shocked. "But your mother is the cause of all my happiness," Lady Anne said. "She brought me out of a dreadful melancholy, encouraged my talent and created such a work of art. I am so grateful for my portrait. I am certain that it ensured my husband's affection."

Mrs. Bennet had turned her face to look out the carriage window, silently swallowing back her tears. "Now, Lady Anne, he was in love with you, not the painting."

Georgianna, hardly one for confrontation, spoke her

piece. "I lived in isolation, terrified of speaking to anyone, seeing only my brother and my housekeeper until your mother came and started the 'singing cure,' as I call it. I danced at my first ball because of your mother's so-called meddling and manipulation. Lizzy, you cannot think..."

"But can't you see?" Lizzy cried. "She brought us all here today to make this happen; you, Georgianna, giving lessons and Lady Anne providing patronage?"

"All Mother did was to provide the opportunity," said Lydia. "They made their own decision."

Mrs. Bennet, bolstered by this show of support, said gently, "Lizzy, if you decide you do not want to be involved at the school, and fear your husband would censure you too severely for it, then please do not feel obligated."

"Yes," said Georgianna. "I can talk to my brother myself, he rarely denies me what I ask."

"Of course we can do the event," said Lady Anne, "perhaps a concert by Georgianna and an art display by you, Mrs. Bennet, and the student work. Lizzy, you and Darcy would at least attend the concert in support of Georgianna. I know he would come to hear his sister play, whether he approved of the school or not."

Lizzy looked at each woman: Lady Anne, flushed and excited about a new project; Georgianna feeling confident; Lydia looking perplexed; and her mother's face full of concern.

She burst into tears. When the carriage pulled up to the Gardiner apartments, Mrs. Bennet asked that Georgianna, Lady Anne and Lydia go inside for tea so she could talk to

Lizzy privately.

"Lizzy, you are unhappy."

"Not unhappy, but I feel so torn. I want to please my husband and fit in and make him proud. I feel like I am not doing anything right."

Mrs. Bennet moved to sit next to her and took her in her arms. "My advice to you is to stop trying. He married you for who you are."

"But he will shoot me a look, a raised eyebrow, a frown, so I know I have made some faux pas."

"Are you his puppet or his wife? You will have a miserable life if you continue in this vein, always questioning yourself, looking for approval from him or others. You need to return to Lizzy the quick-witted; Lizzy the well-read, satirical puncturer of the pompous, wherever she sees it. Trust me, you will be respected and perhaps even feared."

"Feared?"

"Yes, feared; many a time I was the butt of that wit, and its sting is sharp. However, don't neglect the development of compassion."

"What do I do when he gives me that stern look?"

Mrs. Bennet thought a moment, then smiled, "Stick out your tongue. It shows him you are aware of what you are doing, and he can't control you, and yet it is playful and saucy. If you are in a situation where you can't do that, raise your eyebrows and wiggle them right back at him."

Lizzy started to laugh. "We will look a fine pair, making childish faces at each other at these tedious dinner parties."

"You must complement each other. You bring charm and wit to the match; he brings his serious, responsible nature. You both have good hearts, so work to complement each other, not to change yourself."

Lizzy leaned forward and kissed her mother. "Have you always been this wise? Why have I not noticed it?"

"You had to grow up a bit."

"Was I awful?"

"Dreadful!" laughed Mrs. Bennet. "Now, let's join the others for tea."

"Mother, I do want to help with the school, it's just that I'm also …" She hesitated, searching for the right word.

"Jealous," said Mrs. Bennet.

Lizzy's eyes widened. "Yes, I don't know why. I have everything I want or need."

"But for Mary," said Mrs. Bennet, "there will be other opportunities, a possible independent life not available before. I understand, Lizzy. But I think we should all foster this new possibility, for I believe we all of us will benefit."

CHAPTER LIII

Though her parents had kept the news from her of Wickham's desertion, Lydia received her own news about her husband's whereabouts. A letter had been sent to

Longbourn, which the Collinses had forwarded to London. Wickham was in a hospital up North. The doctor has sent word that he was gravely ill and would not last a month.

Lydia prepared to visit him, attended by her father. Wickham's lifestyle of copious drink had finally caught up with him. His liver was failing. Mrs. Bennet cautioned her husband to hold his temper and allow Lydia to have her goodbye.

The biggest shock was Wickham's appearance, bloated and yellow—Lydia hadn't expected that. Her father stood watchful in the doorway as she approached his hospital bed.

Wickham turned at her presence and spoke faintly. "I wanted someone who really loved me to be near me at the end. I know you really loved me, Lydia, and I did not deserve it."

Lydia, with a strength and compassion that amazed her father, took Wickham's hand and sat quietly by his side. She stayed by his side for two days until he passed.

Mr. Bennet paid for a simple stone and a plot nearby. Lydia, in her newly purchased widow weeds, cried for her lost youth and the memory of a charming young man brought to this.

The carriage ride back to London was shared with an elderly gentleman, Mr. Leeds, and a Mrs. Hampton, a recent widow herself. She consoled Lydia as best as she could, but seemed more interested in conversing with Mr. Bennet.

Lydia stared out at the countryside and longed for her mother. She thought Mrs. Hampton looked ridiculous in her cheap red satin gown edged with black lace, and she did not like the beauty mark the woman had pasted on near her lip. But Mr. Bennet seemed more accommodating, and soon he and Mrs. Hampton discovered that they had writing in common. She was an aspiring lady novelist. She asked Mr. Bennet if he might peruse her manuscript once they'd reached London. She gave him her card.

The plans for the school benefit were in full swing. Thanks to the efforts of Lady Anne, the event had become something to attend as part of the London season. Georgianna was to give a concert. Mrs. Bennet's students' work was framed and ready for display. Lady Anne brought the portrait Mrs. Bennet had painted of her to add to the display, and Georgianna brought hers as well. Her students made quite a fuss over Mrs. Bennet's work. Headmistress Elders, upon seeing the painting of Georgianna at the piano, pronounced it a magnificent piece and reiterated her gratitude to Mrs. Bennet for her time teaching the students.

Lord Worthing planned to bring some artists from France, as well as some titled gentry that he was entertaining. The young ladies coming out for the season in London, along with their mothers and dowager aunts and potential suitors, had all responded to the invitation to attend the benefit concert and art show. The event had been advertised to the general public as well.

Lady Anne and Colonel Fitzwilliam, Lizzy and Darcy, and Jane and Bingley were amongst the guests. Lizzy looked happier and more relaxed as she mingled. Darcy seemed nothing less than excited about his sister's concert and placed his program on a pair of chairs in the front row to assure his place. He perused the student artwork and made appropriate comments of praise to each artist. Lord Worthing's guests were completely charmed by the school. Mary, practicing her French, gave them a tour.

One of the artists in Lord Worthing's party sought out Mrs. Bennet. "Madam, you are the artist who painted the young woman at the piano and the one of the young woman as a fairy queen?"

Mrs. Bennet acknowledged it was she.

"Madam, I invite you to come to France to join a new artist's colony. You are painting in a more modern style that will change the way portraits are viewed."

Mrs. Bennet laughed, thinking the gentleman was just being polite. "Well, I also do landscapes and still lifes."

"Here is my card. If you decide to come, there will be a place for you."

Mrs. Bennet was taken aback by this small, strange man's intense manner. "Thank you very much, but I have a husband and a widowed daughter. I am not free to make my own arrangements."

"The accommodations are rustic, small apartments, but what is being created is important. You should be part of it."

Mrs. Bennet looked for her husband to introduce him to this man and to hear the comments he made about her work. For here was someone validating her talent in a way that made her heart beat faster, treating her as a real artist.

She searched the room and couldn't find Mr. Bennet. When she turned back to the small man, he was already heading into the concert.

Mrs. Bennet saw her husband conversing with a tall, buxom woman in a shiny green gown edged with bright pink lace. She crossed the room to retrieve him for the concert.

"Miriam, this is Mrs. Hampton, an aspiring novelist. We met on the carriage ride back from the North."

"Welcome," said Mrs. Bennet. "Are you coming in for the concert?"

"Oh, no," faltered Mrs. Hampton, "I came just to see… to see the school, and to ask your husband to look at my novel."

Mrs. Bennet, always a supporter of her husband's talent, said, "He is a very good writer, and I'm sure his suggestions will be helpful. Do you have the novel at hand?"

Mrs. Hampton blushed. "Indeed, I do."

"Give it to me for safekeeping, and I will make sure Edward reads it. We hope to turn out many quality lady novelists from the Abbey."

Mrs. Bennet extended her hand, wanting to make this woman comfortable. She could see that she was not gentry, but there were many from the general public attending the concert.

"Are you sure you won't join us for the concert?"

"No, thank you, Mrs. Bennet. Thank you, Mr. Bennet. I'll best be on my way."

As they turned to go into the concert, Mrs. Bennet said, "Edward, why were you so silent? I'm sure if you had extended the invitation to join us she might have."

"Not everyone enjoys a classical concert, Miriam," he retorted. He held the entrance door open for his wife, glanced over his shoulder and gave a slight nod to Mrs. Hampton as she retreated.

The benefit was a great success. At the end of the night, Miss Elders reported more titled families had become patrons and that applications for next year were increasing.

CHAPTER LIV

"We must start looking for new living quarters," Mrs. Bennet said to her husband as she was preparing for bed. "My brother will be returning soon. There is a cottage nearby the school that might suit; it would be affordable with the revenue from your work and since the Abbey now has adequate patronage, I will ask Miss Elders to consider increasing my teaching days in exchange for a salary. Lydia might stay on to assist my brother, and he could provide her with a stipend. Or you might want to continue to assist him in the warehouse if he needs help. I'm sure he will need help with all the extra exotic things he has purchased."

"I don't really want to work for your brother, Miriam,"

he replied gruffly.

"Well, it was just a suggestion," she harrumphed.

Mrs. Bennet found herself unable to sleep. Her head was spinning with ideas about living situations and the offer made by that odd gentleman from France. She propped her feet up and began to read Mrs. Hampton's novel. Not being a novelist herself, she was hesitant to pass judgment, but the convoluted plot of pirates and governesses was hard to follow. She pitied her husband having to labor through this.

Mrs. Bennet reflected on her family's adaptability after leaving Longbourn. The move to London had, for the most part, gone smoothly, though she sometimes felt slightly amiss without her usual things surrounding her.

Tonight, for example. She went into the kitchen to make herself a warm cup of cocoa, reached for her special mug and sighed, seeing it was not there. She would have to make do with her brother's smaller teacups. She missed her large mug, so perfect for a late-night cocoa indulgence, with its sturdy handle and hefty ceramic weight. It had seen her through many nights of insomnia. But she felt safe in the knowledge that it, along with most of their things, was in storage at Netherfield, and she looked forward to the day she would be reunited with the essence of her home.

She kept a small box with some sketchbooks and a few keepsakes for comfort at her writing desk. Feeling lonesome for Longbourn, Mrs. Bennet opened the box and sifted through sketches of the girls from their toddler days to their girlhood.

As she looked over the drawings, she laughed to herself.

She could see that even then she had captured each girl's character: here was Jane, daydreaming with a faraway smile; Lizzy, with a wry twist to her mouth and an arched eyebrow, always the critic; Mary, with a furrowed brow, bending over her books; Kitty in a pout; and Lydia perched precariously in a tree, tilting her face to the sun. She looked at the drawings again using her artist's eye rather than a mother's.

She realized that her talent was strong, but now there was a difference. Her technique had deepened. She possessed a new confidence of stroke; there was a boldness and passion to her painting. She was no longer content to just depict her subjects' character but to search for their soul.

She lifted the poems and letters written to her by Edward and misted up as she reread, remembering their young love. He was so passionate, wooing her with words of love, promising her a poem a day. He used to leave her little verses tucked under her pillow or in her vanity. She could not remember the last time she had received any notes from him other than a list of things to buy at the butcher. *Well, Valentine's Day is coming up, perhaps I should make more of an effort,* she mused. She usually painted a small card for him and he penned a few cursory comic verses for her.

This year she resolved to do better. She decided to present a small portrait of him in profile. With his graying temples and aquiline nose, he still was a handsome man. This would be a good way for her to demonstrate her love and affection for him, to show him she still found him attractive. She sighed, realizing that her teaching duties at the school and her portrait commissions did make it difficult to balance her wifely duties and her art.

She rifled under the letters to feel for her mother's cameo brooch. It was an overly large pin carved with the alabaster Roman head of Flora, hair piled high and entwined with roses. It was not to Miriam's taste, but she fondly recalled her mother's words as she'd fastened it upon her shawl to keep her safe from the cold. "This large cameo is intricately carved, Miriam. It took some time for the artist to carve it; let it serve as a reminder to you, dear one, to carve out some time for yourself and your art. My mother gave it to me. Flora is the goddess of flowers, and my mother understood that my art is my garden."

The brooch was not there. She searched the box twice, shaking out each drawing and letter. *How odd,* she thought. *I know I have not worn it.* It was not an article that would tempt movers or household staff to steal. *Perhaps I gave it to one of the girls or they borrowed it.* Just to be sure, she returned to her bedchamber and checked her vanity box on her dressing table. There were her pearls, a small gold bracelet and various hairpins, the small locket Mary wore to Jane's engagement party, but no brooch. She would check with Lydia tomorrow, she decided. With Mr. Bennet snoring heavily at her side, she finally drifted off to sleep with lurid visions of pirates and kidnapped governesses in her head.

The next morning, after breakfast, Mrs. Bennet still felt anxious about her mother's brooch. She was hoping that

Lydia had borrowed it, as she often went into her vanity for hairpins, ribbons, and the tortoise combs.

"Lydia, did you by chance borrow my cameo brooch?"

"What brooch, Mama?" Lydia started to clear the dishes from the table.

"A cameo. It was my mother's."

Lydia put the dishes down on the sideboard, turned and studied her mother. Mrs. Bennet, in her agitation, was picking distractedly at the embroidered flower on her napkin. Lydia crossed the room to sit next to her mother.

"I have never seen it, Mama. Did you perhaps pin it on a suit or shawl?" she asked gently.

"No, I never wear it. It is not to my taste, but I keep it in memory of my mother." She attempted to keep her voice light, but at the mention of her mother, her voice quavered and her eyes misted.

Lydia, with a look of concern, took her hand. "Perhaps you gave it to Kitty, Lizzy, or Jane for a wedding keepsake? You know, 'something old, something new, something borrowed, something blue.'"

"No, dear, I would remember that. No matter." She patted Lydia's hand. "It is not of great value just a sentimental one for me."

Lydia hugged her. "It is important to remember your own mama. I will search our things, enquire of my sisters, and ask Jane to check our belongings in storage. I will ask Lizzy to write to Charlotte too, to search among the cupboards at Longbourn."

Well, Mother, Mrs. Bennet thought as she made ready to

leave for the Abbey, *even though I might have lost your brooch, I think you would still be proud. I have followed your advice and managed to carve a little time for myself and my art.*

♦♦♦

CHAPTER LV

Because of Mrs. Bennet's display at the school benefit, she found herself with several commissions for portraits. She spent an extra day at the Abbey each week to accommodate her subjects. In addition, some of the students' parents requested formal portraits of their daughters. Some wanted it done in the simple gray frock, but others took the opportunity to have a more formal portrait done.

Lydia was busy in her uncle's establishment. Mr. Bennet still assisted with the management of the warehouse, but had more free time as Mr. Gardiner was preparing to return and had stopped purchasing items. Mr. Bennet's latest book was being read at dinner parties by all. Lizzy reported that she often smiled to herself as the readers remarked upon the cleverness of the writer and the beautiful illustrations. Some were having wedding gowns run up based on the drawings.

Mrs. Bennet again brought up the subject of the cottage nearby to the Abbey. "Edward, we must meet with the landlord and come to some terms. My brother is due back next month."

Mr. Bennet seemed indifferent. "Whatever you decide, Miriam. If being near the Abbey is easier, then so be it."

Mrs. Bennet stifled her irritation, but she put his disinterest down to embarrassment regarding the entail. She wrote to the landlord of her interest.

In preparation for her commissions, Mrs. Bennet frequented Quigley's Painting Supplies. Mrs. Bennet loved Quigley's because they had a room behind the store where Mr. Quigley employed strong young men who built the wooden frames and could stretch and attach the muslin for her canvas. When she was at Longbourn, she had always asked the farmhands to help. Today, she needed three canvases prepared. As she stood at the doorway with her back to shop, she heard Mrs. Hurst and Lady Caroline enter.

"Why are we here, Caroline? I don't feel quite safe in this part of London," said Mrs. Hurst irritably.

"Nonsense, I have it on good authority this is the best place for painting supplies. Amelia has become an avid artist under Mrs. Bennet's tutelage. We want her to continue her art during school holiday."

"Oh, oh, speaking of Mrs. Bennet, I have a piece of juicy gossip," chortled Mrs. Hurst.

"Now, now," said Caroline, "she is practically a relative,

with our brother married to Jane. Is it a scandal that could harm us?"

"No, not us."

"Then do tell."

"Well, it seems Mr. Hurst had stopped for tea in an establishment he doesn't usually frequent. His carriage wheel was being repaired and he went into this side street tea shop to wait."

"Yes, yes, what does this have to do with Mrs. Bennet?"

"Guess who was in the tea shop? Mr. Bennet, with a woman whom Mr. Hurst described as one step away from a brothel, very shiny gown with cheap lace, and strong perfume. You know Mr. Hurst knows quality lace when he sees it."

"And?" sighed Caroline in exasperation.

"Well, Mr. Hurst says they were sitting very close, she was holding his hand and they were deep in conversation. Mr. Hurst couldn't resist, and he didn't want to be rude, in case Mr. Bennet saw him, so he went over to them. Mr. Bennet jumped up quickly and tried to act respectable, introduced the tart as a Mrs. Hampton, an aspiring lady novelist, even held up a manuscript for show. Says he's offering her consultation. Mr. Hurst told me it looked like he was offering her more than that," giggled Mrs. Hurst.

Miriam kept her back facing the doorway; she slowly stepped further into the back room to avoid being noticed by the women. Her stomach felt as if it had been pierced with a knife; she couldn't catch her breath. One of the young men noticed her ashen appearance and rushed to her side. She sat down slowly and sipped the glass of water offered.

Mr. Quigley, working the front of the shop, had overheard the women's conversation and hurriedly wrapped their purchase. He found Mrs. Bennet seated in the back, looking crestfallen.

"Ma'am, them cats don't know nothing. Mr. Bennet's a published poet, isn't he? He was probably just helping that poor soul."

Mrs. Bennet looked at Mr. Quigley gratefully, gathered her belongings, and said, "I'm sure you're right, Mr. Quigley. The canvases are stretched. Can the fellows put them in the carriage for me?"

Later that night, Mrs. Bennet furtively went through her husband's pockets. She found a card from the tea shop, copied down the address, then replaced the card in his pocket.

At dinner, she announced that the carriage held three canvases that she would take to the Abbey tomorrow, as she had a portrait appointment that afternoon. "What are your plans, Edward?"

"I think I will check in at the warehouse, escort Lydia to the shop, and then take myself for a long stroll through the streets of London. I am seeking inspiration for my next project."

That morning, Mrs. Bennet packed the carriage with her overnight bag and various painting supplies, and made a great show of leaving, admonishing Lydia to make a good dinner for her father, and reminding Mr. Bennet to wear his wool scarf to avoid a chill.

At one o'clock, she pulled the carriage into the wheel-repair shop near the tea shop and asked the gentleman to make sure all wheels were secure.

Through the window of the tea shop, she could see Mr. Bennet sitting with Mrs. Hampton, a manuscript prominently displayed on the table but clearly unopened. She watched Mrs. Hampton lean over to flick a piece of lint off her husband's collar, and with that gesture, she knew the truth. That gesture, done so often in a wifely context, demonstrated an intimacy, a sense of ownership and ease in their relationship. With her heart pounding, she entered the shop. Mr. Bennet looked up in surprise.

Mrs. Bennet crossed the room rapidly and took Mrs. Hampton's hand in a firm grip. "So nice to see you again, Mrs. Hampton."

Mrs. Hampton was speechless. Mr. Bennet, his face paling, started to rise.

"How is the novel coming?"

"Fine," said Mrs. Hampton faintly.

As Mrs. Bennet looked down, she noticed that her mother's brooch was pinned to the bodice of Mrs. Hamilton's lurid yellow gown. A wave of nausea rose and she could taste the bile in her throat. She smiled tightly and spoke through gritted teeth. "Do be careful of that large cameo. So distinctive; I have one exactly like it. I wouldn't want you to tear your lovely gown. It could rip your lace apart." Mrs. Bennet swallowed hard, thinking of more than lace ripping apart. It was all she could do to restrain herself from yanking the brooch free from this tawdry woman.

Mr. Bennet rose fully then, and came to his wife's side. "Miriam, what are you doing here?"

"I needed to make sure the carriage wheels were secure before my journey. There is a carriage shop nearby. I wanted a spot of tea, and they directed me here."

"I am here consulting on Mrs. Hampton's novel."

"Yes, I see that," said Mrs. Bennet dryly. "Mrs. Hampton, I have read your novel and was quite confused as to which pirate goes with which governess, but I am sure my husband can help you sort all that out."

She turned to leave. Mr. Bennet insisted on accompanying her back to the carriage shop, all the while babbling about the poor quality of Mrs. Hampton's novel. Mrs. Bennet got up into the seat, grabbed the buggy whip and flicked it at the horse. She missed the horse and stung Mr. Bennet's hand instead. He cried out in pain.

"Oh, Edward, I am so sorry. Have I cut you to the quick? Then it is only as you have done to me."

Large tears welling up in her eyes, she flicked her wrist again and the horse trotted smartly to the road.

"Miriam, what is it?" Miss Elders had seen her dismount from the carriage in distress. She'd sent the students out to unload the carriage, and now she knocked upon the studio door. Mrs. Bennet turned to hide her tear-stained face. "The girls are on their way with the canvases. I will have them drop them off outside the door, and I will bring you some tea."

"I need something stronger," said Mrs. Bennet in a muffled voice.

"Cognac, then," said Miss Elders, "it's medicinal."

As Mrs. Bennet sipped her cognac, Miss Elders supplied a sympathetic ear. "Though I have never married, I know the state requires much compromise. Perhaps this is just a rocky part of the road, and you will continue to travel together. You have so much history together. I am sure he is full of remorse."

Mrs. Bennet lifted her chin in determination. "I have supported all his endeavors, raised the girls, smiled through his scorn and occasional shows of contempt, soothed him when I was having success, lest he feel jealous, encouraged him artistically, even collaborated with him to help with his success. I thought of him as my true hero. He is no longer that. I can never look at him the same way again."

"What do you plan to do?"

"I plan to stay here and complete as many commissions as I can. If you do not mind, I will occupy the room I use when I must stay the night, now on a more regular basis."

"Of course, that is fine."

"My excuse will be the amount of work I have, plus my teaching schedule. Edward will come looking for me. I will direct him to meet with the landlord of the nearby cottage and encourage him to take it."

"Then you plan on forgiving him?"

"Not at all. I plan to live in France."

"What!" gasped Miss Elders.

Mrs. Bennet nodded decisively. "I was offered a place in an artist's colony by that visiting French artist. I will accept. I think that is the perfect solution. Mary is studying French, and she can come to me during the holidays and summers. Edward will be in the nearby cottage to watch over Mary. I will take Lydia with me. She needs a change, the poor girl."

"Won't Mr. Bennet not take the cottage if he knows you will be leaving for France?"

"I don't plan to tell him until he has the lease and is well ensconced in the dwelling. As he has deceived me, so shall he be deceived. Once the commissions are complete, I will book passage for myself and Lydia."

CHAPTER LVI

Mr. Bennet did come to the Abbey to seek out his wife. "Miriam, you have not been home for six days."

She avoided her husband's gaze and continued to paint. "I have been inundated with commissions lately."

He looked down at the paint-spattered floor, shifted his weight uncomfortably, cleared his throat, and said hoarsely, "Your brother is due back soon. What will he think about your absence? You must come home, if not for me then for propriety's sake."

"Propriety's sake? Propriety's sake?" Mrs. Bennet slammed down her paintbrush and turned to confront her husband. "Edward, if you were so worried about propriety you would not have been drawn to such a vulgar creature. I might have understood if the woman had a modicum of talent or even beauty. The low level of her talent and tawdry appearance is an insult. Caroline Worthing and Mrs. Hurst were quite amused by it all, and I am sure have spread their amusement to all willing to be amused." She bit her lip to keep it from quivering and took deep breaths, trying to prevent the sobs rising in her chest.

"Miriam, you must not put stock in what those viperous women say."

"Why not? Edward, it is the truth."

"Miriam, you must understand. I was just flattered by the attention. You were always so busy with the school and your commissions."

"So your dalliance was my fault?" She felt a rush of cold anger and disgust overcome her. "And giving away my mother's brooch? How dare you go through my things searching for a trinket for your mistress! Your obsession with thrift knows no bounds." She shook her head in disbelief.

He, knowing what was required, acted the penitent and slowly lowered his knee to the floor. "Please forgive me. I didn't know it was your mother's brooch. You never wear it. She is not my mistress. It was her birthday, and I just wished to present her with a little something that would soften my criticism of her attempt at a novel." Mr. Bennet looked up at his wife. Though he appeared contrite, she noted a slight sneer on his lips. "She lacks your astounding ability to flourish in adversity. Not all women have your indomitable strength and a yearning for independence. Some need and bask in the protection offered by the male sex."

Mrs. Bennet stiffened and took a step back. "Edward, do you wish your freedom?"

"No, of course not!" He stood and began to pace, for certainly he knew the value of a good wife over a cheap entanglement. "Miriam, we cannot afford another scandal. You must come home."

"There is no scandal in my staying at the school for now. The scandal that you so fear is wrought by your own low liaison. I have these commissions that must be completed. Staying here allows me to avoid the furtive looks, false smiles and the pity of the shopkeepers."

She snorted. "Though for men, it is different. For you there is the conspiratorial wink, the shared smirk, and an occasional glass raised in silent toast. For women, there is the appraising glance to see in what way she is deficient. To quote the famous bard, whose writings you so love, 'If we two be one and thou dost play false I do digest the poison of the flesh being strumpeted by thy contagion.'" As she spoke the final words, she let out a strangled cry, unable to hold back her tears.

"Miriam, Miriam, please, please, we must mend this." He moved to embrace her. She recoiled from his touch.

Mr. Bennet, searching for a way to make his case, nearly

fell to his knees again. "Miriam, remember the end of the Bard's speech? 'Keep then fair league and truce with thy true bed, I'll live distained and thou undishonored.' Please stay at my side. Your presence will avert any gossip. Think of the girls. You cannot stay permanently at the school. That would cast a pall over the school's reputation."

Mrs. Bennet could see the truth of her situation. A married woman had little recourse or power if betrayed by her husband. Society assumed she would ignore any peccadillo and carry on in the wifely role. Mrs. Bennet dried her eyes and pretended she agreed with him.

"Edward, I think it best if we start anew." He nodded fervently, and she pressed ahead. "I think new beginnings require a new residence. However, I need some time, Edward. I will remain here and finish these commissions until the cottage is ready. The excuse of readying the cottage while completing my commissions will provide the reason for my absence."

Mr. Bennet, grateful for the reprieve, went with alacrity to secure the lease.

CHAPTER LVII

The Gardiners had returned. It was a busy month. Lydia oversaw most of the move while Mrs. Bennet stayed at the school and feverishly completed her commissions. Jane and Charles brought the furnishings kept in storage at Netherfield. Mr. Bennet was quite pleased with the cottage and said it inspired him to write.

Mrs. Bennet decided to give her husband a chance to redeem himself. She wanted to believe that what he said was the truth. That nothing had occurred, just a mere flirtation. She vowed to put her anger aside and try to accept him back into her heart. The smirks of Caroline and Mrs. Hurst presented a hurdle. However, she met them with a smooth and pleasant countenance, and their wagging tongues eventually ceased.

She settled into their cottage. Edward was starting to write some short stories based on the characters he observed around London. Some were humorous and some were poignant. Miriam continued with her classes and her commissions. All was comfortable—perhaps too comfortable. She did not long for the drama of getting her girls settled, but she'd always thought that once her birds had flown, she would have more time to reconnect with her husband.

She examined her heart to see if she was holding onto resentment of his flirtation. She did still feel hurt, but she masked it from her husband. Yet she did think it odd he did nothing to appease her: No flowers, no special attentions, no tokens of affection were proffered, and no real apology beyond the excuses he'd uttered when he came to the school. He seemed grateful she was there, ate with great gusto the meals she prepared after coming home from the school. He then usually retired into his den to work on more stories, sometimes coming to bed in the early morning hours.

So the effort to rekindle their romance was left to her. St. Valentine's Day was coming and, instead of just the one portrait, she set about secretly capturing her husband's likeness from many angles. It was a good project, one which helped her to observe all his good qualities: his kindness to Lydia; his furrowed brow as he concentrated, pen in hand; the curve of his face as he slept. All this attention to his being caused her to fall in love with her husband all over again.

She steeled herself against having any expectation that he would surprise her with anything elaborate. Even his usual practice of a simple love poem for her would be enough.

She casually showed him her box of old drawings one evening, exclaiming as she lifted an old love poem of his. "You were such a good writer even then, Edward!"

He read his old poem and laughed. "I think I was a bit of a moon-calf."

"Yes, but you were my moon-calf." Miriam leaned forward for a kiss and was rewarded with a pat on her shoulder and a dry peck. Edward rose from his chair and took the old poem with him into his study. Still she remained hopeful.

The cottage was not large and did not require daily help. Miriam did most of the cooking, and between Lydia and herself they managed to keep the house tidy. As Mrs. Bennet was dusting Mr. Bennet's desk, she noticed the imprint of a poem on his blotter, the words were slightly blurred but still readable.

For my Love who gazes at me in admiration
I wonder am I worth such a gaze.

Miriam sucked in her breath; it was clear Edward had noticed her studying him for his portraits.

A simple man of letters am I
As I peruse the page,
Knowing what I offer is love
But not a living wage.

This caused Miriam a twinge of regret, remembering a barbed comment or two she'd made in the past about their scarce income.

You look to me to be your hero
The one to save the day.
Pleading with me to never leave
Promising happiness if I stay.

Miriam chucked to herself and shook her head over the male ego. It was he who had pleaded with her to stay.

A life together is what you desire,
Resuming our passionate ways
To find my way through this labyrinth of obligations and duty.
Mastering this maze.

To meet your admiring eye again, hoping to be worthy of your gaze.

Miriam sighed wistfully. It seemed they both wanted the same thing, to reconnect, reenergize and create a life together, bringing their passion back to each other. She vowed she would do all she could to make him happy. Her beloved husband so clearly wanted to find his way back to her through the labyrinth of daily life.

CHAPTER LVIII

On Valentine's Day, at breakfast, Miriam presented Edward with her portrait of him. It was a collage of finely penciled sketches of him in various poses, all on one page.

Mr. Bennet gasped as he unrolled the parchment. "Miriam, this is truly wonderful, very touching. I have not forgotten you either. See the box at your plate."

"What could this be?" She laughed in delight. She opened the small square box. It was her mother's cameo. Mrs. Bennet was overcome with the retrieval of the cameo and the significance of that retrieval. She looked up at her husband. This was his apology, finally given, a new beginning for them.

"And that's not all, Miriam, as befits our Valentine's tradition I have included a poem." Miriam fished a small, folded paper out of the box. There on the page was a short comic limerick.

There is a Missus who loves to paint
Strong fumes do not cause her to faint
She can draw you true
Oh that you may rue! But
Your likeness is no cause for complaint.

Mrs. Bennet sat very still. Instead of feeling the heat of anger, she felt her body grow cold and numb. She pressed her lips together and tried to blink away the tears starting to form. She now understood the significance of the stanzas in his poem, the pleadings to never leave, and the happiness if he stayed. Seeing now that it was not a mere reversal of fact by the male ego, but a true recording of another woman's words. He was seeing Mrs. Hampton again. That was the significance of the returned cameo.

"What's wrong, my dear?"

Mrs. Bennet spoke slowly and deliberately. "Edward, did she enjoy the poem?"

He looked at her in alarm. "What poem?"

"Please, Edward, I saw on your blotter the imprint of a love poem you had written that I thought was intended for me."

"Miriam, I... it was just a.... something to appease her. I had to get your cameo back..."

"It was quite a deep declaration of love you gave her for the brooch."

"Once I realized the significance of the brooch to you, of course I had to get it back. The poem was... the poem..." Mr. Bennet faltered, cleared his throat, searching for a proper explanation. His shoulders sagged in resignation, realizing he had been caught out, trying to have the love of his wife, the comfort of a home, and the excitement of a new admirer.

Her voice now thick with emotion, Mrs. Bennet finished his sentence for him. "The poem was clearly expressing who has your heart, for I know how difficult it is for you to write of your feelings. I foolishly thought it was for me, and I planned on teasing you that you had returned to your 'moon-calf' ways."

"Miriam," he said looking down at his plate, "I do value you."

"Not enough, Edward, not enough."

"Please."

"Please? Please what? Please you? Please the girls? Please society?" Mrs. Bennet remembered the original plan she had discussed with Miss Elders. "This time I am going to please myself and accept the offer from France."

His eyes widened in horror. "You can't, Miriam, it will look...."

She stood, her small figure trembling but infused with purpose. "It will look fine. You will stay behind to watch over Mary. I will take Lydia with me. I will announce it at our Easter luncheon."

CHAPTER LIX

Mrs. Bennet returned to her studio at the Abbey, giving the excuse that she had many commissions to finish before the end of Spring term. Lydia met her in her studio to pack her things. "Mother, you have been here almost three weeks working, but the portraits are lovely."

"Thank you, dear. Lydia, I fear being cooped up in a country cottage is not fair to you."

Lydia sighed. "I was thinking of asking Uncle if I could stay on in London."

"If you would like that, that would be fine, but I have another idea. How would you like to go to France?"

"What! Oh Mother, France! I would love that!"

Mrs. Bennet squeezed her hand. "I have been offered a place in an artist's colony, and you may accompany me."

Lydia frowned. "What about Father?"

"He can stay here and write, and watch over Mary. Mary can visit us this summer. She can practice her French."

"It sounds thrilling."

"Don't say anything just yet, will you? When we are all together next week I will announce it."

Mrs. Bennet had planned a small Easter luncheon. Lizzy and Darcy, Georgianna, Lady Anne and Colonel Fitzwilliam, and Jane and Charles would be there. Kitty and Officer Denny were also coming. The Gardiners, the Philips, and Miss Elders would also be in attendance.

There was a small, charming garden at the back of the cottage. Mrs. Bennet brought out her remaining linens and china, and luncheon was served outside.

All raised a glass to toast the new dwellings, the beginning of spring and new ventures. Then a toast was made with a wink to a secret author's success with a recent book that was all the rage. By now most of the family had sussed out the identity of E.B. A toast was raised to the Gardiners' return, and finally a toast was raised to the success of the Abbey school, and to Mrs. Bennet's many recent commissions.

Mrs. Bennet rose and proffered another toast. "A toast to Lydia's and my trip to France. Because of my painting, specifically the ones of you, Georgianna, and you, Lady Anne, I have been invited to become an artist-in-residence at a new artists' colony in France."

There was a stunned silence, then a burst of chatter.

Mrs. Philips seemed to be weeping with happiness. "Oh, my, France, just think of it! My little sister in France!"

Miss Elders clapped her hands and exclaimed it was terrific representation for the school.

Mrs. Gardiner, who was of French parentage, was thrilled, wanting to know the exact address as she had relatives for Mrs. Bennet to contact. Mary burst out in French excitedly, hoping to be able to visit and practice her newly acquired language. Charles exclaimed that he'd always wanted to take his bride to Paris. Lady Anne congratulated Mrs. Bennet as a true artist and allowed she was envious.

Only Jane looked at her mother in distress. Lizzy seemed

overwhelmed by the news, and Darcy was frowning. Kitty burst into tears, for she had missed Lydia and her family.

Mr. Bennet rose to his feet, raised his glass and said stiffly, "Congratulations, my dear."

Mrs. Bennet called for quiet. She kissed her sister, shook her brother's hand. She calmed Kitty, saying she could visit in the summer with Mary. She told Charles she would be delighted to see him and Jane in France. She turned to Darcy and said, "It is most respectable, you needn't worry. It was Lord Worthing's friend who contacted me. Lady Anne, perhaps you could submit your flower illustrations to the colony committee and at some point join us."

"When are you to set sail?" asked Robert Denny.

"Next month, so I would like to spend some time with my girls before I leave." Kitty was planning to stay in London with Jane and Charles. Pemberley was close enough so Lizzy could come in for a visit.

Kitty and Lydia stayed in the kitchen to help washing up. Jane walked with her mother into the garden.

"Mother, Caroline hinted at something about Father. Is that why you are going?"

She patted Jane's arm. "I am going because it is a tremendous opportunity."

"But if there was no trouble with Father would you still go?"

She thought for a moment. "Yes. It just made it easier."

"What if I—" Jane started crying. "Please say you'll come back when it's time for my confinement."

Mrs. Bennet stopped and faced her. She placed her

palms on her cheeks and kissed her forehead. "I wouldn't miss it for the world, dear Jane."

"What is going to happen now?"

"I don't know." She reached to smooth back a lock of her daughter's hair. "All's well that ends well, isn't that what they say?"

Mrs. Bennet had time with each of her daughters. Lizzy made no secret that she was affronted that her mother was abandoning their father; she vowed to have Mr. Bennet at Pemberley often. Kitty hoped to be able to visit in the summer.

For the next three weeks, Mr. Bennet wandered about the cottage appearing slightly disheveled, unshaven, with a rumpled waistcoat and ink-stained fingers. It was clear he was still in a state of shock over her departure. He tried to start several conversations with her, but she always found herself too busy at the school or preparing for the trip or visiting with the girls to spend any time with him.

He tried to make jokes and entice her with an upcoming artistic endeavor where they could collaborate again, he the prose, she the paint. He suggested that when Mary visited for the summer, he would accompany her and maybe write a novella about the Englishman trying to adapt abroad with her illustrations. Mrs. Bennet did laugh at that and said it was a good idea, but of course her apartments would be quite cramped with Lydia, Mary and Kitty. He would have to find other lodging.

He knew then that the young woman he'd married, who wore her heart on her sleeve, bore his children, farmed with him, cooked for him, encouraged him artistically, supported and believed in his talent, was unable to mend her heart, and had plucked it forever from her sleeve, putting it out of his reach.

Mrs. Bennet looked out her window onto the beautiful golden color of the leaves starting to change. She gathered her supplies and set up right in the middle of the meadow. She liked the new technique practiced by many artists in the colony.

Lydia had become a favorite model. There was a beautiful rendition of her dancing in a man's arms, she in her red hat, he in his straw one. Lydia had fallen for the artist, and Mrs. Bennet did not have the energy to combat her or lecture her.

Here in France she had time to reflect on all that had passed and all she had accomplished. She had done her duty as a mother to the best of her ability. Her daughters were for the most part settled: Mary now pursuing the life of an academic, Lizzy growing into her role as mistress of Pemberley, Kitty delighting in the role of an officer's wife, and dearest Jane rosy with the bloom of impending motherhood.

As for Mr. Bennet, he did not do well when left on his own to manage a household. He resided now with Lizzy, where he could retreat into and avail himself of all the treasures in the vast library of Pemberley.

She had been a faithful wife, a true supportive partner to her husband's endeavors in farming and his writing, and a good mother who offered love, advice and care when needed. But she was most proud of her ability to forge her own career as a respected painter, and earn her own living, a difficult task for any artist.

Mrs. Bennet looked at her surroundings, grateful that, for every cherished moment of her journey, she was now where she'd wished to be so long ago, alone with her easel and box of paints, her brushstrokes creating a lush meadow alive with wild flowers and golden-throated birds with beautifully colored feathers.

THE END

ABOUT THE AUTHOR

Ms. Salois has been the Artistic Director of Vantage Theatre since 1994 and is now the Executive Director. As a Director and Producer Ms. Salois has brought over 38 plays to fruition. She created a three-way partnership with Vantage, San Diego Repertory, and La Jolla Playhouse bringing Anna Deavere Smith's New York production of *Let Me Down Easy* to San Diego in association with Arena Stage's national tour. She produced Lynne Kaufman's award winning *Be Here Now The Journey of Ram Dass* at The OB Playhouse and for the San Diego Fringe festival and she recently brought Joel Drake Johnson's 2015 Nominee as Best Off - Broadway play *Rasheeda Speaking* to a new theatre space she created in La Jolla.

She has written and directed for television, *So This is Washington* and *West of Hedon*. She has also written for the theatre. She is a co-author of the plays *The Importance of Being Earnest the Musical!*, *The Holy Man* an adaptation of Susan Trotts novels, and *Macgregor*.

As an Actor she has performed in professional theatres as well as film and television in New York, Los Angeles, Massachusetts, Washington D.C. and San Diego She received her Baccalaureate from Lowell University and her Masters from Georgetown University.

She resides in La Jolla with her husband, is the mother of two grown daughters and writes fiction under her married name Salerno.

Made in the USA
Charleston, SC
30 September 2016